LET US PREY
A Gotcha Detective Agency Novel
by
Jamie Lee Scott

Copyright © 2011 by Jamie Lee Scott

This book is a work of fiction. The names, characters, places, and incidents are products of the writer's imagination or have been used fictitiously and are not to be construed as real. Any resemblance to persons, living or dead, actual events, locales or organizations is entirely coincidental.

All rights are reserved. No part of this book may be used or reproduced in any manner whatsoever without written permission from the author.

* * * * *

ACKNOWLEDGEMENTS

I must first and foremost thank Scot Dierks for his never ending patience with my writing endeavors over the years. Thanks Scot for all the extra hours you work at the restaurant so I can live my dream. You are my heart and soul, and the love of my life.

Next, I would never have gotten to this point without my lovely critique partner and fabulous writer, Bente Gallagher. She is the author of the DIY mystery series by Jennie Bentley. Thanks Bente for your unwavering faith, and for reading my work from the beginning.

Teresa Watson for her tireless efforts as my editor, for making the story read so much better.

I would never be at the point I'm at without the superb "treefort" who include Jeanne Bowerman, Kim Garland, Mina Zaher, and Zac Sanford. Thank for all of your support and for letting me rant.

And last, but not least, the employees at our restaurant who listened patiently as I brainstormed plots and characters.

CHAPTER 1

When you work as a private detective, there are two things that are certain; you'll be bored nearly to death by a long stakeout, and you'll have to pee at some time during that stakeout. I was approaching the "have to pee" stage when my cell phone rang.

"Speak to me."

"Nice, very professional," Charles said.

"I try. What's up?"

"I've got Jackie coming to relieve you. I have sort of an emergency at the office. The client is on her way now." There was an undertone to Charles's voice that put me on alert.

Before I could respond he hung up.

I'm Mimi Capurro, and I own Gotcha Detective Agency. We're a fledgling agency on the Central Coast of California. I'm a former Secret Service agent. I left the job to start a family with my husband, Dominic, but the family plans hit a major road block when Dominic died in a plane crash a year after we married. Gotcha is my way of trying to move on, and I've put all of my time and energy into growing the business. Some days are easier than others.

Charles Parks is my right-hand man. He's from the Naval Postgraduate School in Monterey, California. I met him while I was protecting a former first lady. Charles is not only one of my best friends, but he's a genius with computers, business, and defense.

Jackie Baccarin, who was coming to relieve me, was my best friend. Normally I would never recommend going into business with friends, but these were friends with talent. Jackie could pee in a freaking coffee can without ever leaving her stakeout post. Now that's talent. And like me, she needed an outlet. She'd lost her husband too. Only she'd killed hers. Not literally, it's just that as far as she was concerned, he was dead.

I saw Jackie's car come around the corner, so I fired up my 1982 Toyota pickup and headed out. Gotcha has a fleet of cars for different occasions. Since my Land Rover would have stood out like a purple cow in this neighborhood I had the Toyota. And by fleet of cars, I mean we had our personal cars and three that belonged to the company. Thank God for people who trade in their junker cars and the auctioneers who sell them. All three cars cost $1,500, total.

Some P.I. agencies specialize and only do insurance work, or track down deadbeat dads. Gotcha isn't picky; we're a fledgling company and can't afford to be picky about the cases we take. Since I have a specialized background in the Secret Service, we also provide bodyguards, or professional protection.

I drove around the back of the Victorian house that had been converted into offices, and parked in the backyard/parking lot. This house had belonged to Dominic when he ran his produce brokerage company. It was while doing business for that company that he was killed.

Every time I opened the kitchen door I swore I could smell the Blue Mountain coffee he was so fond of. But that label hasn't been brewed in the house since I took over, so I know it's just a memory. I feel the glitch in my heart to this day, and it's been more than two years since his plane went down.

I thought I could sneak into my office and do a quick clean up and pee, before my client arrived.

Yeah, that didn't happen as my new clients were sitting in my office when I walked in. I'm not big on surprises, so I shot Charles a look that told him as much.

Charles, who'd been sitting at my desk, casually rose to his feet when I entered the room. "And this is Mimi."

The ladies looked in my direction just as I was adjusting my face from a scowl to a smile. I walked forward and shook hands with both women.

The older woman looked to be in her forties. She had large brown eyes like topaz gems and wavy, medium-length hair the color of rich cream. She stood tall with a muscular build. Her skin was tanned, which clashed with her gray suit. I shook her hand first.

She took my hand in a firm grip. "I'm Lauren Silke."

I'm pretty sure I had a fan-girl moment, but I did my best to hide it. I was shaking hands with the New York Times bestselling author of the Sophie Nolan vampire series. I had every book in the series. Well, I didn't have the latest, but as soon as it hit bookstores I would.

"Wow, I'm a big fan." I just had to say it.

"Thank you." Lauren indicated the waif standing beside her. "This is my assistant, Esme Bailey."

I turned to the girl with the large sapphire eyes. Her fine, straight, black hair was worn in a precise bob. She was tall and thin and a shade too pale. Her hollow cheeks and thin red lips made her look even thinner. I had to envy her style with her black thigh high boots and mini skirt.

"Esme. Hi."

Esme gave me an overenthusiastic handshake.

"Oh, thank you so much for meeting us at the last minute. Charles has been such a doll in your absence.

And he assures us that taking us as a client will be no imposition. I'm so sorry for the last-minute meeting."

Was this girl on crack? Her movements were steady and fluid, but she spoke so fast I could hardly keep up. And when she said Charles had assured them I'd take the case, the words really began to blur as my mind whirled.

I glared at Charles again.

"Well, ladies, now that you've met, I'll just go grab you some coffee and cookies." Charles nearly ran from the room.

Charles, a fop if ever there was one, wore creased khaki slacks and a lavender polo shirt. I could see the lavender in his argyle socks as he left the room.

I'm pretty sure my Doberman, Lola, heard Charles say cookies because she stood from her bed in the corner of my office, performed a downward dog, and trotted to the kitchen. She didn't even acknowledge me.

I went around my desk and sat. "Okay, so exactly what is it I'm taking on here?"

Lauren settled back in her chair, and as she did I noticed something a little off about her coloring. I couldn't quite place it.

Esme sat forward on her chair, her long legs twisted like spaghetti noodles. She seemed anxious.

"Okay, so you know who Lauren is?"

I smiled. "I do."

"Oh, good, that will make this faster. So you know about Sophie and the vampires. Well, then, um, you also know that in the last book, Lauren killed off a long-running character. I mean she had to, there were just getting to be too many characters to keep track of. But I digress.

"Okay, apparently some of her loyal fans aren't thrilled with the story line lately. And this last weekend Lauren was speaking at a paranormal writers conference—"

"I was on a panel. Not really speaking. My presence was considered to be a great draw for some reason."

"And, long story short, she got the shit beat out of her in the bathroom. By a lady claiming to be her fan of all things." Esme was wide eyed, and now nearly tipping off the chair.

Lauren glared at Esme but said nothing.

That was it. The makeup on Lauren's face was thick. Very thick because it was covering bruising. And when I looked close I could see just a bit of red on her eyeball.

"Oh my God. How on earth did that happen?"

Now Lauren sat forward in her chair. "I went to the bathroom, and this lady apparently followed me in. We were the only two in the bathroom, and I didn't think anything of it. I mean why would I?"

Esme interrupted. "And the woman waited until Lauren was in the stall and had her pants half down, then she kicked in the stall door."

"Did you have any idea who she was?"

"Not a clue," Lauren said.

"Anyway, she knocked Lauren out cold."

I leaned forward. "Holy shit."

Lauren laughed. "That's exactly what I thought when I came to. But the woman was gone. I vaguely remember her saying she was pissed off about something, but I can't for the life of me remember what she said."

"Did anyone find the woman, or walk in while this was happening?"

Blushing now, Lauren said, "No, a woman did come in moments later and found me on the floor with my pants down. God it was humiliating."

Esme laughed. "But good publicity."

"Huh, I didn't read about it." Then I wondered where I would possibly have read about something like this happening.

"The conference was in Seattle. It was in their paper." Esme reached into her Coach briefcase and handed me a clipping of the article.

I glanced at it and put it on my desk. "So how do I fit into this?"

"Lauren's book tour for Prey starts tonight. Yeah, tonight. And she needs a bodyguard."

"Tonight?" What the hell did Charles get me into?

Right on cue, Charles reentered the office with a tray of coffee and snacks. He placed it on the table between the two women.

"I wasn't sure what you liked, so I made plain black coffee, but there are several creamers." He pointed at a plate on the tray. "And we have hazelnut, orange, and mocha biscotti."

"So Charles, you are going to provide Ms. Silke with executive protection tonight?"

Esme was giddy. "Oh Charles, really?"

"Not me. I've cleared your schedule, so you'll be available to travel to San Francisco with Lauren tonight."

I stood. It took everything I had to not reach across the desk and grab Charles by the collar and yank him toward me. I took a deep breath before I spoke. Being a small, new business, we needed the clientele, but I felt like Charles had manipulated me. Wouldn't be the first time. Or the last.

"Fine. I'd be happy to accompany you tonight. I'm sure Charles told you about our fees?"

Esme regurgitated what Charles had quoted in my absence and I nearly choked. The quote was nearly three times our normal fee.

I coughed, then said, "And this works for you?"

Lauren said, "If we can schedule you for the week, we can double the fee."

"The week?"

"Well, Lauren has five engagements this week. And with the attack at the conference and the flurry of negative and nasty comments on Facebook, Twitter and her blog, we think it's best she has someone watching her back so she can give the proper attention to her fans."

"Do you have the itinerary for this entire week?"

"I don't have it on me. I have to call Lauren's publicist this afternoon to get the details on times, flights, and all that. We weren't sure we were going to honor the tour dates if we couldn't get a bodyguard."

Esme reached back into her briefcase and handed me a hardcover book.

I looked at the stunningly erotic cover of Prey. When I opened the cover I saw it was autographed already.

"Wow, thanks."

Esme smiled. "No problem. This is going be a great week."

Neither Lauren nor Esme touched the coffee and biscotti. And I immediately started preparing for the job ahead, having no idea what I was getting myself into.

* * *

I'd never been to a book signing, but I think it would have been considered a hit. There was a line out the door of the bookstore in San Francisco that trailed down the block. Lauren talked and laughed and signed for three hours.

I had no idea how fanatical fiction fans could be. More than half of the fans dressed as characters in Lauren's books. Well, their versions anyway.

Toward the end of the signing Lauren said, "You didn't get to meet my biggest fan. He looks exactly like I pictured Lawrence when I created his character. The guy is great, a little creepy, but dedicated. I don't think he's missed a signing in California since my first book. Weird he wasn't there tonight. Esme always points him out when she's with me. I swear she knows him, but she says she doesn't."

"Sorry, I didn't see anyone who looked like that."

"Weird he wasn't here."

After spending an hour at Lauren's house that afternoon, the drive to and from San Francisco, and the signing, I was exhausted. So when our driver pulled the car up to Lauren's house to drop her off, I was ready to be home and in my nice warm bed.

"Oh, the itinerary," Lauren said, as she gathered up her handbag and briefcase. "Come on in and I'll get it for you. Sorry it wasn't here this afternoon. Esme was supposed to leave it in the foyer."

"I've got an early morning. Can you just email or fax it to me?"

Lauren looked a bit annoyed. "Sure, but I'd rather you take the printed version. I think the plane tickets are here too. Well, the confirmations anyway."

"Okay." I did my best to sound cheerful.

When I looked at my watch, it was after midnight. I really didn't feel like going into her house, but I followed her inside. When Lauren flipped on the lights, the itinerary was suddenly the last thing on our minds.

CHAPTER 2

Sitting in the middle of the dining room table was Esme. Not all of Esme, just her head, eyes wide open, staring from the crystal bowl. Her hair had been cut into a short spiky chopped mess, and blood had pooled in the bottom of the bowl. Her body had been positioned in a chair next to an antique cabinet with her hands cupped in her lap, collecting pools of blood that had seeped from her neck. Her legs were twisted in the same twist tie I'd seen in my office that day.

I looked around the room. Everything looked the same as it had when I'd been there in the afternoon. The table was set with a series of white Nortaki china, crystal goblets, and a table runner across the middle. The runner was under the crystal bowl containing Esme's head. The last time I'd seen the bowl it had been empty. I avoided looking at the head and tried to concentrate on the details of the room. I'd never been to a crime scene so I didn't really know what I was looking for, but there didn't seem to be signs of a struggle. I looked behind Esme's body and saw a slight darkening of the brown walls where blood from Esme's neck had sprayed the surface. Other than the blood, the room looked pristine. Pristine if you didn't consider the trail of blood from the body to the head on the table. It looked like a set up for a horror flick or a bad joke. Only the acrid smell of expelled body fluids made the scene real.

Lauren wrapped her arms around her middle and bent forward, the remains of her fast food dinner spewing forth onto the floor. Holding her hair back with one hand, she spit vomit onto the hardwood floor. Her mouth hung open and spit dribbled from her lips. It seemed she couldn't catch her breath as she dropped to her hands and knees. She didn't seem to notice the chunks of her dinner under her hands.

"Oh my god, oh my god," she said. Sucking in a deep breath, she vomited again. This time she didn't try to pull her hair from her face.

I stood silent, stunned. I followed cheating spouses, did skip traces, took photographs of people committing insurance fraud, and I stood guard to protect people, but I wasn't a cop, and I'd never seen anything like this. Between Lauren's barfing, and Esme's decapitated head I didn't know how to keep myself from fainting. Finally, I looked up, which helped me swallow the bile building in the back of my throat, and concentrated on the ceiling for a moment.

Watching Lauren, and smelling the regurgitated fish filet, was too much. But I couldn't vomit. I had to get my head together. Call the police. But I couldn't move. I was the professional here, right? Oh, I so didn't want to be the professional. I wanted to go back to the car and have a do-over. Lauren started to stand up, and I regained my composure, trying to be the consummate professional.

"Don't touch anything. I'll call the police," I said.

She barely got herself into a sitting position on the floor rocking back and forth, whispering. I couldn't hear what she said. I leaned closer, and choked back my vomit when I smelled hers.

"What?" I said.

"Henry. Where is Henry?" She wiped the vomit from her hands onto her skirt.

I pulled my cell phone from my hip holster and dialed 911. I put the phone to my ear and listened. It seemed like an hour before the dispatcher answered.

"911, what's your emergency?"

"There's been a murder."

"Ma'am, are you okay?"

"Yes," I lied. "A woman was murdered, and we just got home and found her."

"Ma'am. What's your name?"

"Mimi Capurro. I'm here with the owner of the house. She isn't doing so well."

"Has she been injured?"

"No. She found the body. She's not handling it very well." I looked back at Lauren who was still rocking and mumbling.

"What's your location, ma'am?"

Why do they always ask that, when they know where you are? Then I remembered I was calling from my cell phone. I gave her the home's address.

"Okay, I have a car on the way. Is anyone else in the house with you?"

"I don't know. I'll go check."

I crept down the hallway, switching from the handset to my Bluetooth headset. I heard the dispatcher snap at me. "No, ma'am, don't go anywhere. The police will be there any minute. They'll look for anyone else in the house."

Knowing full well the killer could still be in the house, I didn't even know if we were safe, so I pulled my nine millimeter from my shoulder holster and climbed the stairs.

"Ma'am, are you there?" The dispatcher sounded more concerned and less confident now.

I didn't answer. I was trying to climb the stairs quietly, and I wasn't really listening to her.

"Ma'am. Stay put. The police will be there any minute. Ma'am?"

She sounded distraught now, so I felt compelled to say something. I whispered, "Call me Mimi, please. I can't stay put, I have to see if the husband is alive. I may be able to help him, if he's still alive. I'm okay, I have a gun."

Now that was the wrong thing to say. The dispatcher went on alert.

"Mimi, did you say you have a gun?"

"Don't worry. I'm a private detective. I'm licensed." Not that I'd ever had to shoot anyone before. But I could if I had to, I was sure of it.

"Please Mimi, stop where you are. I need you to stay put until the police arrive." I'm pretty sure she was screaming at me, but I'd blocked her out.

I climbed the rest of the stairs and plastered my back against the wall, creeping along until I reached what I hoped was the bathroom door. Reaching across the door and turning the handle, I pushed the door open and flipped on the light, pointing my gun in front of me. The room was empty. I breathed deep, grabbed a hand towel from the counter and headed to the next room.

Again I led with my weapon. With the hand towel in my free hand, I twisted the doorknob and pushed the door open. I waited, and when no one jumped out at me I crept into the room. I thought I could see a body on the bed. This had to be Henry. I flipped the light on. If he was dead, he wouldn't care. If he was asleep and I woke him, I didn't care. He didn't stir.

Henry lay on his back, the bed still made. He was fully dressed, in a blue pinpoint cotton shirt with black slacks, and a black belt, his shoes next to the bed. I looked closer, but saw no movement in his chest. Shit,

shit, shit. I didn't want to touch a dead body. Wrist or neck? I cringed and put my fingers to his throat.

There was a pulse, a good pulse. Damn, he slept the sleep of the dead. I shook him. No response. At least he was alive. He was alive and safe, but he creeped me out, so I scooted out the door and on to the next room.

I opened doors, flipped on lights and did a quick check of the remaining rooms on the second floor. All were lavishly decorated, and all were empty.

At the bottom of the stairs I turned right and entered what appeared to be a formal living room. Like the rest of the house it looked like a photo spread from *Architectural Digest*. Robin's egg blue on adobe walls, rose chintz fabric on the sofa and chairs, and an oriental rug that had to be custom made for the space. I'd never seen a rug so large. All of the seating was positioned on the rug, with mahogany cabinets lining the walls. I saw a door on the far side of the room and headed for it.

The door led to the kitchen, which looked like it occupied the entire length of the back of the house. The floors were slate, topped by oak cabinets with dark cement countertops. It was spotless. The only thing that didn't look right was the back door. The door was Dutch, solid on the bottom, with a paned window on top, and the top didn't look like it was fully closed. I started toward it, but stopped. I thought I heard a car. Amateur detective hour was over.

Before I got to the dining room, the police arrived. I heard the tires on the gravel drive. I went to the door, which was still open, with my hands in the air. I didn't want to get shot, and I wasn't sure if they'd think I was the intruder.

"I'm the one who called," I said. "I'm Mimi Capurro."

To my relief, they didn't have any weapons readied as they exited their patrol car. They left the headlights on, making the two officers mere silhouettes in the night. But as they climbed the steps of the porch, they became Kevlar-wearing, pistol-packing, grim-faced policemen.

Both men were Latino, and both were about an inch shorter than me. But what they had in bulk made up for the height deficit. One of the officers stepped ahead of the other. These guys were young. Baby faced twenty-somethings with rookie attitudes. They approached with stern expressions.

"I'm Officer Martinez," one of them said. He stood with his thumbs in his belt.

I stood in place and shivered as a chill of realization ran down my spine. This was not a dream.

"Are you okay, ma'am?" Martinez's expression softened.

"I'm fine, considering." Even though I wasn't.

I'd been blocking out the image of Esme's head while I was creeping about the house, and pretending that I wasn't scared to death the killer was going to spring out at me. But now the adrenaline rush was wearing off and I was shaking.

I heard the dispatcher in my ear. "Okay, I'm going to disconnect now."

I'd forgotten about her. "Thanks," I said, and disconnected.

I opened the door wider, and the cops walked in.

"Who's been here?"

"Just me, and Lauren Silke, the home's owner. Her husband is out cold in the bedroom upstairs."

"You were upstairs when the murder occurred?" The second officer, who didn't identify himself, asked.

"No, I went up there to see if Lauren's husband was home. And he is, he's in the master bedroom."

Martinez pushed past me. "Ma'am, I need you to stay put. Did you touch anything when you went snooping?"

Snooping? I resented the way he implied I was a busybody. I thought about it. "The front door. I used a hand towel to open the bedrooms upstairs. I had to check on Lauren's husband." I couldn't believe I was defending myself.

Lauren's moaning became louder and echoed toward the foyer. I turned and ran toward her.

Lauren still sat where I left her. "Oh God, what am I going to do?" Lauren murmured.

I turned my head and took a deep breath, then leaned close. "I checked on Henry. He's okay."

She turned on me. "Then where is he?"

I recoiled. "He's passed out in your bedroom."

"Didn't you wake him up?" She was whining now.

"I tried. He won't wake up," I said. I accidentally inhaled, smelling the acid on her breath. I backed away.

Turning to the officers, I said. "She's a little shocked."

And so were they. Both stood still, staring at the table, or more specifically, Esme's head. The unidentified officer said, "Fuck!"

Officer Martinez spoke into his radio.

Involuntarily, I followed their gaze. For the first time, I saw the weapon. A sword, with a swath of blood, lay on the chair near Esme's head.

Two more cops arrived. The homicide unit. The woman, Natalie Simon, I knew from other business dealings. She had blonde hair brushed into a ponytail with dark roots showing, no makeup, gray slacks, and a T-shirt. She was cute, roots and all, the kind of cute which ages well. The male detective was, holy testosterone, one of the last people I ever expected to see wearing a badge.

CHAPTER 3

I couldn't have imagined I'd ever see the man in front of me again. Nick Christianson, wow, a blast from the past. I didn't know if I wanted him to be in my present.

Nick's clean smell took me away from the murder scene and back to my college days. He always had a freshly showered smell, not weighed down by cologne. I love cologne on men, but in subtle amounts, and Nick didn't even need that.

He'd been my on-again and off-again lover in college. He'd come from Ohio to play football for the junior college, and we'd turned to each other when our respective relationships went to hell. We talked, had sex (what I thought was great sex back then), and went on our merry way. We even ended up at the same university, San Jose State, where Nick was a star defensive back, and I was nobody after the school cancelled their track program. There went my scholarship. But Nick still had his.

I thought he was the most handsome guy I'd ever seen. A six-three Adonis in his football uniform. His olive skin and wavy black hair made his blue-grey eyes sizzle. And that wasn't the only thing sizzling. He claimed his heritage to be Greek and Irish. Talk about hot. In the beginning I always wondered why he was with me, this guy who had every girl in the school ready to lift her skirts, was with me. At San Jose State, I didn't have to wonder anymore, since he never spoke to me.

I studied Human Performance, with an emphasis on prevention and care of athletic injuries, so I saw him almost every day during football season and spring training. He didn't ignore me as much as avoid me. I missed our talks. I knew more about him than anyone, and then I didn't know him at all.

Looking at Nick now, he'd changed very little. He looked older; naturally, he'd had a rough fifteen years. From college, he'd gone on to play for two different NFL teams. After six years with the NFL, he'd violated their drug and alcohol policies, and they booted him. Can we say stupid? After that, I'd lost track of him. Not that I was keeping track exactly, but his name and face had been in the sports section almost daily while he tried to fight the charges.

I'd had a long day, and with the adrenaline hangover ensuing, I felt nauseated. If I had to see Nick again, I wanted to look my very best. Between the head on the table and Nick standing in front of me after all these years, I'd reached my daily limit. I turned and barfed into the potted palm. I hardly even noticed the liquid that had splattered onto the floor and my pants. My stomach roiled again before I even lifted my head.

Nick turned to his partner. "Natalie, get her out of here, she's fucking up my crime scene."

Natalie put her arm around my waist and walked me out to the porch. "That was a pretty gruesome scene in there. Are you alright?"

"Other than embarrassed, I'm fine," I said. Puking always made me sweat and I felt wet, sticky, and gross. I pushed away from Natalie.

She handed me a piece of Big Red chewing gum.

"Thanks." I popped it in my mouth, and chewed the taste of puke away.

"Why don't you sit out here," she said, as we headed to the porch.

"No, I want to stay. Lauren Silke is my client."

"Client?" Natalie said.

"Yeah, I'm her bodyguard for the next week. She's had some threats and an altercation, so she hired me as a bodyguard for her book tour."

"We'll have to talk more about this. I'm going back in," Natalie said. She helped me onto the wicker rocker on the porch.

"I'm better, I'll come too." I pushed myself up. Not so smart of me. I sat back down.

"I really don't want you back in the house," Natalie said.

"I don't really want to go back, but I need to stay with Lauren. I won't touch anything."

"How about just loitering around the doorway?"

I nodded. "Hey," I said as she turned to go. "Where's Oliver?"

Oliver Bernardi, her usual partner, was as old as dirt, and had likely retired.

"He took his wife to the Bahamas. Can you believe it?"

I shook my head. I couldn't imagine Oliver in anything but a polyester suit and fat tie. The thought of him on the beach with his wife made me smile. Or maybe it wasn't actually the thought of Oliver, but the thought of Nick in Oliver's place.

"So I get stuck breaking in the new guy." She rolled her eyes toward the house.

"New guy, huh?" Feigning ignorance is my forte.

"Just transferred from SFPD. Burglary/Homicide. He's cute, but he's an asshole."

Didn't I know it? "I didn't really notice," I lied.

"Knows it all, and then some. Hey, I gotta get back inside. Stay by the door, okay?"

Being nosy, I slowly stood up, waited for the dizziness to subside, and walked over to the front door and leaned against the door jamb.

"Ms. Silke, can you stand up?" It sounded like Martinez.

"Get her up and outside," Nick said. He sounded pissed, and not in the mood to deal with Lauren's moaning.

"I'll help," Natalie said.

Martinez and Natalie, on either side of Lauren, came toward me. Lauren sagged between them, making it an effort to move. They deposited her on a bench next to the rocker.

"Talk to her while I check the rest of the house," Nick said to Natalie.

"Her husband is asleep upstairs. Third door on the right," I offered from my position by the door.

"We've got it from here. We'll question you later if needed." Nick's words were clipped.

In all this, our driver had remained in his car. Weird. He was still here, and he never got out to see what was going on? Feeling better I trotted down the stairs to talk to him.

"Hey, you okay in there?" I tapped on the window.

He startled awake and rolled down the window.

"You okay?" I asked again.

He rubbed his eyes and yawned, then said, "Cops told me to stay in the car, so I did."

He was a better man than me. I would've been in the house, right behind them. I told him to head home. I'd get a ride from the cops. Or maybe I'd stay. Hell, I had no idea what would happen next. He got out and handed me my bag and briefcase. I thanked him, and he drove off.

I went back up to the porch and heard Lauren speaking slightly more coherently.

"We just got back from San Francisco. She was there. Like that. She was there," Lauren stammered. Sweat soaked her hair, and rolled down her forehead.

"Where's your husband?" Natalie said.

"Upstairs?" She looked up at me. "You went to get him. Where is he?"

I stood on the top step, not daring to come any closer. "I told you, he's out cold. Does he always sleep so soundly?"

"He usually doesn't sleep much at all," Lauren said.

The uniformed officers came out onto the porch, Henry staggering between them. He was awake, but barely. They placed him on the rocker next to Lauren.

Lauren leaned forward. "Henry, what did you take?"

Henry didn't answer.

She looked at me. "This is all my fault."

"What makes you say that?" Natalie said.

"What?" Lauren asked.

"How is this your fault?" Natalie said. She squatted down in front of Lauren.

"The scene. In the dining room. It's staged just like a scene from my newest novel, Prey. Did you see the hair? Esme had a shoulder length bob. That haircut is Sophie's. They even cut her hair."

Now that she'd said it, I remembered. Sophie has a pixie cut, short and choppy, because she cuts it herself. This was getting freakier by the second.

"Sophie?" Natalie asked.

"I write a series about a thousand-year-old vampire named Lawrence who is very powerful. He has slaves and minions, and even groupies. And then there's Sophie, who is a vampire slayer." Lauren paused and swallowed.

"Abel, Lawrence's main follower, is jealous of Sophie, and wants her gone. When he can't get rid of her, he decides to kill her." Lauren took a deep breath and continued, "Anyway, in the scene, Abel has Sophie tied to a chair. He's going to decapitate her and leave her for Lawrence to find. He pulls his sword, but before he can kill Sophie, Lawrence approaches from behind and swings his own sword. He picks Abel's head up and places it in a bowl on the table, then pushes the body against the wall. Abel's body lands in a chair and blood spatters everywhere, awakening the other vampires in the house. He unties Sophie and they leave Abel there, oozing blood for the other lesser vampires to feed on."

Since I had read all of Lauren's books, I could easily visualize this scene. Only in my head it was more gruesome because I was seeing Esme, not Abel.

"Somebody killed Esme because of me. Whoever did this has read my latest book."

"So that narrows it down to..." Natalie was clearly frustrated.

"How many people have read it?" I asked.

"With advance readers' copies, and the books in the stores ready to distribute, Esme and whoever she shared the book with, it could be hundreds of people."

Natalie said, "Not hundreds of thousands?"

I explained. "The book just hit shelves today. That wouldn't leave much time to read the book, plan the murder, and then find out where Lauren lives."

"So whoever knows the scene had to have read the book before the release." Natalie chewed on the information.

Lauren slammed her hand on the bench. "Henry, where were you? How did this happen?"

Henry just sat in the rocker and stared forward. I was pretty sure he didn't even blink when Lauren slammed her hand down.

"We'll find who did this," Natalie promised.

"Mimi, what am I going to do?" Lauren whined.

"We are going to have the CSU team go over your house tonight. Is there a place you can stay?" Natalie said.

I could almost see Lauren's brain trying to focus on the question. "We'll stay in a hotel. But I'm not going back in that house. I'll go shopping tomorrow and get some new clothes."

Natalie stood. "As soon as the CSU guys are done, I'll get some clothes for you. Let us know where you are staying, and we'll send an officer over." She handed Lauren a business card.

"I'm in no condition to drive." She looked to the driveway. "Did my driver leave?"

"I'll call you a taxi," I said.

"No, I'll call the service and they'll send another car. But Mimi, I do need you to get started on this right away."

"On what?"

"You have to find out who did this. I have to know who did this to my Esme. And, oh God, we have to tell her mom." Lauren began sobbing. She dropped her head in her hands and wailed.

"Lauren, I'm protecting you on your tour. This is a police investigation. The police will notify the next of kin." I said, not wanting any part of a murder investigation.

"You don't understand. I can't finish the book tour. I'll be a wreck," Lauren whimpered through her hands.

Nick stepped onto the porch. "I just have a few questions for you, then the officers here can take you to a hotel. But I think it's best you keep to your planned schedule. As long as we can get in touch with you if we need to."

Lauren looked up toward Nick, "Excuse me?"

"Keep your normal schedule. If we need you we'll call you," Nick stated casually as if this weren't a murder, but something as minor as a broken finger.

"Are you kidding me?" Lauren spat.

"No. It will keep the publicity down, and help us do our job with less interference."

Looking puzzled, Lauren said, "Okay."

"Martinez? Can you please take Mr. and Mrs. Silke to whatever hotel they'd like to stay at for the night?"

Martinez and his partner helped Lauren and Henry to the patrol car. Bet they weren't looking forward to that drive, because Lauren had to smell just peachy.

I waited until they were loaded up and pulling out of the driveway before I said anything. Once the car was out of sight I said, "Um, I'll need a ride too."

Nick looked at me with what could have been a scowl, or possibly gas.

CHAPTER 4

"I had no idea fiction readers where such fanatics," Charles said.

"I didn't either."

"So do you think a fan killed that cute little Esme?" Charles seemed concerned.

"I have no idea. I can't imagine even the biggest lunatic would kill someone over a work of fiction." But then again…

"Well, that one lady was lunatic enough to punch out Lauren. Which was good because we got a much needed client, but bad because look where we are now."

We were sitting at the 1950s Formica dining table in the breakfast nook of Gotcha's kitchen. Charles wore khaki Dockers, with monochrome argyle socks and leather tasseled loafers. The temperature was only supposed to be sixty-five, so he wore a pale blue rugby shirt. He crossed his ankles and rested them on the table.

Gemma had apparently just dragged herself out of bed when I'd called her into work. She arrived wearing a pink long john shirt, and surgical scrub bottoms. It was entirely too cold for the flip-flops she had on her feet. Gemma's one of my junior detectives, and she doesn't have a P.I. license because the state of California requires an inordinate amount of hours under supervision before you can apply.

"Give me all the gory details," Gemma said. Her golden brown, shoulder-length curls bobbed as she hopped up to sit on the kitchen counter.

I told her about walking in and seeing Esme's head on the table and how her body was posed, giving all the details, except the part about Nick Christianson.

"Esme seemed like such a happy girl. Even when Lauren snapped at her, she took it in stride. I can't imagine anyone would want to hurt her. But what did I know, I'd only met the girl twice."

"I'm curious, does seeing her like that change the way you see her in your mind?" Gemma said.

Good question. I know most people like closure. You know, open casket, to be sure the person is really dead. I've always been a closed casket kind of girl. I wanted to remember the person as they were in life. I avoid funerals as much as possible. Until the last couple of years, I'd been pretty good at it. I'd only been to my fifth grade teacher's and my grandmother's funerals. When Dominic died, I didn't have to worry about what I'd see. They never found his body.

Dominic and I had been married a little more than a year when his plane went down on a charter flight to Idaho. He'd been with one of his clients, and Dominic, the client, and the pilot all died. No bodies were recovered. A part of me died with Dominic, and it's been a long road back.

Seeing Esme must've brought those thoughts back. I dreamed of Dominic last night for the first time over a year.

"Sort of. I have to make an effort to see the live Esme," I said.

"I don't think I'd be able to get the decapitated head out of my mind," Gemma said around a piece of cinnamon toast.

"I'll bet her head was flying before she even knew the sword had sliced her," Charles said. He swiped his arms in front of him, as if he held the sword.

"You are a sick puppy," Gemma said. She hopped off the counter and poured herself a cup of coffee.

"Hey, top me off," I said.

Gemma brought the pot over and topped off my cup. Then she eased toward Charles and brushed her breast on his shoulder as she filled his cup. Charles flinched, putting his hands up to fend her off. Gemma laughed.

Gemma, with her tanned athletic body, had never met a man who didn't want her, until Charles. She was sure she could convert him, if only he would accept her advances. Her lifetime goal was to get Charles to have sex with her, I was sure of it. I'd bet she got tired of the challenge before he gave in.

Gemma creeped him out. He hated when she touched him, much less rubbed her body parts against him. I kept telling him to reciprocate, and she'd give up. Maybe even suggest a threesome with the love of Charles's life. Charles wanted no part of it. The whole scene was fun to watch most days, but irritating on mornings like this.

"Gemma, get off him," I snapped.

She rolled her eyes and put the coffee pot back on the burner.

"So what happens now?" Gemma said.

"You, my dear, get to fly to Los Angeles, and then spend the next several days with the lovely Ms. Silke," Charles said.

"Yup," I said.

"By lovely, you mean she's a real pain in the ass," Gemma said.

Charles and I smiled.

"No, but she'll be really freaked and probably very jumpy. Just be aware."

Bored with Gemma, Charles turned to me. "The cops are bringing Esme's laptop over this morning. The one she used at work."

"Oh?"

"Just so happens, I'm the best computer forensics agent around."

I stuck my finger down my throat and lurched forward.

"Whatever. They are backed up, and I always take their overflow. You want me to process it here, or at the school?" Charles said.

Charles was a graduate of the Naval Postgraduate School in Monterey. Being in good standing, he had access to all of their computer forensics equipment. I had a fair amount of money invested in my own equipment, so I'd just as soon have Charles do the work in house.

"Do it here. I want to know what's going on, even if I'm not making money on the deal."

Charles grinned. He made a lot of money on the side. The man was a computer genius. Gemma, Jackie, and I were barely able to download songs onto our iPods, so we were completely dependent on Charles and he knew it. He also loved it.

"I thought you'd say that. Some cop is going to drop it off. Hopefully soon."

"Guess I'd better head home and get packed. Anything I need to know before I leave," Gemma said.

"Square your cases with Jackie," I said. Jackie's forte is stakeouts, but she's also a great decoy.

"I don't have much going on. I just finished with finals, so I've only been serving papers."

Gemma was taking criminology, forensics, and investigative techniques classes. She still had a lot of hours of actual work time to put in before being eligible for her P.I. license. Now that school was out, I'd have her work some skip traces, and a lot of GPS tracking. She was too young and too impatient for stakeouts. She had eyes behind her head when she was working, so Gemma was the perfect bodyguard. She had a black belt in Tae Kwan Do, so she had plenty of practice both in offensive and defensive maneuvers. Lauren would be in good hands.

"Have eyes behind your head, just like in all protection jobs," I said.

"Yes, Momma Mimi," Gemma said sarcastically. Everyone who worked for me was a smart ass. It's probably why I hired them.

"Most of Lauren's fans are normal. I don't know if you've ever been to a book signing, but they attract all walks of life. Be suspicious of everyone."

"That's a given," Gemma said.

"Why ask if you know it all already?"

"I like to make you feel important," Gemma said.

Charles dropped his feet off the table and laughed.

"Shut up," I said to Charles, and then I threw a dish towel at Gemma.

"That was a good one Gemma," Charles said, still laughing.

Gemma grabbed the towel and threw it at Charles. "It wasn't that funny."

Charles sobered. "A girl just got her head lopped off, and we're here joking over morning coffee."

"Nothing we can do about it now. She's dead," Gemma said.

"Only thing we can do is find the killer," I said.

The atmosphere cooled considerably.

"I'm going home and pack," Gemma said.

"I gave Lauren's publicist your home address. The car will meet you at your house."

"Sweet. My parents will be excited to see their daughter climb into a limo."

"It's not a limo, it's a town car," Charles said, doing his best to burst Gemma's bubble.

"Oh, whatever," Gemma said.

"Don't let Lauren out of your sight," I said.

"So I go to the bathroom with her, too?"

"Yes, even if you're in the hotel room. You check before she goes."

"Got it. See ya." Gemma turned to leave.

When she grabbed the handle on the back door of the kitchen, a man came up the steps. Gemma opened the door, holding the door with her left hand and the wall with her right, effectively blocking the entrance. No one ever came to the back door.

"Can I help you?" Gemma said.

"Is Charles Parks around?"

"Oh, yeah, a hot guy, I should have known you'd be looking for Charles," Gemma said.

"I need him to sign for a computer I'm dropping off," he said.

"Jesus Christ, Gemma, let him in," I said.

Gemma stepped away from the door, and I wished I could take back my words. Nick Christianson stepped into the kitchen.

"What are you doing here?" Nick said.

"I own this place," I said. My voice could've iced my coffee.

He looked past me. "Charles?"

Charles was struck dumb. He scanned Nick from crotch to peepers.

I would never admit it aloud, but Nick looked good. He wore grey slacks with polished black shoes and a grey v-neck sweater that complimented his eyes. Nick's wavy black hair looked windblown, or maybe just finger brushed. I'd bet Charles had mentally run his fingers through it already.

Charles stood, and stepped very close to Nick when they shook hands. Charles did the "I can grip your hand harder than you can grip mine" squeeze. Men.

"You are?" Charles said.

"Detective Nick Christianson."

"Well, detective, do you have the computer, or is this a social call?" I said.

Nick looked at me like he just barely remembered I was in the room. I stood and pushed between Nick and Charles. I felt a jolt as my skin touched Nick's.

He backed up. "The computer's right here." He raised the laptop case with his left hand. Charles took it.

"Thanks, we'll get right on it," I said.

"We? I'm releasing custody of the computer to Charles," Nick said.

"That's what she meant. I'll get right on it," Charles said.

Nick had Charles sign papers for chain of custody. Charles grazed Nick's arm as he handed the papers back.

"Do I call you or your lieutenant when I have the report written?" Charles said.

Nick handed him a business card. "My cell number is on the back. Natalie and I are headed over to Santa Cruz to talk to the victim's mother, so leave a message if I don't answer."

"You're going to talk to Esme's mom? Does she know yet?" I said.

"She doesn't know anything yet. We're going to tell her about her daughter's death without going into the gruesome details if possible," Nick said.

"Natalie is really good with families," I said.

"So I've heard," Nick said. He turned to leave.

A small part of me was sad to see him go. I didn't keep in touch with many people from college. It felt good to see him, but the tension between us was palpable.

"So Mimi, do you have some time tonight?" Nick asked.

Goddamn it if my heart didn't skip a beat. "For what?"

"I'd like to talk to you about the murder. We didn't get a decent interview last night."

"Not tonight. I'm having dinner at my mom's."

Nick's eyes flickered. He had liked my mom, and she liked him. God knows how, but he had charmed my mother. She had invited him for dinner regularly when we were still in junior college. I'd come home and Nick would be sitting at the kitchen table while my mom cooked fried chicken and mashed potatoes. I almost mentioned we were having chicken tonight.

"Do you think maybe you can skip the dinner?" Nick said.

"Nope."

I could, but it wasn't worth the wrath I'd get from Mom. Not that we didn't speak to each other almost daily. I just didn't want to disappoint my mom by cancelling our dinner plans.

"Nope?" Nick said, his tone mocking.

"Lunch tomorrow," I said. I didn't want to do that either, but I had to give an official statement. Lunch was better than the cop shop.

"Lunch is good. Georgio's?" Nick said.

For an asshole, he had a good memory. Georgio's is my favorite restaurant. I have other favorites, but Georgio's is the best in town, and it's been around forever. I felt a tug at my memory. Nick and I had only enough money to split meals back in the day. It would be weird to have a lunch I could actually afford, with Nick.

"Georgio's it is," I said. "Eleven, so we beat the lunch crowd."

"How about one, after the crowd?" Nick said.

"Fine."

And he walked out the door.

"What's with you two?" Charles said.

"We used to be friends," I said. I didn't intend to elaborate, so I poured myself more coffee and headed to my office.

Charles followed, like a gossipy school girl. "Oh, no. There's more to it than that. Spill."

I had no intention of spilling anything, except maybe my coffee. I sat at my desk, and Lola put her head in my lap. I scrubbed her behind the ears, then wrapped my fingers around her snout and kissed her on the lips. "Hello, baby." I let her settle her chin on my lap, and opened my laptop to type up my notes from the murder scene.

Charles patted Lola on the head. "Come to papa," he said. Lola, the disloyal floozy, sauntered over to rest her chin on Charles's knee as he sat on the edge of my desk.

"Get off." I shoved him with my foot.

Charles maintained his position on the desk. "You've slept with him."

I thought for a minute. No, technically I had never slept with him. I could answer in all honesty. "No."

"Whatever. You've had sex with him." He paused. "Wow, it must have been a long time ago."

"Another lifetime," I murmured.

"Huh?" Charles said.

"Don't you have a computer to crack?" I said. I started typing.

Charles stood. "This isn't the end of it. If I have to, I'll ask Nick."

I wanted to protest, but it would only fuel his curiosity. I said, "You have his number."

CHAPTER 5

After a long day, I was ready to have someone else cook for me. Not that I cooked on any other days.

My mom lived in an apartment on the north side of town. She moved there soon after the divorce. My dad, succumbing to a mid-life crisis at age thirty-six, maxed out the equity on our home and started an electronics store. About a year after opening the business, he took medical leave from his real job (a firefighter), closed the doors on his business, bought a Corvette, and drove to Florida. Other than the divorce papers and child support payments (which ended a long time ago), no one has heard from him.

My mom had painted, re-carpeted, bug bombed, and air-freshened our house to get the smell of my dad and his cigarettes out. In the end, she sold it, invested the profits into a retirement fund, and was enjoying apartment life.

I lived with Mom until I left for college. I have to agree, no plumbers to pay, no lawn to mow, just keep the place clean. It wasn't too bad for a couple of single girls.

I loved coming back to the apartment. Mom had painted the kitchen pale yellow to brighten the already bright room. We sat in the dining area, looking out at the street from the sliding glass doors. This was where most everyone entered and left the apartment. Otherwise, they had to go to the main entrance, ring the buzzer, and walk half a block to get to the front door.

My mom started every morning by vacuuming the apartment, much the same as she'd done in our house. With her being a neat freak, I didn't have to clean anything but my bedroom. I loved that.

I'm not sure if my mom was born obsessive/compulsive about cleaning and grooming, or if my dad made her that way. I don't think I'd ever seen my mom without her makeup and hair done before the divorce. Now she wore minimal makeup on her olive skin, and kept her black hair short, so she didn't have to make weekly salon appointments.

I sat and watched the traffic go by while my mom finished shaking the ingredients for her secret fried chicken recipe. Shake 'N' Bake could learn a thing or two from my mom.

"Talk to Ann lately?" I said.

"She's coming home next month."

My sister, Ann, and her family had moved to Arizona five years ago. Her husband owned a construction company, and had wanted to take advantage of the influx of snowbirds moving to Lake Havasu City, Arizona. He'd done the right thing, they were getting rich. Ann was two years older than me and had two darling kids, Ashley, fourteen, and Ben, eight. Better than my hellion sister deserved. She'd been a handful as a teen, and now she was a Martha Stewart clone.

"Too hot to work in July, I guess." I went to the kitchen and pulled the chicken from the refrigerator.

"Speaking of hot, remember Nick Christianson? I saw him at the grocery store last week," she said.

I dropped the pan of chicken on the floor. "Shit."

"Mimi, watch your mouth."

"Whatever." She'd said a lot worse in her time. I picked up the pan. Only one piece of chicken landed on the floor.

"Did you hear me? Nick. You remember Nick?"

I composed myself, and began dredging the chicken in mom's flour mixture. "Think I could ever forget Nick?"

"I know he was a pompous ass, but he was a cute pompous ass."

I laughed.

The grease was good and hot, and I placed several pieces of chicken in the skillet. As it sizzled, I said, "I saw him last night."

"Last night?" My mom stopped fussing with the chicken.

"At a crime scene."

"A crime scene? What were you doing at a crime scene?" Mom was freaked.

"You really don't want to know."

"Oh, yes I do," she snapped.

"It wasn't because of me." I got defensive.

"Then why were you there?"

I told her about Lauren Silke and the book tour, and then gently, without so much detail, about Esme.

She stood silent and still. "I really don't think this PI thing is such a good idea."

How many times had I heard that one? "I wasn't in danger."

"How do you know that?" She flipped a piece of chicken and it splattered grease. "Damn it."

"The crime wasn't about me. It was about Lauren, or Esme, or vampires. Hell, I don't know, but it wasn't about me." This wasn't helping her calm down.

"Some day it will be about you. And I'll have to come identify your body." Tears welled in her eyes.

"Not this again," I said. "Besides, on top of the dead body, it wasn't pleasant to see Nick in that situation. I had barfed and everything."

"I'd think just looking at Nick would be pleasant. He's aged very well." She'd loosened up at the thought of Nick.

Good God, Mom, take a cold shower already. But at least she wasn't bitching at me about my job.

"Yes, he has." I admitted. "But Mom, the past is the past. Besides, he's probably married."

"Nope," she said. She rolled the chicken over, to brown it evenly. "I asked. He never did marry."

I took a bottle of chardonnay from the refrigerator, pulled the cork and drank straight from the bottle. I sighed. "It's funny, I never expected to see his face again. I'd almost forgotten about him."

"Stop that." She swiped the bottle from me and poured the wine into a glass. "We never forget the ones who broke our hearts."

"He didn't break my heart. We were friends."

"Friends with benefits."

"Mom!"

"Mimi, I'm not stupid. I know you had sex with that boy. Hell, if I was young enough, I'd have had sex with him. He oozed sex appeal, and he still does."

My mom and I were only twenty years apart, and since she'd been single for much of my teenage and adult life, we talked. Well, I talked. I didn't want to know anything about my mother's sex life. Eeeewwww! Even now that I'm an adult, I can't even think about the subject. And my mom with a much younger man? Let's not go there.

"That was another lifetime," I said.

I put the fried chicken on a plate while my mom made gravy from the drippings and flour. And when I pulled the bowl of mashed potatoes from the oven, I could smell the butter she'd mixed in. Nothing was better than fried chicken and mashed potatoes with my mom.

We ate the chicken with our fingers, and nearly licked the plates. I missed nights with my mom. But she had a steady boyfriend now, and it looked serious. I broached the subject while we ate our Jell-O pudding dessert.

"So, speaking of sexy. How's Luke?"

My mom blushed. "He's wonderful."

They'd been dating for more than a year and still acted like they'd just met. They held hands and touched each other constantly. If I wasn't so happy for my mom I'd be embarrassed. Now my sister, on the other hand hated change, and Luke was change, so she hated him.

If my mom missed her weekly call to Ann, it was Luke's fault. Actually, anything that took attention away from Ann was suddenly Luke's fault. But Luke was good for Mom, and I loved him for that.

"Why isn't he eating with us?"

"Oh, he thought we needed the girl time. He's coming over later."

"When are you two going to move in together?" I prodded.

"When are you going to go out on a date?" she retorted.

"Fine." I gave up, not wanting to have this discussion.

"I have Nick's card. Maybe I'll invite him to dinner. Won't he just die when he comes back here, after all these years?"

I nearly spit Jell-O pudding all over my mom's floor.

By the time I started home, the fog had rolled in on an otherwise sunny day. I punched buttons on my cell phone until I had it tuned to Pandora Radio, then I plugged the headset into the stereo of my Land Rover

Discovery. John Mayer radio serenaded me all the way home.

The best thing about dinner with Mom, other than the company, was leftovers. She always made too much and sent me home with gobs of food. Lola danced around at my feet as I put the Gladware containers in the refrigerator. She was hoping for a late night snack later. That wasn't happening.

I let Lola out in the small fenced yard behind my house and got in the shower. For a couple of hours I hadn't thought about vampires, Esme, or death, but now I was overwhelmed by it. I wish I hadn't met Esme before the murder. I kept thinking of the potential she'd never achieve. And in death, I'd probably learn more about her than I ever would have if she were still alive.

I hadn't heard from Lauren or Henry since last night. I hoped they'd gotten settled in the hotel before Lauren had to catch her plane.

I put my head under the showerhead and let the water engulf me. I didn't know anything, and the cops weren't going to share. The cops. Nick. I didn't think anyone could get under my skin after Dominic died, but suddenly there was Nick.

And my mom hadn't mentioned Nick in fifteen years, then whammy, she brings up his name. Surprisingly, I hadn't choked on my food.

I forced myself out of the shower when the water turned cold. I dried off and dressed in an old T-shirt. When I took the towel off my wet hair, I could see a good half inch of roots. The roots didn't bother me so much as the grey. I didn't want to have grey roots when I had lunch with Nick. I wanted to look my very best. Aren't you supposed to color your hair before you wash it? So what, I was going to color my roots.

I just happened to have a box of medium brown hair color stashed in my medicine cabinet. I blow dried the hair near my scalp only. It'd take another half hour to blow dry all of my hair, only to get it all wet again when I rinsed and conditioned. I applied the color, being careful to keep the goop only on the roots. I looked in the mirror. The hair near my scalp stuck straight out for about an inch, the rest hung like mangled spaghetti. I could just see Nick knocking on my door about now. I had to laugh.

When I let Lola in she sniffed the air, trotted past me to her bed in the living room, and shoved her head under her blanket. I had to agree, I did stink.

I sat in the kitchen and tried to read Lauren's latest novel, Prey. I was careful not to rumple the dust jacket or crease any pages, as this was an autographed copy. With each page Esme's corpse became more and more vivid, and I hadn't even gotten to the slaying scene. It was the first time I'd ever put down one of Lauren's books voluntarily. Maybe I'd do some cleaning instead.

I have a small, 700-square-foot house, which is too big for me, and I have a hard time keeping up with the cleaning. I looked at the overflowing laundry hamper and decided to stuff the clothes inside rather than start a load. Besides, I'd used up all the hot water with my shower, and I needed some to rinse my hair. For once, I wished a part of my mom would rub off on me.

Instead of cleaning, I tried to think of things I could do to get ready for tomorrow. I needed to get started on the investigation. I'd see who Nick had talked to and interviewed, and then I'd try to talk to them too.

Then it hit me: look up Lauren's website. I set the timer on the stove so I'd remember to wash out the coloring. I didn't want to lose track of time, fry my hair, and be bald in the morning.

I did a Google search, and found the official website. It opened to a black page graced with a large image of the cover of her newest novel and smaller images of her previous novels below. She even offered an excerpt from Prey to entice the readers to want more. The designs on the earlier jacket covers were sexy. Each cover had a detailed close up of a woman. The images were artist's sketches, but they were so life-like. They also became gradually more erotic as the Sophie Nolan vampire series continued. The Prey cover suggested violence and sex, showing a woman's neck and chest. A corset barely covered the woman's nipples, and long dark hair draped along her neck, slightly covering a dripping wound.

She had all of the usual links, about the author, contact information, frequently asked questions, Twitter, Facebook, and a blog.

The timer buzzed just as I finished reading her author page. She had been vague, telling only a little more than the jacket covers of her book. Lauren was born and raised in Ringling, Oklahoma, and moved to Santa Cruz just before high school. She went to college at the University of California at Santa Cruz. She was always fascinated with ghost and vampire stories surrounding Santa Cruz. She loved to walk the beach at night and imagine vampires on the periphery. She has worn a cross on her neck since she was fifteen. Blah, blah, blah. Not all that interesting.

I tore my attention from the author page, rinsed and conditioned my hair, then planted myself back in the chair to read through her Facebook and Twitter feeds.

I didn't bother to dry my hair, since I knew I'd be up late, surfing Lauren's site. My hair would be dry by the time my head hit the pillow. I wanted to check posts and comments on her blog and Facebook. Maybe there was something there that might be linked to Esme's murder. Wow, Lauren had thousands of followers on Twitter and even more Facebook fans. I'd have to check out that Twitter thing someday.

I started with the blog, reading the posts and comments, looking for something out of place. She shared her progress on her latest novels, and gave hints as to what her new series would entail. Her imagined world, in which Sophie lived, was very real to her.

There was one very long rant, which seemed out of character for Lauren. In the rant, she chastised all the people who criticized her writing, and the world in which her characters lived. She wrote, "If you don't like it, then don't read it. But if you keep buying my books and reading them, then I must be doing something right." Okay, so I paraphrased. I looked at the date on the post. Two weeks ago.

In all fairness, if you aren't into sex and violence in your reading, then she's right, don't read her books. The Sophie Nolan series is very violent and erotic, and Lauren made no apologies. As well she shouldn't, since the book covers spoke volumes about the content.

I thought I'd get through the blog in a hurry, and then move on to Lauren's Facebook page, but there were thousands of comments to sift through. If I had any interest in becoming a writer, the site would have been interesting. Lauren presented a wealth of information about the publishing industry. She answered the emails in her blog, so others could comment, and ask more questions. I thought this time-consuming task was admirable. Then I wondered if maybe Esme was responsible for writing the blog and social media posts.

I began feeling like I was on a stakeout. In other words, absolutely nothing was leading me anywhere, and my mind started to wander, and I had to pee. But then a photo on Facebook caught my eye.

CHAPTER 6

I got to the office early the next morning and found Charles already at work, staring at the screen of the computer he was dissecting. I walked up behind him, taking small steps on my toes. I wanted to scare him. Lola made sure that didn't happen. She raced past me and pushed her cold, wet nose at Charles's arm.

He scrubbed her behind the ears without looking away from the screen. "Hello, my lovely."

"Hello," I said.

He looked up. "Oh, hey, good morning. Don't you look sharp?"

I'll admit I'd spent some extra time getting ready. I pulled my freshly colored hair into a high ponytail, and took extra care in applying my makeup. I wanted to wear my most form-fitting outfit, but since I had a few extra pounds gripping tightly to my ass, I chose a knee-grazing A-line dress in black, with large yellow rose cutouts. The top of the dress was fitted, so it showcased my boobs, and diverted attention from other parts.

I sat my ever-widening butt on the side table and put a sling-back black pump on Charles's chair. I leaned in to read the screen.

"What's the scoop?" I said.

"I just got started. I hacked into her Blackberry software. Look at this, she abbreviated everything."

I looked at the page. There were acronyms, symbols, and abbreviations for almost every entry.

"ITM BK w/ SO IHOP," Charles said.

"In the morning, breakfast with whoever SO is, at the IHOP pancake place," I said.

"Well, that was an easy one," Charles said. He scrolled down the page to another entry.

It read: MC Fri, br Sab swd.

"Not a clue," I said.

"Me either," Charles said.

"Maybe Henry would have an idea," I said.

"Or you could call Lauren," Charles offered.

"No. Just call Henry, and if he's not in, we can call Lauren."

"I figured you'd say that, so I called and left a message on his cell phone."

"You have his cell phone number?" I didn't even have it.

"I have everyone's number. I have Esme's address book from her Blackberry."

"Everyone's number?" I said. "You don't have her phone."

"I don't need it, she syncs everything with her laptop."

"Oh." Good to know.

"Just because I love you, I printed off all the contact information from her address book." He handed me a stack of papers. "Don't tell the detective. He'll be pissed I gave you the info first."

"Not a problem." Of course I wouldn't tell. He'd have the information soon enough. And it's not like I was jeopardizing his investigation by getting a jumpstart.

I flipped through the pages. She had every contact needed: Publishers, web designers, agents, writers, restaurants in nearly every metropolis and several smaller towns, hair salons, bookstores, coffee houses, and then just names. No wonder Lauren would miss Esme. It looked as if Esme knew everything, and then some about Lauren and her needs. Not that she wouldn't miss Esme as a person, and a friend. Right?

"Looks like I have some work ahead of me today."

"See you in a few days," Charles said.

"Huh?"

"When you get through that list." He pointed at the stack in my hands.

I needed coffee before I embarked upon this task.

"You want some coffee?"

"I've already been through a pot and a half. If I have anymore, they'll have to insert a catheter so I can get through this hard drive."

The visual rolled across my mind. I shuttered.

"Well, I'm making a pot if you change your mind."

"I'm good." Charles said, absentmindedly as he stared at his computer screen.

"Hey, if you get a chance today, take a look at Lauren's Facebook page and see if any of the pictures catch your eye."

Charles looked up. "Because?"

"I don't know, there's just some weird stuff with people dressed as vampires. I swear one of the people is Esme."

I went to the kitchen and started a pot of vanilla flavored coffee. While the pot brewed, I debated changing my clothes before lunch. Was a skin-tight bodice and strappy shoulders the impression I wanted to make? Hell, yeah! Even with the few extra pounds (thank God they gripped my hips and thighs, which could easily be disguised) I looked good in this dress. Four-inch black heels helped finish the look. I poured fat-free half and half into my cup with a dash of sweetener, then pulled the coffee pot from the maker before the pot was full and filled my cup.

In my office, I sipped from my cup as I went through the pages of contacts, crossing off out-of-town restaurants, bookstores, coffee houses, vintage clothing boutiques, office supply stores, publishers (other than Newton Publishing, Lauren's publisher), and agents.

I kicked my shoes off under the desk, which was Lola's cue to get up from her bed, track the enemy and kill it. She crept up to my shoe, moved in and snatched it. When she had it in her mouth, she shook her head hard enough to kill her prey and then flung it across the room. It's funny, no matter how many times I've seen it. If I make noise, she gets distracted and stops, so I watched in silence for a few moments before returning to my list of name and numbers. The shoe was now dead, so Lola went back to bed.

Next I went through the list and highlighted phone entries that seemed to be personal names, either business or friends. That narrowed the list to about forty-five. From there I narrowed the list to female names, marking them with a star. Down to twenty-five. Females like to hear themselves talk. Don't deny it, you know it's true. So I figured if anyone was going to proffer the information I needed, I'd start with the women.

After an hour's worth of calling I had garnered nine disconnected numbers, eleven voicemails and three actual people. I hung up on the voicemails. Of the actual people I reached, only one knew who Esme was, but it was a jackpot.

Susan Osgood was Esme's best friend.

"Hi, Susan?"

"Yes." Her voice was shaky.

"I'm Mimi Capurro, I'm calling about your friend, Esme Bailey."

She broke down. "Um, she's not here." Sobs. "She's dead."

"I'm sorry. I know Esme is dead. I'm so sorry. I wanted to talk to you about her death."

"How did you know she died?" She gulped air between words.

"I was the one who found her." I hated telling her this over the phone.

"I thought her boss found her." Susan sobered a bit.

"I was with Lauren when she found her."

"How did you know her?" Susan said.

"Lauren? I was working for her."

"No, Esme."

"Oh, I'd just met her the day she died. She seemed so nice," I said. I explained how I was working with Lauren on her book tour.

"She was my best friend," Susan said, between sobs.

I understood her loss. When you lose someone close, you want to talk to someone, but you cry so hard you can't talk, even if you wanted to. I waited her out.

When she calmed a little, I said, "Susan, do you mind if I come by tonight to talk?"

"Talk about what?" Susan said. She sniffed and then blew her nose.

"Esme."

"Why?" Susan sounded defensive.

"Well, how did you find out about what happened?"

"Esme's mom called me this morning."

"Did Esme's mom tell you how she died?"

"She said she died at work," Susan said. She sniffed again.

"Yes, well, sort of. But I'd rather not discuss this on the phone," I said.

"I took a sick day, so I won't be going anywhere. What time?"

I looked at the area code and prefix on the phone number. Santa Cruz. I had three GPS reports to write, a follow up with the parent of a teen we were tracking, lunch with Nick, and the drive to Santa Cruz, so it would be early evening before I could get there.

"How about seven tonight?" I said.

"Okay," she said, her voice still shaky.

She gave me her address, and I put the information into my cell phone. I thanked her for her time and hung up. I still needed more contacts, but maybe Nick would cough up some details I could follow up on. I didn't want to step on his territory, but Lauren was paying me to assist in the investigation.

I practically skipped to Charles's desk, waving the sheet with Susan's information. I had something, and I wanted to share it with someone.

"Hey, I got a hit. I've got a meeting with Esme's best friend."

"Great place to start."

"I don't know. But it's all I've got for the moment. I only know how to investigate a murder from what I see on T.V. I don't want to waste Lauren's time or money." I was having serious doubts about trying to investigate alongside the police.

"But you'll have more chances to see Detective Christianson." Charles winked.

"Oh, yeah, I should be busting my butt on this investigation to impress good old Nick." I wanted to take the words back as soon as I said them.

"Or busting your butt on a treadmill." Charles reached around and patted me smartly on the side of my rear.

"I'm going to make time to run tonight."

Charles smirked. "Yeah, sure."

I ignored him.

I kept wondering if I was looking in the right direction. What was I going to get out of interviewing Susan? What information could she provide that would help us? Interviewing a person without a plan could be a total waste of time. I didn't know exactly what I was going to ask. The direction of the investigation leaned toward revenge against Lauren. Maybe Esme had confided in Susan about threats or messages. Maybe Esme was scared. I wasn't sure. I looked at my watch. I dreaded my next appointment.

CHAPTER 7

I arrived at Georgio's at about ten minutes before one and waited in my Land Rover doing a stealthy hair and makeup check. My ponytail took a few years off my looks, along with the deftly applied eye shadow and blush. I'd brushed on some nice cheekbones, which made my face look a tad thinner. By the way, I adore the person who invented stay-put lipsticks.

Nick's silver Crown Vic pulled up beside my car and I stepped out before he got out of the car. Okay, I'll rephrase that. I tried to step out of my car. The heel of my shoe caught on the rubber floor mat of the Land Rover and I had to launch myself at the door of the car parked next to me to keep from falling on my face.

I swear Nick moved as quickly as the vampires in the books I'd been reading, since he seemed to be standing in front of me before I could regain composure.

"Sensible shoes," Nick said.

"I wasn't trying to be sensible."

"Obviously." He stepped back and headed to the restaurant.

As I followed him to the restaurant I couldn't help but notice he'd dressed up for the occasion. That is unless he always wore Ralph Lauren dress shirts and slacks. I stepped past him, smelling the faintest hint of Hugo Boss cologne.

"Thank you," I said. At least he was polite enough to hold the door.

In a weird way, it felt like we were 19 years old again, but with more money, and nicer clothes.

Georgio's still looked like it had when we were in college, cozy Italian, with murals of gondolas gliding along the river, white table clothes and blond wood chairs. The hostess sat us at a table near the front of the restaurant where it felt like being seated in the dining room of a private home.

"Time warp," Nick said.

I felt the same, but words caught in my throat. "Uh-huh."

"Want to split a plate, for old time's sake?"

He had a lot of nerve. He hadn't spoken to me in over a decade, and now he wanted to bring up old times. "We have no old time's sake."

He ignored me and looked at the menu.

It didn't take long for the waiter to take our order. In moments he was back at the table with a bread basket and our salads. There was an uncomfortable silence.

I pulled open the napkin and placed it on my lap. "So you wanted to grill me about Monday night."

"I just wanted to get an official statement." He pulled a recorder from his pocket.

I told him about the trip to San Francisco, and how we walked into the house, finding Esme's head, and then her body. I even told him that I'd looked through the rest of the house.

"Right before the uniforms arrived I went through the formal living room, and the kitchen. Did you see that kitchen?"

"Bigger than my apartment," Nick said, stuffing a forkful of salad into his mouth.

"I know, bigger than my house too. If I cooked I'd be jealous." I pushed the remainder of my salad toward Nick. "Want the rest?"

"Sure."

"When I went into the kitchen, the back door was open."

"Are you sure? When I went through, the door was closed."

"I'm absolutely positive that door was open," I said. "The bottom was closed, but the top part of the door, with the window, was ajar. I know it was."

"That just doesn't jive." Nick looked puzzled.

Our lunches arrived. Nick had Penne Carciofi Arrabiato, and I had Chicken Marsala. We thanked the waiter, and I picked up my fork and knife and cut into my chicken. Nick fiddled with the shrimp on his plate.

I swallowed my mouthful of chicken, most of it anyway. "Did either of the officers, or Natalie, go through the house?"

"No. Just after you and Natalie left, CSU arrived while I was in the kitchen."

He still hadn't touched his food. I wanted to reach across with my fork and eat it for him. As good as my chicken tasted, a bite of shrimp would taste better.

"So you think the killer was still there?" Holy shit, I walked through the house alone, and the killer may have been there.

Nick thought about it. I couldn't help myself. I reached across the table, and took a bite of shrimp. Oh, goodness, it did taste delicious. And it brought Nick to. He pulled the plate closer to him, and picked up an artichoke heart and chewed as if trying to decipher what he'd put in his mouth.

"If he was, how did he get there, and how did he leave?" Nick was still chewing as he spoke.

"True. The location is fairly remote. But he could've parked down the road."

"We checked all the cars along the road. And CSU scanned the yards."

"Do you really think Lauren's right? That it was someone trying to get back at her?"

"We don't have enough to go on to form a theory just yet."

I reached across to steal another bite.

Nick slapped my hand. "If you wanted shrimp, you should have ordered it, instead of a stupid chicken."

"Fine." I rubbed my hand.

Nick grabbed the spoon and placed a mound of shrimp, artichoke and olives on the side of my plate. "Now stop picking at my plate."

Some things never change. He never did like sharing, even when we barely had money for one plate. I fought back a grin.

"So what else can I tell you?" I said.

"The dispatcher said you went through the rooms."

"Not really. I went to the bathroom upstairs to get a towel. I didn't want to leave prints when I opened the doors."

"Not like there wouldn't be at least a dozen prints on the doorknobs already," Nick said.

"I was looking for Henry. I guess I wondered why he didn't come down when Lauren started wailing."

"Olivarez said he was out cold."

"I actually thought he was dead. I went into the room, and flipped on the light. He didn't even respond, flinch or anything. As much as I didn't want to touch him, I checked for a pulse. He had one. Obviously." I shoveled in a mouthful of marsala chicken.

"We took a blood sample from him. He said he never sleeps like that. In fact, he rarely sleeps at all," Nick said.

"That's what Lauren said."

"What's the deal with them?" Nick said.

"Who?"

"Lauren and Henry."

"I just met them myself. Lauren didn't talk to me much on the way to and from the signing. She was on her phone, or working on her laptop. She said she had a deadline."

"None of this makes any sense."

"I know. But Lauren's fan base is different. Like Star Trek geeks, or role-playing fanatics."

"What?" Nick was genuinely puzzled.

"Okay, remember the movie *The Rocky Horror Picture Show*, from the late seventies, or was it early eighties?" Oh, I was dating myself.

"I've heard of it, but never saw it."

"Well, the Lighthouse Theatre in Monterey used to have a midnight show. That was after the Eight Twelve on Cannery Row burned down. Anyway, people used to come dressed as the characters, Frankenfurter, Magenta, Columbia, and Riff Raff."

"What the hell?" He put his fork down and wiped his mouth.

"Those were the main characters in the movie. Oh, and Brad and Janet."

"And you know this because?"

Okay, so I'd been a fan of this cult movie. And not only did the freaks dress up, but they brought props, and danced to the "Time Warp." I wasn't going to admit it to Nick, but I could still dance the time warp. It's just a jump to the left… And before I go any further, no, I didn't dress in character. I'd seen the movie more than a hundred times, but I wasn't going to admit that to Nick either.

"I used to go with my friends, every once in awhile. It was great fun," I said.

"You aren't normal, are you?" I think he really meant it.

"Normal is boring."

"Uh-huh," Nick said. He picked up his recorder. "Wow, we've wasted a lot of tape."

And time, I thought. He hadn't learned anything, and neither had I.

"So what I'm trying to say is that her fans really get into it. They dress the way they think her characters would look."

"And you think they'd do the things that are done in the books?"

"Hard to say, since we don't live amongst werewolves and vampires," I said.

"Just one more avenue to explore."

"What happened at Esme's mom's house?" I said.

"I hate that part of the job. Thank God for Natalie."

"She probably hates it, too. She's just more compassionate than you are."

I expected a rebuttal, but he said, "True."

"Well?"

"Well, nothing. She and Esme hadn't been close for awhile. I guess Esme had moved out a few years ago, and they rarely spoke."

"Did they have a falling out?"

"From the mom's point of view, Esme had it coming. She said that Esme had come on to her boyfriend. She didn't want her daughter having sex with her boyfriend, so she chose the boyfriend and kicked Esme out."

"Oh, the mom's a real winner, huh? Do you think Esme was really flirting with the boyfriend?"

"A real Susie Homemaker. And I have no idea about Esme. I haven't put together enough of a back story to know anything." Nick said.

"Did she give you any ideas about who might hate Esme enough to brutally murder her?"

"She didn't know shit. I thought she put on a good act, but I don't think she cared all that much. She did the tissue to the eyes, but they weren't even wet. She probably couldn't wait for me to leave so she could find out if Esme had a life insurance policy."

Ouch. That said a lot about his view of the woman.

"What did Natalie think of the mom?" I asked.

"Not much. But it hardly matters. Oliver is back, and I'm on my own on this one."

Not really, I thought. I'll be behind you all the way. Like it or not.

"Esme was what, maybe twenty-three?"

"Something like that." Nick said.

"Did you see her clothes?" I remembered the Coach briefcase she'd brought to my office. And her clothes were off the rack, but off a very expensive rack.

"Sorry, Mimi, I wasn't really interested in her clothes. Not really a label hound."

I almost laughed as I looked at the Polo logo on his shirt.

"I just meant that either Lauren paid Esme quite well, or the girl had and incredible credit card bill."

Nick looked at me. "I'll look into that. I'll have to run a check on her bank account and credit cards anyway."

"You know she was a vampire freak, right?"

Again I got a perplexed look. This was a whole new world of weird for Nick.

"A vampire freak?"

"Likes all things vampire. By the way, did you know Esme worked a lot of late hours and had a room in Lauren's house?"

"It's a huge fucking house. You and I could move in and never even be noticed," Nick said.

"Have you checked her room?"

"Until now, I didn't even know she had one. I'm sure the CSU guys went through the whole house."

Nick flipped open his phone. He hit a speed dial number and waited. "Is the crime scene tape still up?"

I wished like hell I could hear the other end of the conversation. Not because it was interesting, but because I'm nosey.

"No, no. I want you to leave it up."

Sounded like my lunch date was about over.

"Keep the officer there until I get there." He hung up.

"Well?"

"I gotta go." Nick stood and pulled his wallet from his back pocket. "I want to check out Esme's room at the house before they release the scene."

"I'm coming with you."

"The hell you are," Nick said. He threw a twenty dollar bill on the table and walked away.

Twenty dollars wasn't going to cover our meals, plus a tip. Then I thought about it. He plopped down just enough money to cover his meal and a tip. Not that I'm cheap, or expect a man to pay my way. Never mind. I tossed another twenty on top of his.

The only question now - how was I going to get back into that house to see Esme's room?

CHAPTER 8

I arrived at the house about three minutes behind Nick. I waited on the shoulder of the highway, guestimating the time it would take him to drive up to the front of the house, talk to the officer, and get past the fence. I figured it pretty damn close, since I saw the heel of Nick's shoe disappear into the house as I turned into the drive.

I parked my car behind Nick's and hitched my dress up as I stepped out of the car. I let one stiletto-clad foot settle on the gravel drive long enough to get the young police officer's attention. Forget impressing Nick, who'd barely noticed my summer dress and too high heels, I'd turn my sights on the uniformed hunk.

By the time I stepped fully out of the car, Uniformed Hunk was at my door. I straightened and adjusted my dress. I'd already made sure I had plenty of cleavage, and now I bent slightly forward to afford him a better view.

"Oh, hi Officer. I'm with Detective Christianson," I said, using my best jazz and whiskey voice.

"You don't look like a detective to me."

I read his nametag. "Officer Beal, I'm a private detective." I showed him my credentials, provided by the state of California.

"So?"

"So I'm working with Detective Christianson on this case." I stepped forward, brushing my breast against his shoulder in my best Gemma impersonation.

He stepped back, nonplused. I continued walking toward the house.

"Stop right there," Officer Beal said.

I pretended not to hear him.

"Ma'am. Stop or I'm going to arrest you."

So I was a little rusty with my feminine wiles. I was going to have to work on that. It always worked on decoy jobs. It was the extra ten pounds. That's why Nick didn't notice how cute I looked, and now I couldn't even talk my way past a young officer. Shit. I was going on a diet.

"Okay, okay. Just go ask Nick. He'll tell you I'm with him." I stamped my stiletto in the dirt.

"Do not step past this tape, or I'll arrest you," Beal snapped. "I'll be right back."

Or I'll arrest you. "Fine," I said.

But it wasn't fine. I wanted in that house. I had a right. Lauren had hired me to help find Esme's killer. I didn't want Nick in there by himself, finding something I should have looked for on Monday night. I had access to the damn house before the cops got there, and I didn't even think to look for the room where Esme stayed.

I thought about lifting the tape and walking around to the back of the house. I wanted to see where the back door of the kitchen led. Then I thought about spending even an hour in holding cell A, B or C in the Salinas Police Department and decided to wait where I was.

Nick emerged from the house. "I told you, you weren't coming with me."

Officer Beal followed closely behind, grinning like a cat. I could almost see a mouse's tail wiggling at the side of his lips, just before he dropped it in front of Nick as an offering. Little suck up.

"Nick, this is my case. Lauren wants me here." I detected a bit of a whine in my voice and I hated myself for it.

"I really don't give a shit what Lauren wants. This is an open investigation. Go home."

But he hadn't turned away, so maybe I still had a chance. I said, "Come here."

He rolled his eyes and bent under the tape, coming toward me. I grabbed his arm and held him close. I tried the breast maneuver on him. He knew what was under the dress, so maybe I'd have more influence. I held my breast against his arm as I whispered in his ear.

"I promise to be a good girl. Come on, for old time's sake?"

"I thought we didn't have an old time's sake," Nick said.

Open mouth, switch feet. I swear, if I didn't have one foot in my mouth, I had the other. It's no wonder I haven't had a real date since Dominic died.

I pushed my breast a little harder into his arm. "Two sets of eyes are better than one."

I didn't know what else to say. And I'll be damned if I was going to beg. I stepped back and let go of his arm. I looked into his gray eyes. For a moment, I was 19 years old again. For a moment I wanted to be with Nick in my bedroom, not Esme's. He must have felt something, too. He reached into his pocket.

"They've already released the scene, they just haven't taken down the tape." He handed me a pair of latex gloves. "And leave your shoes on the porch. I don't want you breaking an ankle on the stairs."

"So I don't even need your permission to come in?"

Nick grinned. "Nope." He walked back to the house.

I muttered, "Asshole."

I followed several paces behind Nick and stopped to kick my shoes off at the door. I swear I heard my feet say, "Ahhh." I focused on the staircase, avoiding looking at the dining room, as I entered the house.

I hadn't gone into all the rooms on Monday night. And if I had, I didn't have time to scope them out. A body of a full-sized man was easier to spot than most evidence. Investigating murders wasn't my specialty. On the other hand, investigating Nick's backside as we ascended the stairs, well, let's just say I had to grip the railing with both hands.

"Are you going to check out all the rooms? Or just Esme's?"

"I'm sure CSU already looked at it, along with the rest of the house. I just want to get a look at Esme's for my own peace of mind. See if I can get to know her a little better."

The room was still dark even though it was early afternoon. The drapes hadn't been opened, and the room was dark. Nick nodded toward me.

"Got your gloves on?" Nick snapped the end of his left glove.

"Uh huh." I did now.

"Open the curtains, so we have some light in here."

I slipped around the double bed to the far wall and pulled the cord to open the drapes. In the light of day, I could see the drapes were a heavy navy fabric with a sheer navy liner. The shock of sun awoke the room, and we saw a sparse space with a dresser, a double bed, and a nightstand with a reading lamp.

Esme had stacks of books on either side of the bed, including several of Lauren's novels. I moved to the stack and picked up the first book. I turned to sit on the bed.

"No."

I jumped.

"What?" I said. I tossed the book back on the pile.

"Don't sit on the bed. Can't you kneel on the floor?"

Fine, so I sat on the floor in my black dress and crossed my legs like a pretzel, then tucked the fabric of my dress to cover my crotch. I picked the book back up.

The Encyclopedia of Vampires. I flipped through the pages and saw nothing significant. I put the book down and opened the next. Doing a quick count, I figured there were fifteen books.

All of the books had an underworld theme. Novels about vampires, witches, werewolves, and numerous stories about fairies, were stacked with nonfiction books on the same subjects. She had a role-playing book on something called the Masquerade. I picked it up.

"What are you doing?"

"I'm looking through the stacks of books. I wanted to see if she had Prey."

"Prey?"

"Lauren said the murder scene was exactly the same as a scene from her new novel. I wanted to read it."

"You haven't read it yet?" Nick said.

"It just came out on Monday. I thought I'd take a look and see what happened after the slaying scene. I started to read it last night, but my mind kept wandering to Esme's head, and I just couldn't stomach it."

"I hate to say this, but that's a good thread to follow," Nick said. "I'll have an officer pick one up at the bookstore."

"Where are Lauren and Henry?" I asked.

"They, or he, packed some things and moved to a hotel in Monterey. The Del Monte, I think."

"Why Monterey?"

"Guess Henry likes it there. And Lauren will be gone most of the time."

I'd have to go talk to Henry. I wanted to know why he was so lethargic that night. Was he drugged?

I decided to get Nick's opinion. "You think Henry was drugged?"

"Don't know. We took a blood sample, but haven't gotten the tox report back yet."

Nick picked through the closet, one piece of clothing at a time, checking pockets, bottoms of shoes, and inside liners of coats. Not that Esme kept much here. At a glance I'd say the closet was less than half full.

"So, my mom said she saw you at the grocery store," I said.

"Yeah, she looks good," Nick said.

His comment could have been taken as crude, but I knew he meant it as a compliment.

"A new lover will do that for a woman."

"A new lover, your mom?" Nick turned to look at me.

"I really think this may be the man for her. He's kind, handy, and I think he's looking for the real thing."

"The real thing, what's that?"

I rolled my eyes. Nick wouldn't know the real thing if it stepped up and grabbed his crotch. "You know, settling down for life."

"Oh, *that* real thing," Nick said. "Is your mom looking for that?"

"Eventually, I think she'll succumb to his nurturing."

I found a wealth of information on psychic phenomenon, werewolves, fairies, witches, and tarot cards. I wondered if maybe Esme had planned to write her own book. I picked up the third book from the bottom of the stack.

You know how, when you lift something, and you expect it to be heavier than it is, and you nearly smack yourself with it? That's what happened. The book was at least three inches thick, and had a dust jacket indicating it was a reference about vampires. But when I opened it, the center of the book had been carved out. The cut out section resembled an archway; flat bottom and arched top.

The interior was lined with burgundy silk. But the book was empty.

"Nice little hiding place."

"Huh?" Nick came up behind me.

"Look at this." I handed him the book.

He did the same thing I did, expecting the book to be heavy. He nearly knocked himself in the head. Then he opened it. "What do you make of this?"

"Well, it had something in it at one time. But what, or who, was she hiding it from?"

"Good questions," Nick said. "Set it aside. We'll get back to it."

I took the book back and put it on the top of the stack. I got up and started looking through the dresser.

The dresser was bare on top, except the layer of dust. I the housekeeper didn't clean Esme's room. I wrenched my head around and looked at my butt and saw a layer of gray dust. I started to brush it off when Nick came out of the closet. Out of the closet, Charles could only wish.

"Want me to get that for you?" Nick offered.

"Ha, ha. No." He'd never touch my butt again. Not in this lifetime.

"I see you're wearing a wedding ring. How long have you been married?" Nick asked.

"Three years, four months and six days."

"That much in love, huh?"

"I haven't seen him in two years, four months and three days." I lifted satin La Perla lingerie from the small top drawer. This girl had expensive taste.

"What's the deal?" He'd stopped rummaging.

"He died just after our first anniversary," I said. I stopped too, and looked at Nick.

"Oh." He averted his gaze, again looking through the drawer.

"You married?" I asked.

"Nope."

"Ever married?"

"What happened?" Nick ignored the question and started opening other drawers. Black socks, black panties, black nylons, black nail polish, lipstick.

"Plane crash."

"I'm sorry." He sounded sincere.

I didn't say anything. I didn't want to have this conversation with him. I didn't want him to even think about me, and I'd do the same for him.

In one drawer, amongst all the black was something silver. I grabbed the handle before Nick shut the drawer. I shoved my hand under the black silk. A pendant.

"Just wait." Nick slapped my hand away.

I saw it. The chain had two silver-toned charms and a vial. I leaned in closer to Nick. God he smelled good. Oh, the pendant. The three charms were an Ankh, a Shen, and a glass vial shaped like a fang.

"What is this?" Nick said. He held the pendant up in the sun, squinting at it.

"The cross shape is an Ankh. The symbol for immortality."

"No shit," Nick said in a questioning tone.

"And the other charm is a Shen."

The Shen resembled a coiled rope, and was found in many Egyptian scrolls. The symbol usually appeared in scrolls with deities.

"Shen," Nick repeated.

"Divine protection," I informed him.

"If you have immortality, why do you need divine protection?"

"Hell if I know." It was a good question.

"Well you knew what this stuff was. Why don't you know the significance of them together?"

"You're leaving out the vial. The three of them may have meaning," I said.

Nick flicked at the vial with his middle finger, like it was a test tube in chemistry class. Some of the brown flecks moved, others were plastered to the glass.

"I'm guessing that's dried blood," I said.

"Yeah." Nick stared at the vial.

Nick set the pendant on the dresser, and continued sifting through the drawers. Just clothes and girl stuff. Then Nick opened the bottom drawer. Empty.

I looked at my watch. I had other cases to catch up on, and then the trip to Santa Cruz. If I hurried, I could stop by and see Henry.

"I've gotta go," I said.

"Can't it wait?"

"No, I mean I have to get going. I have meetings this afternoon."

I didn't wait for his approval. The search had garnered nothing. I was disappointed. What did I think I was going to find, a letter of confession? What did I know about investigating a murder. I was a private eye. I spied on cheating spouses.

I turned to leave. When I got to the door, I heard Nick clear his throat.

"Mimi, stay out of this, okay?"

Incredulous, I said, "What?"

"Your forte is cheating spouses, not dead bodies. I don't need you messing in my investigation."

"And yet you let me come in here with you today."

"I didn't want to have an embarrassing scene in front of Beal out there. You hanging on me, and rubbing your breasts on me like that. What do you think he thought?"

I couldn't look at him. I ran down the stairs.

CHAPTER 9

Not only was Jackie my best friend, but she was also the best detective in the office. She'd nursed me through every heartbreak in high school. She even knew about Nick. And I'd been with her through the only heartbreak she'd ever had.

"So I heard Nick's back in town," Jackie said. She sifted through a mountain of paperwork that had backed up over the last several days.

"Goddamn that Charles. What a big mouth. Please tell me you didn't say anything." I had stopped looking through my files and stared at Jackie.

She looked up. "What? He just asked who he was. And you being my best friend in the whole world, I wanted to brag about what a hunk you had dated. I told him you were long lost lovers, and you dumped him because he wasn't that good in bed."

"Jackie, you didn't!"

Giving me a stone cold stare, Jackie said, "You think I want to go job hunting? I told him I had no idea who the hell Nick Christianson was. But I don't think he believed me."

"Bless you, my child," I said. "Sorry I yelled, but you know how Charles can be."

"I know. That's why he's so much fun to have around. Besides I'll use my Nick card to bribe him when I want something." She laughed. It was a hearty, throaty laugh.

Before Jackie started working for me, I hadn't heard her laugh like that in years. She'd married an investment banker right out of high school. I'll never know why. All her life Jackie had been plump, bordering on fat, and Bradley was her first real boyfriend. He'd banked at the branch where Jackie worked, and they married within months of their first date. He was a chubby, balding geek with no social skills, but Jackie loved him, so I accepted him. Well, sort of.

Not being the type of person to hide my feelings (Nick always said he could read my feelings on my face) I let Bradley know I didn't trust him. Because of my big mouth Jackie and I didn't speak for nearly twelve years. She'd missed my college graduation, my wedding, and the funeral. And I'd missed the birth of her two children, twins Cory and Catey.

In the long run I'd been right. A year after opening Gotcha she came through the doors looking for help. Bradley had absconded with all their money to parts unknown. Jackie wanted to find him so she could divorce him and get her fair share of the money. She used Gotcha's resources and found the little prick herself. She's been working for me ever since.

She sat across from me at my desk and leaned over the table. "I heard you and Nick had lunch today."

I know I said she was chubby, but the Jackie sitting across from me only had fat in the right places now. And by right places I mean she sports a 36D chest. Because she earned it with lots of dieting and exercise she flaunted it. But she didn't flaunt it like the women who'd paid thousands of dollars for theirs. And those D-cups were resting on my desk.

I looked at her chest and flushed. Had I really pressed my boobs against Nick? "It was humiliating."

Sitting up, Jackie said, "How can lunch be humiliating? I don't see any food on you."

I told her about following Nick to Lauren's house, and how I'd rubbed against him. I also told her how he belittled me and told me to stay away from the case.

She tossed her head back, red hair flipping off her shoulders. "Mimi, that's what we do. It's our God-given right to use our feminine wiles to get what we want. Took me long enough to figure that one out."

Then I told her what Nick had said about it being an embarrassing scene.

"Oh, please. He enjoyed every minute of it. I'll bet he's back for more within hours. He just wants you to back off. He remembers the old Mimi. He doesn't know the new and improved Mimi."

She was my best friend because she always knew what to say to make me feel better. My mood lightened. "I don't think he ever really knew the old Mimi either."

"Too bad for him," Jackie said. "Stop dwelling on it. Use some of that energy to find Esme's killer."

"You're right. I've already wasted a lot of energy on Nick. I spent extra time to touch up my roots last night, I wore this summer dress, and I even stumbled around in stilettos." I propped my foot on the desk. "See."

"I didn't say you should look like a dried-up old hag. Of course you should look good. Let him know what he missed out on."

"Yeah, I really showed him my best side when I barfed at the murder scene."

"Oh, shit. What an impression." Jackie laughed.

"One he'll never forget." I couldn't quite laugh about it yet.

"I'll take half of this to my office. You work on this." She pushed a stack of papers toward me. My favorite, reports. "We'll never get this done if we do this in the same office."

"True. I've got to get over to Santa Cruz tonight."

"And I've got to get ready for a date." Jackie flipped her locks with her fingers.

"A date?" I didn't even know she'd met a man.

"Don't get all excited. It's a work date. I'm playing decoy tonight." She held her portion of the files against her chest. "Later."

I was disappointed. Like me, Jackie had no plans to include a man in her future. But I did have a girl in my future, and I had to get cranking on the paperwork before I headed out.

It felt like ten minutes, but when I looked at my watch, it had been a couple of hours. I'd gotten through a good portion of the mountain Jackie had pushed toward me. I had just enough time to change clothes and head out.

The drive felt so familiar, though I hadn't been over this way in years. As a kid we went to Santa Cruz several times each summer. And then as a teenager, it was a great place to hang out at night, have a bonfire on the beach, and drink a few beers. Oh, not teenager, I mean when I was in my early twenties.

Nick and I had our share of nights sitting in the sand by the fire. We loved going to the beach and boardwalk.

The voice on my GPS unit directed me to Beach Street. As I turned onto the street memories came flooding back. The saltwater taffy being pulled on a machine, skee ball in the arcade, and miniature golf. I could almost smell the grease from the fried artichokes as I cruised past Surf City Grill.

Even though it was nearly seven, the streets were busy. A decent day in June and the boardwalk was hopping. I looked up just in time to see a hard, tanned body cross in front of my bumper. Clad in surf shorts and aqua shoes, he slapped his palm on the hood of my car. We made eye contact. Suddenly, I wished I was twenty-something again. He smiled and flipped his straight blonde hair from his forehead, then he jogged toward the beach.

I looked at my black slacks and flats and wished I hadn't changed clothes. At least with my summer dress and pumps, I would have given off enough pheromone to warrant two seconds of eye contact.

I think my sex life (or lack thereof) was looking for a kick start. Alas, I had an investigation to conduct. Sex and sexy twenty-something surfers were not in my near future.

Approaching the Coconut Grove Ballroom, I could hear the rumble and screams of the Big Dipper roller coaster behind me. Ahead were rows of beach volleyball courts.

Several kids sat on the wall separating the beach from the sidewalk, shaking sand from their shoes, while parents stood by with coolers and towels. Back in the day, I would have been one of those kids, but with skin like a cooked lobster. And my sister and I would be peeling skin from each other's backs for days. Oh, thinking back, that was gross.

"You have reached your destination," GPS girl offered in an English accent.

I pulled into the dirt lot and looked at the building. The sun, sand, and salt air are hard on buildings. This building, which had shops downstairs and apartments upstairs, was in need of repair. I got out of the car and had second thoughts about going up to meet Susan. Not because of the idea of grilling a grieving friend, but because of the stairs.

As I grabbed the railing, it wobbled in my hand. So, if the step broke the handle wouldn't even begin to keep me from falling. Oh, no, it would be going down with me. I stepped slowly and carefully, not getting in a hurry.

The landing didn't feel much sturdier. I stood on the rotting plywood and knocked on the door. Waiting, I looked at my knuckles. Chips of paint had broken off as I knocked and stuck to my skin. I was brushing at my hand when the door opened.

"Mimi?" The girl had cracked the door about an inch.

"Yes. Susan?"

Susan's blond hair looked like she'd used her fingers to comb it up into a messy ponytail. Even with long, wispy bangs I could see she had large blue eyes that were bloodshot and swollen. She wore no makeup, and her bare skin showed the scars of teenage acne. As I scanned quickly down the rest of her body, I realized she'd made up for the bad skin by having a flawless body. The deep tan of her skin looked as if it had recently seen the sun, with a hint of pink overlaying the bronzed flesh. Flesh that was taut and curved, Susan sported a body that had been honed to near perfection. Her pert boobs popped under her strappy tank top, and a dancer's legs extended below the men's boxer shorts she wore. She made me want to run about ten miles, just to pretend my body could someday look that good.

She opened the door wider, and stepped behind it. "Come in."

In I went. And stunned I was. There was no way this was the same apartment the exterior suggested. The walls had been painted in a faux finish to look like white-washed paneling, and deep aqua curtains hung from floor to ceiling on the far wall. From what I could tell, the closed curtains covered the only exterior windows. The floors were polished pine, covered with carpet squares in a woven grass pattern.

An antique armoire adorned the wall next to the door, and an exquisite table graced the middle of the room. I saw Lauren's novel on the table.

Overstuffed armchairs faced a caramel-colored leather couch and flanked the coffee table. Accents of pale teal and aqua were scattered about the room in the form of pillows, throws and glass. This room was as well dressed as Esme had been when I met her.

Susan sat in one of the armchairs, and gestured me toward the couch. I sat on buttery soft leather and swore I was going shopping for a new couch.

"I'm sorry to bother you. I know you probably don't want company, or to be answering questions," I said.

She tucked her knees up to her chin. "I don't mind. I loved Esme. Anything that might help."

"How long have you known Esme?"

"Seems like forever, but we met in high school. We were best friends."

"You were?" I must have looked puzzled.

Esme was tiny, with short black hair and a very Goth look. Susan, with her shoulder-length blonde locks and tanned skin didn't seem like the type to hang with a girl like Esme.

"Look, Esme and I weren't as opposite as you think. Yeah, she was popular, and I wasn't, but we both had secrets." Susan had gone on the defensive.

"Secrets?"

"She was embarrassed about her home life and so was I. Neither of us wanted people to know where we lived. So we had secrets. In high school you are judged by where you live and who your parents are."

That made sense, but I still couldn't see them as high school chums.

"Esme was a cheerleader. She had every boy wanting to take her to the prom. But I can guarantee you; no boy was ever going to be picking her up at her house."

"Why was that?"

Susan dropped her feet to the floor and leaned forward. "Esme's mom was a drug addict. They lived in a rundown shit hole and Esme was humiliated by it. No one, well no one but me knew where she lived."

Esme, a cheerleader, I'd never have guessed.

"So you met in cheerleading?"

"Ha. Yeah, no. It would have been a bright morning in a vampire's coffin before I'd have been voted in for cheerleading."

I felt really lost.

"Look, I was a puffy marshmallow in high school. That was until I met Esme. We lived in the same complex¬. And we were the only girls in our school to be living in subsidized housing. I didn't care if everyone knew, but Esme did. So, at first, I blackmailed her into being my friend."

Nice girl.

"Blackmailed her how?"

"If she wouldn't be my friend, I'd tell everyone about her mom. And about where she lived," Susan boasted. "Once Esme and I started hanging out we became real friends. She taught me how to eat right, we ran together, and she taught me how to look like I had money, even though I was as poor as she was. We bonded."

I didn't know what to say, so I said, "Short black-haired Esme, and long-blonde haired Susan were the two girls to take to the prom."

"Esme has. I mean had…" Susan stopped talking. She put her face in her hands and sobbed.

I let her. I knew the grief of losing a loved one. I knew how it felt to want to talk about them, but not being able to reminisce without breaking down. I waited.

"Sorry," she finally said. She wiped at her eyes and blew her nose so hard she put a whole through the tissue.

I got up and handed her the box of tissue from the table. I sat.

"What I tried to say was Esme's hair is blonde. She's only been a freak since she met Sebastian."

"Sebastian?"

"Yeah, have you talked to him? Sebastian Zidonis was her boyfriend. He probably saw her talking to another guy, and killed her himself." Susan straightened as if she meant to go after Sebastian.

"Why do you say that?"

"Sebastian is a looker. I mean he's hot. But he's really insecure, and very jealous. He didn't even want Esme going out with me. Called it whoring around. I can see him going off the deep end. Maybe he saw Esme with someone and just lost it."

Quite a revelation. Had Nick talked to Sebastian? I had to go back over my list and find Sebastian's phone number.

"Does he seem like the type?"

"Does anyone? I mean, hell, he plays that stupid game where they stalk each other and have confrontations in the streets. I guess he could see it as a game."

"What game?"

Once again, Susan sat up straight. She looked around the room, as if she expected someone to appear. "Look, if I tell you, you can't let them know you heard it from me."

"Okay?"

"The players. You can't let them know that I know." She looked around again.

I was sure we were alone, but I looked too. She had me spooked.

"What?"

"The game isn't a secret. They play it on the streets here in Santa Cruz on Friday nights. They dress up in vampire garb and skulk around the streets. It's called the Camarilla."

She sat back. I breathed. I felt her tension ease.

"The players are secret. Awful things have happened to those who give up the secret of the Masquerade. You can only be invited by another player, and even then, you can't reveal your identity in the Camarilla to outsiders. Sebastian invited Esme. That's when she got hooked on the vampire freak thing, and started working for Lauren Silke."

I nodded, hoping she'd continue.

"It's a cult I tell you. If they knew that Esme talked, she'd be, well, I guess she already is." Susan breathed deep, and kept taking rhythmic breaths to keep from crying.

"Surely no one would kill over the secret," I said.

"Probably not kill, but she'd be out, and then Sebastian could no longer associate with her because she knew his identity."

I couldn't believe this. I'd heard of live role playing games, like World of Warcraft, but a secret society, with punishment for revealing secrets? Not likely. I didn't say as much. Susan had enough on her mind without me doubting her.

But it all led back to Sebastian. First his jealousy, and then the fear of being revealed as a member of the Camarilla. Was there a chance that Esme's death had nothing to do with Lauren?

"So before she hooked up with Sebastian, she was, for lack of a better word, normal?" I said.

"Yeah, normal. And believe me, we looked good together. We could have any guy we wanted. Not to be conceited, but once she got me into running and lifting weights, I was a whole new girl."

Looking at the athletic body curled on the chair in front of me, I couldn't imagine Susan as fat. I couldn't imagine Esme as a blonde. Go figure.

"So why Sebastian? Why the Goth, vampire thing?"

"Sebastian was mysterious. He wasn't interested in a cute little blonde girl. So she wanted him because he didn't want her. Esme usually only wanted what she couldn't have."

Been there, done that.

"And you think Sebastian has a violent streak?"

"With Sebastian you never know. Between the two of them it was always off and on: she'd be pissed at him, or he'd be pissed at her. He's bigger than her, so he could probably hurt her easily."

I thought about this. "Esme seemed like a self-assured girl. Would she stay with a guy who was violent?"

"You'd have to see Sebastian. I wish I had a picture to show you. I think he could get away with anything and a girl would stay with him. He's beyond hot."

"Hm," I said. "Do you know if anyone hated Esme, or wanted to do her harm?"

"I didn't see much of her lately. She worked all the time. Stayed in Salinas a lot. But that could have been because Sebastian lives there too. But she could be conniving when she wanted. I could see her pissing someone off. Esme was a schemer."

"Conniving how?" I had a hard time picturing this side of Esme, even though I'd only met her briefly.

"Little miss do-all, be-all, end-all. She put forth a front that made her look so sweet and innocent, but when your back is turned, she's doing what she can to suck the life out of you. Maybe the vampire thing really was appropriate." Suddenly Susan wasn't so teary-eyed.

And this girl had just told me she was best friends with Esme, sad that she had passed. Now Susan almost seemed angry. "I thought you were friends."

"We were. She was my best friend. Like they say, 'Keep your friends close, but keep your enemies closer.'"

"I don't get it." This girl was weird. I didn't quite know what to make of her change in attitude. It was like she'd flipped sides in a split second.

"I think we were both friends and enemies. We needed each other more than anything. Both of us had our issues, issues that no one else understood. We were raised by drug addicts, and if that doesn't teach you to trust no one, I don't know what will. We loved each other, but we didn't trust each other. I guess we both knew what each other were capable of doing. You learn to survive in the kind of families we had."

"Did Esme talk about work much?" I wanted to ease the tension Susan had created.

"Oh, all the time. She was so lucky to find such a great job. Lauren and Henry could be very demanding, but they paid her well for it. Me, I run my tail off and kiss butt all day at my job and I don't get paid nearly as well as Esme does, uh, did."

"She ever mention violence or threats?"

"You mean toward Lauren?" Susan picked at a dry tissue.

"Anything. I'm just trying to get a feel for Lauren's readers."

"I think that was Esme's favorite part of maintaining Lauren's blog and Facebook pages. She'd come home and tell me about how someone ripped Lauren a new one for Sophie being so promiscuous. Or try to correct her on the ways that vampires live and feed. I mean read any paranormal series and they all have their take on what a vampire's life is like. Esme just laughed. She'd say, 'They know this shit is fiction, don't they?'"

"Sometimes I wonder," I said.

I wanted to get a better idea of Esme by her things, like at Lauren's house. "Do you mind if I look in her room?"

"Actually, it's my room. Esme stayed mostly with Sebastian or Lauren this last year. I took over the bedroom. She just kept necessities in the bathroom, and lived out of a suitcase when she was here."

This made no sense. Why had Esme spent so much money to furnish this apartment if she was never here? And come to think of it, the décor seemed a little light for Esme. I would've expected black interior and dark fabrics.

"You said she hadn't been living here lately. Did you have a falling out?"

"She got caught up in the vampire world, and then got the job with Lauren. She loves that job." Sniffle. "Loved. Even without Sebastian, she loved the life, and loved the money. She was moving on. But I'd always be here for her. It's still our apartment. Besides, I think everything in the apartment belongs to her. Or belonged anyway."

I was still on the money comment. "Money? I didn't think an author's assistant made that much."

"Apparently Lauren pays better than most. Look at this place. I can't even afford IKEA, and all this is the real thing. We'd go antique shopping on weekdays, when I didn't have to work. I'm a banquet server at the golf course."

"I noticed she dressed well."

"Oh, yeah, she'd take junkets to San Francisco just to buy clothes. Had a personal shopper and everything." These thoughts seemed to cheer Susan a little. She grinned.

Her attitude lightened considerably. Maybe she really did miss her friend. But just moments earlier she'd been bashing her. Or maybe she was only telling the truth about Esme's personality, and what shaped it.

If she wasn't going to let me in the bedroom, I'd at least try to get a look at the bathroom. Never underestimate the power of medicine cabinet snooping.

"I'm sorry. I drank an entire bottle of water on the way here. May I use your bathroom?"

"Sure," she said, pointing. "It's the door next to the kitchen."

I went into the bathroom and locked the door. I figured I had about two to three minutes to do my thing before Susan got suspicious. I was pretty sure I'd been in the bathroom less than a minute when I heard a knock.

"What are you doing in there?" Susan's voice sounded anxious.

CHAPTER 10

After the bathroom snooping, I grabbed my handbag from the living room and couldn't get out of that apartment fast enough. Was it guilt? I doubted it. But I suddenly didn't feel comfortable. I'd barely been in there enough time to pee, if that's what I had been doing, before Susan was banging on the door.

If Esme hadn't been staying there, why were her prescription bottles still in the cabinet? They weren't expired. As soon as I got in my car I looked at the photos I'd taken with my cell phone camera. Paroxetine and Dalmane belonged to Esme. The bottles with Susan's name included stuff I'd never heard of: Tranxene, Lorazepam, and Skelaxin. There was one I had heard of, Halcion, which I knew was for insomnia. I'd have to get my hands on a Physician's Desk Reference.

I looked at my watch. I still had time to stop by Henry's hotel before I headed back home. Leaving Santa Cruz, I got on Highway 1 toward Monterey. Forty minutes later I was driving up the hill toward the hotel's entrance.

On the drive over I kept questioning my impression of Esme. To me she seemed like a well-adjusted girl with a penchant for vampires. Even with her gothic look, she still acted like a caring, responsible adult. Was Susan painting a true picture, or giving me a side of Esme that I couldn't disprove? I wondered what the boyfriend would say about Esme. Was Susan jealous of Esme? That wasn't much of a stretch.

By the time I arrived, the sun had disappeared behind the golf course fairways and the fog had rolled in. I pulled into a space next to the handicapped parking. When I got out of the car I could feel the damp air on my skin and smelled the combination of freshly cut grass and salt air. The atmosphere was chilling, so I jogged up the stairs to the lobby following the landscaping lights that put off an eerie glow from the fog.

The lobby screamed understated elegance and modern minimalist. I almost missed the reservation desk, as the blond wood of the counter blended with the wall behind it. But the black bowl on the counter gave me a clue as to the direction I was headed.

"May I help you?" The young man seemed to appear from nowhere.

"Yes, I'm here to see your guest, Henry Silke."

He tapped the keys of a keyboard. Then tapped some more. "May I enquire, is Mr. Silke expecting you?"

"Yes." I lied.

"And your name?"

"Mimi Capurro."

He tapped a few more keys and scrolled down a list with his finger. "I see. Here you are. Room eleven-sixteen." He pointed. "Just down that hall."

I looked in the direction he pointed and thanked him before heading that way. Wow, I was on some sort of special guest list.

From the sign on the wall, eleven-sixteen was at the far end of the hallway to the right. As I turned I saw a door open. A man came into the hall. I looked up to see Brad Pitt walking toward me. Well, so he wasn't really Brad Pitt, but he sure as hell looked like him. He didn't look at me as I drooled after him, thank God, but my gaze was glued to his ass as he strolled past. I'm sure I smelled CK Man cologne.

I took a deep breath, inhaling his scent, and used every ounce of energy I had to not turn around and follow him. If I did follow, I could take down his license plate and find out who he was. Charles was always good for that kind of snooping, and he'd do it for me. No, I had work to do. I kept moving forward to Henry's room. As I got closer I realized that Brad had come from Henry's room. Huh?

The door was slightly ajar and I knocked lightly.

"Come in." Henry called from deep in the room.

The reception desk must have let him know I was on my way.

"Uh, hello," he stammered. He had pulled the sheets up around his body.

I grinned. Trying to look perfectly comfortable, I said, "How are you holding up?"

"It's been hard. Lauren's been calling a lot." He sat up on the bed. "Would you excuse me?"

"Calling for what?"

"She wanted to know if we could get back into the house. Had Esme's body been released, so her family could plan a funeral? They won't, you know." He said all this sitting up in the bed, trying to maneuver out of it.

"They won't what?" I wasn't following.

"Her family. They won't plan a funeral. She'll be lucky if they even claim the body." He was still maneuvering the sheet around himself.

"From what I've heard, they'll want to know when they can cash the life insurance policy."

"That's about right. So Lauren asked if I could make arrangements. As a twenty-something, Esme didn't talk about death, only the undead. I think we thought we were immortal at that age too."

I remembered the charms. The ankh was a symbol for immortality. "Do you think that's why she wore the ankh?"

Henry struggled a bit more. "No." His answer didn't invite further questions.

I moved past the desk, where the flat screen television was showing The Weather Channel, and looked out the window. I again smelled the faint aroma of CK Man.

Henry finally yanked the sheet loose, wrapped himself, and shuffled to the bathroom. He smelled like soap, so I knew the smell wasn't his.

Oh, boy, did I have bad timing. Or good timing, depending on how you looked at it. But what was I looking at? Had Brad come from Henry's room? It was nearly nine o'clock, so maybe Henry was ready to turn in. My imagination was having a really good time. I could have carried the scent of cologne in from the hallway.

Henry came back into the room. He wore a white T-shirt and red flannel pajama bottoms. He looked cute. Henry wasn't a big man. In fact, when I first met him on Monday, he'd been dwarfed by Lauren. Esme would have been a better fit for him, as tiny as she was.

Getting a closer look I saw Henry's eyes were bloodshot and swollen.

"Everything okay?" I sat on the chair next to the window.

"Not since Tuesday." Henry flopped on the bed nearest the door. A piece of his comb-over spilled onto his forehead. He didn't seem to notice.

I wanted to move the hair for him. "I'm sorry about everything. And I'm sorry I haven't gotten over here earlier. You know Lauren has asked me to investigate?"

He nodded. Another hair dropped down.

"Is there anything compelling you want to tell me about that night?" I asked.

"I'm not sure. What do you already know?"

"I don't have much. Actually I don't have anything. But I did talk to Susan, Esme's best friend. She didn't give me much, but now I have a few questions for you."

"I've already talked to the police several times." He looked drained.

"I only met Esme briefly. I wanted to ask questions about her work for Lauren."

"Like what?" Henry snapped.

"She was Lauren's assistant, right?"

Henry nodded.

"What did that entail?"

"She did everything office related. She scheduled Lauren's appointments, kept up the website, monitored the blog and the websites, answered Lauren's emails, answered calls, and she sometimes traveled with Lauren." He said this in monotone, as if repeating it for the hundredth time.

"Did she ever seem manipulative, or devious?"

Henry snickered. "Esme? All the time."

"Really?" Maybe he'd confirm what Susan had said.

"She had to be to live with and work for Lauren. She sometimes had to be Lauren. And if that's not devious, I don't know what is."

"And she liked her job, right?"

"A little too much. She'd moved in for God's sake. Lauren took advantage of it, and had Esme working late hours whenever she was on deadline. Lauren writes three different series, so she's always on deadline. But Esme was entranced and didn't care as long as she got to focus on the vampire series."

"What about the website and the blog? Did Esme ever indicate there might be physical danger?" I felt like I was going nowhere with this investigation, asking the same questions over and over.

"That's the thing, I really think Lauren was mostly anonymous. Even our neighbors don't know who she is. We tell everyone I'm an investor working from home, which is true since I invest Lauren's money for her. Most people actually think Esme works for me. How would they find her?"

"Do you think Esme could have bragged about working for Lauren, and someone tracked down your residence?"

Henry considered this. "You know Esme was a vampire freak, right?"

"Yes." I hoped the one word answer would prompt him to tell me something.

"She was a normal girl. Other vampire freaks aren't so normal. We, they come in all shapes."

"I know," I said. "Have you ever heard of the Camarilla?"

Suddenly he didn't look so drained. "What do you want to know?"

That was easy.

"Susan said it was a secret society of role players in a vampire game. She seemed to think it was an exclusive club of sorts." Did I promise I wouldn't mention her name? I don't remember.

"She's blowing it out of proportion. The only reason we're secretive is because many players don't want their employers or customers to know about their involvement."

"We're?" Did I hear him correctly?

"We, as in Esme, Sebastian, uh, The Prince, and me. And many others of course."

"Okay, so it's a role playing game. Who cares?" Who cares if you have a vampire fetish?

"You don't understand. There are doctors, lawyers, and business owners amongst the players. Imagine a patient's misgivings if he were to find out his doctor dressed as a vampire and played games in the dark."

"What's the game about?" I really was trying to understand.

"We are a diverse group of kindred put together to decide our own fate," Henry explained.

Yeah, that explained everything.

"Currently, the Kindred are in an uproar since the arrival of two Elders, Francis and Girard. They are battling for the possession of a magical scarab that has the power to bring vampires back to life. They pit Kindred against each other, creating strife."

Sometimes when you overhear a conversation about a soap opera you think the people are talking about real life, and this was how Henry was talking. "This is a game, right?"

He sighed. "Yes. There're elaborate character traits and we have a character sheet for each character. It includes their features, strengths, vulnerabilities, and magical powers. The Storyteller keeps the sheets safe, so no other character knows all the details since they can be used as leverage in the game. Each character belongs to a clan and these clans can be pitted against one another. Do you see?"

No, not really. "Alright, I'm getting it. Do you bite each other?"

I could hear the disgust in his voice. "The game is played with hand signs, denoting challenges, timeouts, and even invisibility. There is absolutely no physical contact. Our rules: Don't touch, no weapons, and know when to stop. If you're thinking the Camarilla had something to do with Esme's murder, you are wrong. We aren't violent." He stood and paced the area from the bathroom to the window, stepping within a few feet of me.

He continued, "That's the problem. The perception of violence. And that's why the City of Santa Cruz is trying to stop the game." I felt his agitation.

"Sorry Henry, I just don't understand the role playing thing." I wasn't about to share *The Rocky Horror Picture Show* part of my life.

"We decide disputes and combat with rock, paper, scissors."

I laughed. "So no fangs, no duels, no stakes through the heart? What's the appeal?"

"No real fangs anyway. It's the seduction of being someone else one night a week. Leaving the screaming brats, the bitchy wife, the nagging husband, the job stress, and becoming that character can be addictive."

I finally got it. Who didn't want to be someone else every once in awhile? To be a member of the living dead wouldn't be my choice, but what the hell, to each his own.

"Anyway, the Camarilla has a complex background that you probably aren't interested in. And I won't bore you with it. The gist is that everyone strives for power over the Kindred and will backstab and double-cross to achieve that power." Henry sat back down on the bed.

"Sounds like quite a rush. But I still don't understand the need for secrecy."

"Like I said, some of the players could lose business if their patients or clients had a problem with their involvement." He leaned forward, resting his elbows on his knees.

"Don't you think they'd notice if they saw their doctor walking along the street, wearing a vampire costume?" I know my doctor well enough. I think I'd recognize her.

"Some of the costumes are very elaborate, with makeup and wigs, so no, they wouldn't recognize anyone." Henry seemed sure. "Other than that, it's not that big a deal."

"Susan made it seem as if a life could be in danger if someone told." She'd sounded scared.

"Maybe Esme spooked her. Esme was quite the storyteller. She really enjoyed the game and took it seriously. That's why we had the dinner meeting Monday night."

Finally, I was going to learn something. "What meeting?"

"Like I said, they want to shut down the game. The Prince, Sebastian, Esme and I were working on a PR campaign to show the game in a better light."

"Why stop the game?" I asked.

Henry turned and stacked the pillows against the headboard. "Complaints."

"Complaints?"

"Santa Cruz is very touristy. With the movie The Lost Boys and the association the city has with vampires, several people have been spooked to see a vampire lurking in the shadows." He leaned back and put his legs up on the bed.

"I get it. I guess I'd be a little spooked too."

"But you see. If more people understood the significance of the game they'd come to Santa Cruz just to have a vampire sighting. Then they'd stay for dinner and drinks, and maybe buy a trinket in one of the stores. We could be good for the city."

This was all very interesting, but where was it getting me. "Twice you've mentioned The Prince. Who is this prince guy?"

"It's not my place to reveal his identity," Henry said.

"Was it the guy who was leaving as I came in?" I wanted to know who that guy was. I wanted his phone number and address. Who cared if he dressed like a vampire and trolled the streets at night?

"What guy?" Henry tensed.

You're not a very good liar. "The Brad Pitt look-a-like who was leaving when I came in."

Henry sat up. I felt like my time here was getting short. "I don't know who you mean. I haven't seen so much as a maid since I've been here. Not even a cop. They made me come to the station. I'm a suspect, you know."

He was in the house, so I figured as much. "Sorry to hear that."

"Look, I've had a very long couple of days. I'm about talked out. The police know everything there is to know about Esme's work for us. And I'd really liked to be left alone." He was back to the same drained Henry that I walked in on.

"Do you think someone followed you home from the meeting?" I was trying to get some more answers before I was evicted from the room, but I leaned forward to indicate I was ready to leave.

"No one even knew we were there. This PR thing was something the four of us cooked up. We haven't presented it to the rest of the players yet." He contemplated a moment, then said, "Well, Sebastian and Esme are sort of Goth, and I guess that could have attracted some attention. But we haven't offended anyone, so no, I don't think anyone followed us home from dinner."

"Does Sebastian know about Esme?" I asked.

"Yes. I called him this morning. Other than the game I haven't seen him around much."

"Do you know why?"

Exasperated, Henry said, "What?"

I repeated the question.

"Of course not. It's not my business. Besides, until now I hadn't thought about it." Standing up, Henry added, "Are you about done here?"

I stood. "Just one more question."

"What?"

"Where did you have dinner?"

"That Italian place on Highway 68. I can't remember the name. Why?"

I assumed he meant the restaurant in Salinas. I couldn't think of any other Italian places on that highway. I'd just been there for lunch. Was that why Nick had chosen Georgio's? He wasn't remembering our meals together. He was getting a look at the place. I was mad at myself for being gullible.

"Can you just give me a rundown on the night's events? Something about that night has to be connected to Esme's death."

"I just don't see how." Henry seemed to be thinking about it.

"Humor me. Just run through the events."

"In a nutshell, we met around eight o'clock. Esme and I rode together, and Sebastian drove up as we were getting out of the car. Esme ran over to give him a kiss. We went inside and got a table right away. Within minutes The Prince showed up. We ate dinner, had some wine with dinner and then Sebastian took Esme home. I stayed on at the table with The Prince to put together some details for a letter to the other players. We wanted to distribute them on Friday night." He scratched his head with his fingers. "That's it."

"And all of you were present at the table the whole time?" I mean, someone could have gotten up to get a bottle of wine from the bar, or gone to the bathroom. "No one came up to your table to say hello to anyone?"

"I didn't recognize anyone in the restaurant that night. The staff probably knows me because I'm fairly regular, but they don't know me." He blinked, then closed his eyes for several moments. "I guess Esme did get up to use the bathroom. She was gone quite awhile, but that's not unusual for a female. God only knows what you ladies do in the bathroom that takes so much time."

"We can't just pee and leave, you know. We have to check ourselves in the mirror. Re-apply our lipstick, literally powder our noses." Like he didn't already know this.

"Women," he sighed.

On the same train of thought but a different view, I wondered, "Do you think you were drugged at the restaurant?"

Henry contemplated a moment. "I'm not positive I was drugged, but I doubt it was at the restaurant. Unless someone in the kitchen had it out for me. No one was ever near my food or wine."

"Are you sure?" I had to push his memory. There had to be something more he wasn't telling me.

"Look, I trust everyone who was at the table on Monday night."

"What about after you left the restaurant?" I asked.

"I went straight home."

"Was Sebastian still there when you got home?"

"No, I didn't see his car." Henry's brow creased. "But he must have come in because there was an open bottle of wine on the island in the kitchen. And there were two glasses. Yes, that's right, because one of the glasses was empty, and the other about half full."

I didn't remember seeing the wine when I peeked into the kitchen.

"I don't know if you know this, but everyone who lives in the house uses the kitchen door entrance. The main hub of the house is the kitchen. There are many nights Lauren, Esme and I have sat around that island trying to fill holes in a plot. And we all drank wine. Lauren is a connoisseur of wine. Or she likes to think so anyway." He laughed. It was the first time I'd heard him let go with an uninhibited laugh.

"Do you have a wine cellar?" Maybe the crime scene guys had already processed that space in the house.

"No, but we do have a rack, and a small wine chiller in the kitchen. It's in the far left corner. And I know you're going to ask, the wine was a *Santa Rita Casa Real Cabernet Sauvignon. 2003*, I think. I poured myself a glass before I put everything away."

I contemplated what Henry just said. I took the hotel notepad and pen and wrote down the name. I tore off the sheet of paper and folded it. Could the Cabernet have been drugged? If Henry got home after the killing, he may never have gone into the dining room. Had the wine been drugged to subdue Esme before killing her? What was the killer's plan? Was there a plan?

"Did you wash the glasses?"

"No, I put them in the dishwasher. I put the wine back in the rack. Believe me, if I'd known there was a dead body in the other room, I wouldn't have touched anything." Henry held his hands up in surrender.

I think I'd know something was wrong in my house before I saw it. The energy would be off. This made me wonder if Henry had ingested something, it may have been before he got home. Maybe the wine exacerbated the drugs, if there were any drugs.

I didn't know how much more I could learn from Henry and he looked to be fading fast. I stood.

"I really appreciate your time. This has all been such a nightmare." I walked toward the door.

"Yes, it has." Henry stood and walked me to the door.

"Good night," I said. As I walked out the door, I glanced into the bathroom. Something caught my eye.

CHAPTER 11

Thoughts of yesterday's interviews played in my head as I drove to work the next morning. I know the guy in the hall had something to do with all of this. I could kick myself for not following him out of the hotel. I should have pretended I forgot something and followed him to the parking lot. I could've gotten a license plate or something. But at the time, how did I know he'd be significant? I still didn't know if he was, but he was definitely in Henry's room.

And the bottle I saw on the counter in the bathroom as I was leaving, I swear it had Susan's name on it. If only I'd had a second more to focus. But it was a prescription bottle and I was sure the name on it wasn't Henry.

Turning onto Central Avenue, all thoughts of yesterday dissipated. There were two patrol cars outside my building. The car in the driveway was parked at an angle and the one on the street had the passenger door open and the lights flashing. To say this wasn't good was sort of cliché.

Since the police were blocking the entrance to Gotcha's parking lot, I drove around the corner and slipped into the closest space on the street. I went around to the passenger side and grabbed my briefcase and laptop. I snapped a leash on Lola before letting her out. She sniffed for a few seconds and started dragging me toward the office. My heart rate peaked as I walked in the front door.

I set my briefcase and laptop just inside the entrance, looking through the foyer to the reception area. It looked like someone had a pillow fight since I'd last been here, the kind where feathers start flying. Only instead of using pillows they used file folders, printer paper, Post-it Notes, paper clips, pencils, pens, and computer discs. I could barely detect a narrow trail of floor.

I let out a breath when I realized I'd been holding it. Holy shit, the place was a mess. Guess I didn't have to ask why the police were here.

Lola was having none of it. She trotted right over the mess and into my office.

I'd never been robbed, or is it burgled? Not as a kid, or in my home, or here at the office. I had no idea how violated I'd feel. Voyeurism came to mind, like someone had gotten a chance to look deep into my private moments. Of course the only thing private about what happened in this building was everything. My business relied on confidentiality. We were so careful not to reveal personal information. Discretion was the bond of the private investigator.

Hearing voices I turned toward the back of the reception room. Charles spoke to the officers as they walked into the room. As always, Charles was the epitome of control. He pointed to the back corner of the room where the safe was tucked behind the mirrors.

"Anything pertaining to an ongoing case is kept in our safe. All the closed files have hard copy and a file on disc. We keep those files here for one year, then they are transferred to a secure storage facility." He pulled the mirror away from the wall. "Do I need to open it?"

The older officer, a man in his late fifties with a thin build but a pot belly said, "As long as it wasn't breached there's no reason to open it."

"My partner says you work on cases for the Salinas PD. Do you have anything you're working on now?" the younger officer asked. This man had a stockier build and no belly, but still looked soft.

"Yes, but I can't discuss open cases, even with you. Suffice it to say the chain of custody wasn't breached and the evidence I'm working with is safe."

I sucked in a deep breath and blew it out when I heard Charles's answer. But still, there were a gazillion files splayed across the floor. How were we going to sort through what was current and what was closed?

"Mimi. Finally. Don't you answer your phone anymore?" Charles admonished.

I looked down for my briefcase. I went back to the door and leaned down to get my cell phone from my bag. I looked and saw eleven missed calls. I'd put my phone on vibrate while I'd conducted my interviews yesterday and forgotten to turn the ringer back on.

I hustled back into reception. "Oh God, Charles, I had it on vibrate. I'm sorry."

"You can see we have a minor disaster." Good old Charles, pointing out the obvious.

"What the hell happened?"

The officers looked at each other and then at Charles, who was obviously the one in control of the situation.

"Someone broke the window pane out of the back door in the kitchen. From there it was easy to unlock the door and come in. I don't know what they were looking for, but Esme's computer is gone. I don't know if they wanted her computer specifically, or just a new laptop."

"And our security system?" What the hell was I paying a fortune for a security system for if it didn't work?

"Yeah, about that. I, um, I left around midnight to have drinks with Alex and planned on coming back, so I didn't set it on the way out. Only I had more than a few drinks and Alex drove me home, not back here."

Wide eyed, I was stunned. "Are you fucking kidding me?"

Charles doesn't even know the meaning of the word sheepish, but he was doing a good impression now. "I know. What are the chances?"

"From the looks of this place, I'd say, oh, about a hundred percent." My frustration was getting the better of me.

"You know this isn't like me." Charles raked his fingers through his perfect hair.

I did know it. Then I remembered what we were working on and gulped. Oh shit, Nick was going to give birth about this one. He didn't want me involved to begin with and now we'd had a major breach. Well, this was Charles's baby, not mine. Nick could take it up with him, if he dared.

"Don't worry. I was done with the computer. I have the hard drive and all the contents removed and stored in the safe. I even had the pages from her PDA filed in the safe. I'm not an idiot." Charles assured.

"Okay." I sighed. "So do we have any idea what else is missing?"

Charles spoke to the police. "Go ahead and take your pictures. I'm going to talk to Mimi in her office. If you need me just knock on the door across the hall." He pointed to my open office door.

I headed to my office. At the door I came to an abrupt halt. I could see the floor in the corner where I kept my filing cabinet was three inches deep with manila folders and paper. All six files drawers were pulled open. One had even been yanked from its rollers. I felt a tightening in my chest as the fury worked its way to my throat. Charles wrapped his arm around me just as my knees gave out.

"Oh, honey, it's not that bad. We'll hire a temp from Manpower and get everything cleaned up in a day or so." He took Lola's leash and guided me toward a client chair and sat me down.

I tried to stand. Irritated, I wanted to pace. Charles gently pushed me back into the chair.

"How will we know if anything is missing?"

Charles grinned. "Absolutely every piece of paper in this office has a computer backup. Not only do we have hard copy backup on CD, but I also backup the files nightly to a separate server. That way if the place burns to the ground we still have everything but the absolute current notes on file."

My cell phone rang. I picked it up and looked at the number. "Unknown." I answered, "This is Mimi."

"Stop now if you know what's good for you," a nondescript voice whispered in my ear.

"Excuse me?" I understood what was said, I just didn't get it.

The voice repeated, "Stop now if you know what's good for you."

I hung up. I couldn't process the call along with everything else.

Charles must have seen the disgust on my face. "Who was that?"

"I don't know. But someone wants me to stop doing something." I tilted my head and raised my brows.

"Stop doing what?" Charles asked.

"I don't know. I'm always doing something I shouldn't be, so you name it." I had to laugh at that one because it was so true.

"Probably a pissed-off cheating husband." Charles dismissed the call like it was an annoying fly.

Before I could comment on Charles's wisdom, Jackie walked in the door. Beyond the horrified look on her face, she looked as put together as always. She wore dark denim tucked into caramel colored boots and a purple T-shirt covered by a tan cotton pea coat. Her auburn hair was pulled to a neat bun at the nape of her neck. She'd recently had her bangs cut. I'd known her most of my life and she'd never had bangs. I still couldn't get used to them no matter how good they looked on her.

"This is so not good." Jackie spoke very slowly.

"Nice observation," Charles retorted. "Got big plans today?"

"Bigger than I expected apparently. What the hell happened?" Jackie stayed in the doorway.

"We aren't sure what the motive was, but someone broke in last night. Whether they found what they wanted or not they wanted us to know they were here," I said. Steadier now, I stood. "They definitely wanted us to know they were here."

"I'll call Manpower and see if they can get someone over here this morning." Charles stepped over papers and folders as he headed back to the door.

I yelled after him. "They have to be licensed and bonded."

Jackie braved another step in the door, and Charles kissed her cheek as he moved past her. Lola tugged at her leash and Charles let go. She went straight to her bed, did three turns and plopped down.

Jackie looked around the corner to my files. "What on earth?"

"My thought exactly. Why not just take what you want and get the hell out?" I walked toward the strewn files. It took every ounce of energy I had not to kick the files across the floor. It'd just make more work in the long run, but boy, it would have felt good in the moment.

"Making a mess of everything will make it that much harder to find what's missing. The longer it takes, the better the chances are that what they took won't matter to us as much," Jackie said. She leaned against the wall with her arms crossed.

"Duh. I should've figured that. But they took Esme's computer. That was pretty obvious." I bent down and pushed paper back into one of the folders.

"Isn't that the one Charles is working on for the police department?" Jackie uncrossed her arms and pushed off the wall.

"Yeah, it was her work computer."

Charles popped his head in the door. "Someone will be here in about an hour. She's got lots of filing experience. But she has a kid in school and has to leave by three."

"Great. One more person will be a big help," I said.

"Oh yeah, one more thing. You know the threats and the nasty messages on Lauren's website and blog?" Charles asked.

"Yeah," I said, a little impatient.

"All of the messages came from the same IP address." Charles turned to leave.

"Hold up. What does that mean?" Me being the computer that I am, I didn't know an IP address from UPS.

"It means that Esme wrote every last one of those hostile remarks, and every threat." He said this so matter of fact I almost didn't catch it.

"What?"

"You heard me. The whole thing was a farce. There were no threats. She probably doesn't even need a bodyguard. Maybe she set up Esme's demise and needed an alibi. That sweet little thing was probably boffing her hubby, and Lauren got rid of her. Setting up the threats could make it look like a crazed fan, and Esme was none the wiser." He ran his manicured fingers through his hair.

"Her alibi would have been the book signing. She could hardly have killed Esme when she was in San Francisco." Jackie loved putting her two cents in.

"Whatever. I don't know why she did it. But she set the whole thing up. Maybe it's the opposite and Lauren doesn't even know about it. Esme could have set it up." He was now examining his fingers, and rubbing something from his thumb. Like a cat, Charles was always grooming.

"You met her. Do you think anything happens that Lauren doesn't know about?" I asked.

"Who knows? Maybe Esme was trying to scare Lauren for some reason." Charles shot his cuffs then turned to leave.

I called after him. "Where are Gemma and Lauren today?"

"Los Angeles. The signing is at seven," Charles called over his shoulder.

I grabbed for my desk phone, but it was on the floor. I picked it up, replaced the receiver, then lifted it and dialed Gemma's cell. She answered on the second ring.

"Put Lauren on the phone," I snapped.

"Mimi? What's going on?" Gemma said.

I could hear noise in the background. A television, radio, I couldn't tell.

"Where are you?"

"I'm in the hotel room. Lauren's in the shower. Hold on." I could hear Gemma put down the phone.

"I'm going to the other room to help Charles. This'll take all day." Jackie left.

"She's just getting out of the shower. Do you want to wait?" Gemma asked.

"Have her call me back. This is very important." I heard Gemma speaking as I hung up the phone.

I shouldn't have been so short with Gemma, this wasn't her fault. Being flummoxed made me testy.

Were there problems between Lauren and Esme? What would make the girl write such awful remarks in a public forum? They seemed to get along well when I met them Monday morning and Esme said she loved her job. I couldn't figure out what was going on. And the way Charles delivered the information was like he'd expected it all along. Maybe I missed something.

I looked at the pile of papers and folders on the floor. Oh, it would have to wait. I started toward the foyer to get my briefcase and laptop when I saw them next to the door. Either Charles or Jackie had brought them in and I hadn't even noticed. I bent down to grab them and saw shiny black feet.

"Mrs. Capurro, may I take pictures in here now?" It was the younger officer.

I stepped away from the doorway. "Sure. Come on in. I'll be working at my desk if that's okay."

"Sure. I'll just be a few minutes." He eased past me.

Setting up my laptop computer on the desk was easy. The intruder had kindly swept the contents of my desk into a pile on the floor. I looked at the pile to the right. In my head I made a sweeping motion. Burglar boy was right-handed. That really narrowed it down.

I couldn't concentrate on anything with papers strewn across the floor, so when the officer finished his photo session I started on the mess.

I'd been picking up and sorting paper from the floor for twenty minutes when my cell phone rang. I rose from my kneeling position in front of the filing cabinet and pulled my phone from the holster.

"Hello, this is Mimi."

"Gemma said you wanted to speak to me." Lauren's tone was stiff.

"Why don't you tell me about the hostile environment on your website these last few months." I said it as a statement.

"What about it?" There was no hint of defensiveness in her voice.

I wondered for a second if she actually knew the threats were fake. But only a second. Nothing went on without Lauren's knowledge, I was certain. I answered back with another question.

"Whose idea was it?"

"Okay, Mimi, I'm really not in the mood for games. What's this about?"

I wasn't in the mood for games either. "Charles informed me this morning that all of the comments and messages on your website were coming from the same IP address. He traced the IP address to the laptop the police delivered. Esme's computer. Do you know what that means?"

"It means that Esme concocted all the crap on the website and blog. So?"

Now I was pissed off. She'd known, and she'd let me think there was really a threat. "So? Are you kidding me? Lauren, this changes everything."

"How's that? I still need protection from that lunatic."

"Oh, really? Is there really a lunatic out there? Or was that a ruse too?" Before she could answer, I said, "Come clean now or Gemma's coming back to Salinas within the hour."

There was a long silence. I could hear what sounded like soap opera dialogue in the background. Just as I was ready to have her put Gemma on the phone, she began talking.

"Look, sales of my last book were down. I didn't know if it was economics, or that people were moving on to other authors or what. Esme came up with the idea to cause a commotion. Conflict sells novels. We decided to invent conflict through the website to garner some attention. It worked. Traffic was up almost fifty percent. If traffic was up, we hoped sales for this next book would be up too. You know, 'Oh, yeah, I bought this book about the time when Lauren was having serious trouble with her fans.'"

I listened, not knowing what to say. This was truly messed up. It made me wonder if something like this was the norm. I mean didn't the controversy over James Frey's book increase sales?

She continued, "It's no different than the public relations department would've done if they'd thought of it first. Who do think writes those five-star reviews on Amazon?"

"I don't really give a shit about reviews on Amazon at this moment. I do give a shit if you've been jerking me around, using me for your book-selling scheme." My face felt hot, and I was yelling, and I didn't care.

"Are you kidding me? The stories in the newspaper will bring you great PR, and you're just the afterthought of the news piece." She was yelling back.

"Put Gemma on the phone." I'd heard enough. I wasn't going to be sucked any further into her fraudulent antics.

Lauren lowered her voice, "Look. The attack was real. I don't know why the woman felt the need to mow me down with her fists, but she did. Maybe she'd been reading the blog, or the Facebook comments. Maybe she thought she'd do more than write a comment. I promise you Mimi, the attack was real."

I took a deep breath. I wasn't sure where I should stand on this. And how did all this tie into Esme's murder? "So we've been on a wild goose chase in Esme's murder investigation, haven't we?"

I heard Lauren take a deep breath. "I really don't know if Esme's death is related to what was written on the website. I can't imagine how anyone would even connecter to me. She works in the background, sort of invisible. Not many people even know I have an assistant. My readers think I update the website and answer all the emails myself. Esme is a great loss for me. Henry told me I already have hundreds of emails to be answered, and the blog readers are wondering why I haven't been blogging from the road. I've always given updates while I'm on a signing tour. So to answer your question, yes, you've probably wasted your time by trying to track down the origin of the messages."

"Shit," I said, under my breath.

"Probably. But I do know this. Whoever killed Esme has read my book. And whoever it was had access to my new book before it hit the bookstore shelves."

By now I was pacing. When I noticed, I changed my pattern and began walking circles around my desk.

I had my phone pressed against my ear so hard it hurt. I switched the phone to my other hand and ear.

"Why didn't you tell me this before? The killer is now days ahead of us." In my head I was trying to decide which direction to take this investigation.

"I did tell you about the scene being from the book."

I sighed. "No, I mean about the online stuff being a PR stunt."

"I know I should have. And for Esme's sake I'm sorry I didn't. Why I didn't, I really can't tell you. Murder is what happens in books and to other people. When it happens to the people around you, you can't believe it. I guess I wasn't thinking right. Between the signings, book sales, the attack, and then the murder, I just wasn't thinking clearly."

"Not to mention, you didn't think we'd figure it out," I said.

"That too." She sounded resigned. "You will keep working with the police, won't you?"

"I just don't know. I have a lot of work piling up. With Gemma traveling with you, and me working the murder, Jackie and Charles are overloaded. If you aren't telling me the truth, I'm wasting everyone's valuable time and money."

"Mimi, I promise. No more publicity stunts. I didn't leak Esme's murder to the press, as you must already know. There hasn't been anything in the papers. I will cooperate fully from here on out. I owe this to Esme. She was my right arm. I will never be able to replace her, as an assistant or as a person."

"I don't know where to go from here. Look, if I find out you haven't come clean, I'm not only going to quit the case, I'm going to make sure you are brought up on obstruction of justice charges. Are we clear?" I enunciated each word carefully, making sure she got the full weight of my threat.

"We're clear," Lauren said.

Charles popped his head in the door and gave me a quizzical look.

"I've got to go." I hung up.

Charles asked, "Who was that?"

"That bitch Lauren knew all along. She let us follow a completely worthless lead." I flopped into my Aeron chair.

Charles sat in the client chair across from me and put his feet on my desk. I didn't have the energy to push them off. "So did you fire her as a client?"

"Not yet," I said. "To tell you the truth, I'd like to solve the case before Nick does."

Charles jumped to his feet. "I knew it. I knew there was something going on with you guys."

"Guess again. There's nothing going on with me and Nick." I rolled my eyes.

Charles sing-songed, "But there was."

I opened my laptop, dismissing Charles.

He pushed it shut. "I know. If not now, there was in the past, and there will be in the future."

I'd had enough. I reopened my computer. "That's where you are definitely wrong. There will *never* be anything between Nick and me. Never."

Charles knew better than to close my laptop again. But he leaned in close. "We'll see."

Noncommittally I said, "Uh huh."

"I've got work to do." He turned and stalked out. At the door he stopped. "You know you look cute together."

Behind the cover of my computer I smiled. As much as I hated to admit it, I liked seeing Nick again. I liked his scent, his smile, and even his sarcasm.

Sitting across from him at lunch yesterday had taken me back to before the bad times.

Suddenly there was a bang and yelling coming from the foyer. I jumped up to see what the commotion was.

Standing in the entry, yelling at Charles, was Nick. So much for the pleasant memories.

"You compromised my murder investigation," Nick shouted.

"I'm not deaf, detective." Charles remained cool.

"No, just stupid."

At that point I stepped in. No one insults my employees but me. And I certainly wasn't going to listen to Nick berate Charles when he didn't even know the facts.

"You either calm down, or leave," I said.

"Mimi, I'm fine." Charles tried to push me aside.

I stood my ground. And I'd be standing my ground from here on out. Nick wasn't going to step back into my life and play alpha male with me, or my staff.

"Nick, you need to shut up and listen to Charles, or I'm going to shoot you." I moved my hand to my shoulder holster. Damn it, I didn't have my gun and holster on.

In a slightly calmer tone, Nick said, "With what, your finger?"

"Just let Charles speak. Uninterrupted."

Nick said nothing. Charles took this as his cue to speak.

"Like I've been trying to tell you, I have everything in the safe. Yes, the computer is gone, but I have all the information that computer contained. And I truly hope the crime scene techs dusted the thing for prints before you brought it to me. If they did, we have nothing to worry about. As of now that computer is just a carcass."

I winced. Charles could have used a better word. This was a murder investigation after all.

"So the evidence is intact?" Nick asked.

I jumped in before Charles could answer. "Yes. So you just wasted all that energy for nothing."

Using a different tone, Nick said, "Were you able to get anything from it?"

Charles's posture never changed. He'd been cool when Nick was yelling, and he was cool now. "Oh, yeah. A whole lot of nothing."

"What he means is we've been chasing the wrong lead. There never were any real threats to Lauren." I was still angry at the woman.

"You figured this out from a computer?" Nick asked, folding his arms across his chest.

"I did some poking around and found out that all of the hostile remarks, threats, and instigation were coming from the same IP address. I pinpointed the address and it turned out to be Esme's computer."

"So all that crap on the website was a hoax?" I could see a crimson color seep into Nick's tanned face.

Here we go again. He's going to blow a gasket.

"In so many words, yes. It was a publicity stunt. They were trying to increase web traffic, therefore possibly increasing sales on the upcoming book." I said as I stood my ground, waiting for the tirade.

"Instead it got Esme killed." He was solemn, almost sad.

Charles piped up. "I don't think so. I don't think Lauren, her books, or her fans have anything to do with the murder."

Incredulous, Nick said, "How can that be? The murder was a replica of that scene in her book."

"So maybe the killer took advantage of the so-called 'publicity' to throw off any suspicion. What else did Esme do besides work for Lauren?" Charles said.

That was it. It wasn't Esme's professional life, it was her personal life that got her killed. And who else would have such an interest in vampires? The Camarilla.

I grabbed Nick by the arm. "Come into my office, we need to talk."

Nick resisted for a moment. I felt the flexing of his muscles and nearly let my guard down, wanting those arms wrapped around me. To save myself the embarrassment of jumping his bones, I kept myself from looking at him until I was safely on the other side of the desk. Yes, a large wooden desk between us was a good thing.

When I did look at him, I could tell he wasn't thinking the same things I was. He was still back on the fact that we'd been following a dead end.

Nick sat in the chair and crossed his legs. "What do we need to talk about?"

"About us." I was joking, but I wanted to get his reaction.

"What us?" He'd put his foot back down and leaned forward, not repulsed like I expected, but intrigued.

Well, that backfired, didn't it? Think fast. I said, "Us working together on this."

"In that case, there is no us." Nick stood.

"Sit down," I demanded. "I have something you'll want to hear."

"I doubt it." He remained standing.

"Fine. You know where the door is."

"What? What could you possibly say that I want to, or need to, hear?"

Drum roll please. "I know what the charm necklace is all about."

That worked. He sat back down. "Okay?"

"Have you ever heard of the Camarilla?" I loved having the edge over him.

"It's a live role-playing game. They play it up in San Francisco. It has a huge cult following. What about it?" But before I said anything, he said, "Vampires."

God, why did he have to know more than I did?

"Fine, so you know about it. Did you know Esme was a player?"

"No shit?" Now I had his attention.

"So is Henry, and Esme's boyfriend, Sebastian. The boyfriend actually got her involved in the game. The charms belong to the players."

"Do you think it's related to her death?"

"Could be. I'm just learning more about the game. I'd like to talk to Sebastian about Esme, the game, the other players, and anything else she might have been involved in."

Nick said, "So would I. I actually like the guy as a suspect."

"Really?" Now he had my attention.

"I haven't been able to get a hold of him. I've left messages, stopped by his apartment, and even went by his office. He hasn't been at work, and hasn't returned my calls." He'd pulled out a notepad and was flipping pages.

"Where does he work?"

He flipped through a couple more sheets of the pad. "That's what I was looking for." He flipped one more page. "Here it is. He works for an IT firm in Monterey. They help set up networks and provide support."

"So what does he do?"

"He provides IT support," Nick said.

"Really? Can you be more specific? And maybe give me the company name?"

He looked at the pad again. "Deriw Support Systems."

I wrote the name down. "And he hasn't been there?"

"I really don't know. Every time I stop by or call, I get the run-around," Nick said.

"Private business?"

"Very private. Unless I have a warrant, they won't even tell me if he's been calling in sick, left the company, or is out on business. Guess they are lawsuit shy."

"He's one of them. The Camarilla vampires. You need to find him."

"You keep coming back to that game," Nick said.

"I'm sure this live role playing thing has something to do with Esme's death. I mean, why else would someone stage it like the scene in a vampire novel? I'm sure she gave advanced copies to her player friends. They have to be freaks too, if they dress up and play that game."

Nick flipped his notebook closed. "The fan angle may not be completely dead. There's always a chance a crazy fan knew more than they think, or found out Esme was posting the messages. Hell, who knows?"

I had a revelation. "Look, you haven't been able to get to Sebastian, maybe I can."

Nick slammed his hands on my desk. I jumped back.

"No. This is a murder investigation. Don't you get that? I can't have you nosing around, contaminating evidence or my potential witnesses." He pushed off the desk and stood. "I've got a meeting to get to."

"Before you storm out of here like the immature boy that you are, I wanted to let you know that there is a bottle of wine at Lauren's house that needs to be tested. And maybe even printed." I still had the one up on him.

"What?"

"Henry said he put away a bottle of wine and two glasses that night when he came home. He said he came in through the kitchen and saw the stuff on the counter. Before putting it away, he poured himself a glass." I beamed with self-satisfaction at knowing this.

"I know. There was a glass of wine on the nightstand in the bedroom," Nick sounded bored.

"Was it drugged?"

"We think so. But I don't have the test results just yet."

"Do you know what wine it was?" I asked.

Nick looked up, like he was plucking the answer from the ceiling. "Red."

"Bummer. Well, see ya." I suddenly couldn't wait for him to leave. I wanted him to want the answer. I wasn't going to blurt it out.

"Are you going to tell me? Or do you want me to guess?" Now he was edgy.

"Fine, it was," I looked at my notes, "*Santa Rita Casa Real Cabernet Sauvignon 2003*."

"Thanks," Nick said, writing furiously in his little pad. "Now stay out of it, Mimi."

Then he stalked out.

As soon as I heard the front door of the building close, I called Charles on the intercom. "Do you have contact information for a Sebastian Zidonis from Esme's PDA?"

CHAPTER 12

I couldn't believe my luck when I called Deriw Support Systems and got Sebastian on the phone. He said he had meetings after lunch, but would be willing to meet with me about one o'clock.

I drove back to the house and dropped off Lola. She didn't need to be running loose in the office with so much paperwork scattered everywhere. She'd probably revert back to her potty training days and see it as an excuse to pee on everything. While I was there, I changed into a black sheath dress. The hem came to about mid-thigh, but was flared just enough to be flattering to my behind. I slipped into the same black pumps I'd worn for lunch with Nick. I even had enough time to straighten my hair and wear it loose over my shoulders. I couldn't wait to meet the elusive Sebastian.

When Sebastian Zidonis walked into the reception area of Deriw Support Systems, my first thought was NBA. Most of the computer geeks I'd met in my life looked like the class nerd. I'd say Charles was the exception, but if you saw his high school photos you'd know he was the class nerd.

Sebastian had a body that had been honed for years. He towered at least a foot above me, and I'm five-seven. He wore Levis, a long-sleeved oxford shirt, and a lanyard with his identification card attached. His face had sharp features with a dimpled chin, and looking in his eyes was like looking into a Jacuzzi, pools of blue so pale they had flecks of white.

I imagined him standing next to Esme, who was the epitome of waif. What a contrast in size, but in looks, they could have been brother and sister: The olive skin, blue eyes, and black hair. Esme's hair was dyed, but Sebastian's look naturally black. He had it cropped short on the sides, with a bit of length on top that could easily grow into a curly mess. A curly mess any girl would want to run her fingers through, including me.

When he put his hand out to greet me I just stared. The paw he offered could cover my face and he'd still have hand left over to wrap his fingers around my head.

"Ms. Capurro?" Sebastian said.

"Mr. Zidonis," I said back. I did take his hand, and he had a gentle but firm grip.

"Wow, you pronounced it correctly." Sebastian smiled. Good lord, everything about him was big, including his grin.

I cocked my head toward the receptionist. "She helped by saying it for me first."

Sebastian glanced at the grandmotherly woman manning the desk. "She may look soft, but she's better than having Dobermans at the door."

"So I hear. I'm glad you were in or I'd never have gotten past her. Thanks for seeing me. I'm sure you're busy."

He stepped forward and put his hand on the back of my shoulder, leading me. "Let's go to my office."

I followed him down a long hall, turned right, then through the first door on the left. I sat without him directing me. I could hear the commotion of people in the hall behind me, but I didn't turn to look.

Sebastian adjusted his pants at the thigh as he sat. The desk between us was clear acrylic and held two desktop computers with flat screens and a laptop. Sebastian closed the laptop as he sat.

"Not what you expected?" He must have noticed me taking in the surroundings.

The office was about the size of my living room, which isn't small, but not too large either. The walls were white; an office-sized basketball hoop graced one wall with a garbage can under it. There wasn't a piece of paper in sight, nor were there any filing cabinets other than the one black two-drawer file under his desk. Since there were no drawers in the desk, I assumed this was where he kept any papers, pencils, pens, clips. I'm assuming, because I wasn't sure those items actually existed in his office.

"Not even close to what I expected." But I couldn't explain why.

"You expected dark, with vampire memorabilia on the walls? Or a vile of blood somewhere?" He spoke lightly, smiling.

"Well, no, but I did expect to see files, paper, maybe a pen or highlighter."

He laughed. It was like his voice, low and throaty. Sexy. I could sit and listen to him talk, or laugh, all day.

"We work with highly confidential materials for major companies. We don't keep anything out where it can be seen. I do have office supplies in my desk if you'd like to see them." He pulled open one of the file drawers.

I have no idea why, but I blushed. It felt like he was revealing something private. It hadn't been that long since I'd been in the same room with an All-American boy. But I guess it had been that long since I thought about what a guy would look like naked.

The All-American image dissolved the moment Sebastian pushed up his sleeves. From where his watch lay to where his sleeves were at his elbows his skin was covered in tattoos. I didn't want to stare, but from a glance I saw a pentagram, blood drops, and what looked like a scepter.

He looked at me looking at him. "Surprised?"

I didn't want to start out with a lie, so I said, "Yes and no."

"If it helps, you're supposed to be. I only roll up my sleeves when I'm not with clients. Tattoos, whether I like it or not, have a stigma."

Could the guy be more easy going?

He continued, "Besides I have to admit, I was surprised by you, too. When Ethel said there was a private detective here to see me, I didn't expect to see a, well, a sexy woman?"

"Thanks? I guess."

Suddenly the room temperature seemed to increase by at least fifty degrees.

This was not going the way I'd planned. I wasn't sure if I should be flattered or insulted. In a flash, I got it. Sebastian knew exactly how good looking he was. And like Nick, he was accustomed to using his looks to put people off center. How old was I anyway? I sure wasn't a twenty-something who'd be pulled in by Sebastian's compliments.

"I'm curious. Has a girl ever told you no?"

Sebastian laughed. "Actually, yes, but not often. I really do think you're attractive."

"Thanks."

"You're a private detective?"

"Yes."

"I'm curious, did you always want to be a private detective? Or was it something you stumbled into?"

I couldn't tell if he was sincere, or mocking me. "I came to it in a roundabout way."

He leaned his tattooed elbows on his desk. "And how was that?"

"I went to college to be an athletic trainer. But I got the chance to apply to the Secret Service and I did that instead."

"Too bad," Sebastian said. "I'll bet there were a lot of young men sorry you didn't tape their ankles."

Out of any other guy that would have sounded creepy, but somehow Sebastian made it sound romantic.

"Long story short, my husband died and I quit the Service. Soon after I opened Gotcha."

"Gotcha?" Sebastian's brows furrowed.

"The Gotcha Detective Agency," I said.

"Cute name," he said. "So you were married. I'm sorry to hear about your husband."

How had this interview gotten away from me? "Sebastian, you are quite the charmer, but just about a decade too young for me to engage you any further. I came here to ask you the questions."

"Get 'em young, treat 'em, rough, tell 'em nothing." Sebastian laughed again.

I ignored the remark. "I wanted to ask you about Monday night."

"You wanted to talk about Esme's death." The preliminaries were over; we were getting to the point.

"You two were an item, right?" I said.

"Wrong," Sebastian corrected. "We hadn't been together for awhile. But we did have connections in other ways."

"The Camarilla." I'd hoped to put him off center.

"Yes. So who told you?" He seemed curious, but not upset that I knew.

"First I heard it from Susan." I saw a reaction. "Then Henry offered up more details."

"Ha, Susan, what did she say?" His voice had tensed. I saw his knee bobbing under the desk.

"Just that you had brought Esme into the game. That a Kindred had to invite any new player into the game. She also said that it was very secretive. Membership included a swearing of silence."

Sebastian rolled his eyes. "There's no swearing of silence. We do have a pact to respect the personal lives of the players. As you've noticed, I don't have anything vampire related in my office. Vampires and the Camarilla are my private life, and I'd like to keep it that way."

"Okay. But you said you and Esme weren't together?"

"Not anymore," Sebastian said. "How do I put this? Esme tended to be gung ho about things. Obsessive even. She took everything on one hundred and twenty percent. That included me. If I didn't know better, I'd think the girl did crack. How else could a person concentrate so much time on large projects?

"Did Esme do drugs?"

"Absolutely not," Sebastian said. "Don't you know about her mom?"

"I've heard a little. Like Esme moved out of the house because her mom accused her of getting too close to her boyfriend. Detective Christianson thinks the boyfriend might have been too chummy with Esme."

"Try the real story. Opal, her mom, tried to sell her for drugs. She needed a fix so she offered her daughter to the boyfriend for money. I don't know how much. Then she begged and pleaded with Esme to cooperate. Esme was old enough to make her own decisions, and she decided it was time to get out before she ended up raped."

My heart sank. How could a mother do that to her own child? "How old was she?"

"This happened about ten years ago, so I guess somewhere around thirteen or fourteen. In so many ways she was old, and in those same ways she was very young."

"Sad," I said. "What about her father?"

"Are you kidding? Opal was like a cat in heat. She could have chosen from a number of men. But half of them she probably couldn't track down." Sebastian looked disgusted.

"Susan said she and Esme were friends since high school, and that Esme lived with her mom during that time. What you're saying doesn't mesh with Susan's story."

Sebastian laughed. "Susan only knows half as much as she thinks she does. Esme came home off and on. She had a good gauge for when her mom was trying to get clean. Even with all the crap, Esme still loved Opal. You know, the mother and daughter bond. I only met Opal once or twice. One of the times was at the house. When Esme went to the bathroom, Opal came on to me. It was creepy. I never told Esme, she didn't need to know. But I never went back there again. That was probably a year ago."

"Could Opal have killed Esme? Thinking there was insurance money or something?" This was a new train of thought for me.

"Oh, yeah, I think Opal would have done her daughter in for the right amount of money." He steepled his fingers and put them under his chin. "But I'm pretty sure Opal had no idea where to find her daughter."

"Are you sure? Susan knew Opal. Do you think she could have slipped and told her?"

Sebastian laughed. "Like I said, Susan thinks she knows more than she does. Right after Esme moved out, Opal went to prison for five years. During high school Esme lived with her aunt. Not a bad lady, but not good either. She also had money and drug issues, but she'd never sell Esme for a fix. Aunt Betty's drug of choice could be made in the kitchen."

"And Esme never told Susan it was her aunt?"

"You've met Susan. Would you trust her?" Sebastian leaned toward me. "Susan cares only about Susan."

"Oh. But I thought they were best friends." Don't best friends share everything? And the girls lived together.

"Esme was Susan's best friend. Esme had tons of friends. Esme is a very popular girl. I'm sorry, she's still an is to me, not a was." Sebastian looked down for a moment.

"I understand." Esme's death was still very new, and Sebastian hadn't even been around right after it happened.

"Not being Susan's friend can be a bad thing. Esme just put up with her."

"But they lived together."

"Sort of. It's Esme's apartment, but Susan needed a place to crash so Esme stayed at Lauren's most of the time. I will never understand why, but Esme felt sorry for Susan."

Susan didn't seem like such a bad person. She did get a little testy about Esme, but part of it could have been the rawness of her loss. Then again, I didn't quite trust her. She'd already been caught exaggerating the Camarilla.

With this in mind, I asked, "The Camarilla? Can anyone join the game?"

"Sure, within limits. We can't let the game get too big. We're already having problems."

"So if I wanted to join, I wouldn't have to be invited by Kindred, or a higher player in the game?"

"I thought I heard you say that before. No. Why, are you a vampire freak?" Sebastian seemed even more interested in me now. Weird behavior for a guy who's ex-girlfriend had recently been murdered.

"Nope, not a freak. But Susan seemed to think it was all very hush hush. And quite the secret society."

"Yes, and Susan was never a player. She was kind of uninvited before she was ever invited."

So Esme had kept Susan from the game. By using the thing, she had kept Susan from talking about it. Esme was smart, and maybe, like Susan said, she was conniving. After talking with Sebastian, I see now that maybe she had good reasons.

"You should stop by when we play. I'd like to get you in a dark place." Sebastian's eyes twinkled.

"Please, let's not go there again." I shook my head and looked away from him.

He leaned back and let go with a solid laugh.

"Do many people outside the game know about it?"

Still leaning back, he put his hands behind his head, lacing his fingers. I swear the tattoos looked like fabric, not skin. There were flowing layers of color, and images of werewolves, vampires, and witches melded into a solid mural. The artwork was incredible, whether I liked tattoos or not. I had to give the artist credit for detailed work.

"I guess quite a few people know of its existence. I mean you can't go into downtown Santa Cruz on a Friday night without running into us."

"Henry said the city is trying to stop the game."

"Henry." Sebastian smiled. "He's always trying to make things right. And this time, with Esme's help, he found a great way to do it."

"Do what?" I asked.

"Make things right. He's the reason we got together on Monday night." He paused. "He did tell you about the dinner, right?"

"Yes, he said you were trying to find a way to show the city of Santa Cruz that the game could be an attraction." I sure was getting a lot of repeat information.

"Yeah. You know the movie The Lost Boys?"

"The one with Kiefer Sutherland?" I knew the movie. Jamie Gertz and what was that other guy's name?

"Yeah. Well, that movie was set in Santa Carla, but it was really Santa Cruz. Everyone knows that. It's an old movie, but everyone's seen it."

"I've seen it too. I loved it." I even remember the boy I went to see it with, Jimmy Donovan.

"So we thought we could capitalize on the history of Santa Cruz. Over the years the city has become synonymous with vampires. Esme had it all worked out. The four of us were the only ones interested in taking it to city hall. We had dinner at Georgio's on Monday night. Georgio's is an Italian place on Highway 68 in Salinas. You know it?"

"Yes, great food."

"Would you like to go with me sometime?" He winked.

I swear his flirting was for real. "Are you that callous? Didn't your girlfriend just die?"

"She wasn't my girlfriend anymore. When Esme became obsessive, I cut off the sex. I hoped it would deter her from calling, sending text messages, and showing up at my house at all hours. Don't get me wrong, I loved Esme as a friend, and fellow vampire addict, but I didn't want to be with her anymore. If she hadn't been so caught up in the Camarilla, I'd probably have asked her not to play anymore."

"So, in the end, your only connection really was the game, and saving it. Why did everyone think you were still together?"

"Because Esme made it look like we were. I didn't want to humiliate her in front of the other players, so I didn't say anything. Besides, there weren't any Camarilla players I wanted to fuck, so she wasn't interfering with anything." Sebastian rocked his chair back and forth. "I was already getting it elsewhere."

"So everyone at the dinner thought you were together?" I asked.

"I guess," Sebastian said.

"Who would they have been?"

Sebastian smiled. Not a genuine smile, but a knowing smile. "Sorry, I'm not going to tell you any names. Besides you already know the others, Henry and Esme. Anyone else doesn't really matter that much."

"But it might," I suggested.

"Probably not." Sebastian looked at his watch.

"At least tell me about dinner. Anything weird happen? Anyone seem tense?"

"No, not really. When I got there Henry and Esme had just arrived. We went into the place together and a few minutes later the other guy arrived."

"The Prince," I prompted.

"Yes."

"So what's his real name?" I tried again.

Sebastian ignored the question. "We ate and had some wine, talked over the project. Esme was going to give the presentation at City Hall, and all was good."

"No one came to or left the table?" The same as I'd asked Henry.

"Sure, Esme said she had to go to the bathroom, but I think that was it. No one came by to say hi or anything. I didn't even see anyone I recognized, other than our party."

"And you all left together?"

"No. I took Esme home. Henry and the other guy stayed on to have drinks at the bar. Henry said he'd like to be nice and drunk before Lauren got home."

So Henry didn't stay behind just to work on their PR campaign some more. Why didn't he tell me that? Well, maybe he didn't want to admit he wasn't looking forward to Lauren coming home after the signing.

"Did you go inside?" I asked.

"Inside where?" Sebastian replied.

"Inside the house, when you took Esme home?"

"Hell no. I told you, I wanted to back off the sex thing with Esme. If I'd gone into the house she would have seduced me, and that was the last thing I needed. Don't get me wrong, I like sex, but not sex with static cling."

"A what?"

"You know, static cling. Some girls stick on like static cling if you have sex with them. Esme was one of those girls. I was trying to extricate myself from her, and going in that house wouldn't have been a good idea. I dropped her at the back door."

Again, I could hear people walking and talking in the hall. This time I looked to see where the noise came from.

"Anything else?" Sebastian looked at his watch. "I have a meeting in ten minutes."

"Just one question. Did you see any cars in the driveway? Or on the street?"

"Not in the driveway. But as for the street, I really didn't pay much attention."

"About what time did you drop Esme off?"

He looked at his watch as if it held the answer. "I don't know, around ten I guess." Sebastian rolled his chair back. "Is that it?"

I straightened, ready to stand, "For now, but may I call you in the future if I have any questions?"

Sebastian stood along with me and came around the desk. I didn't feel any insecurity from him, as Susan had mentioned. I felt only cocky self-satisfaction.

"Call anytime." He had his hand on my shoulder. "I'll walk you to your car. Do you have a business card, in case I think of something relevant?"

I did, and I reach into my clutch purse and pulled one out. When I handed it to him, he touched my hand and I felt myself melt a little. As much as I hate to admit it, I could see us horizontal with the lights out. I'd always wanted to do it with a guy who was different. Sebastian definitely qualified as different. Goodness, I'd been a walking hormone attack this week.

Walking to my Land Rover, he kept his hand between my shoulders, much as he did when we started to his office.

Sebastian suddenly stopped. "Wait here."

He jogged toward a black BMW and I heard the beep-beep of a security alarm. He reached inside for something, and then closed the door, re-engaged the alarm and jogged back to me. "Here."

He handed me a cell phone.

"No thanks. I already have one," I said.

He shook his head. "This is Esme's."

"What?" How on earth did he have Esme's phone?

"I took her home Monday night. It must have fallen on the floor when she got out of the car."

"So you didn't know it was there? No one ever called while it was in your car?" I couldn't believe he hadn't known it was there.

"I left my car at my apartment. I flew out very early Tuesday morning. I found it when I got back last night. By then the phone was dead. I figured I'd give it to the cops when they got around to talking to me. But since you're here, and the next best thing to a cop, I'm giving it to you."

The story was plausible. I'd give him the benefit of doubt.

"Thanks. I'll make sure Nick gets it." I carefully placed it on the console of my car. I stepped in and closed the door. Sebastian remained by my car door, so I rolled the window down.

He leaned down, his azure eyes level with mine. "Ms. Capurro, I think I'd like to see you again."

"Call me Mimi," I said, then rolled up the window and got the hell out of there.

At this point I had no viable suspect, no motives, but plenty of opportunity. Mostly, I didn't know who was telling the truth and who was lying. My cell phone rang.

The caller ID was unknown. I answered anyway.

It was the same voice from this morning. "You aren't listening very well. I see you're still snooping. Stop now, before *I* have to stop you."

CHAPTER 13

Slightly spooked by the call, I drove directly to the cop shop in Salinas. From Sebastian's office in Monterey it was only a fifteen-minute drive. With all of the identical Crown Vics in the parking lot, I had no idea if Nick was in, so I parked at the front of the police station on Lincoln Avenue and walked in through the lobby.

I pushed open the glass door and walked into a busy room. There were three uniformed officers working with civilians and one on the telephone. The walls were a dark blue, with a huge replica of a Salinas Police Department badge behind the reception desk.

I stood in line at the desk. I hadn't been there a minute when Officer Beal walked in. I turned my head as quickly as I could, but he still recognized me.

"Hey, detective," he said, sauntering up very close.

I stepped away from him. "Officer Beal."

He stepped toward me again, invading my personal space. "Here to see me?"

Again I stepped back. "No. Is Nick, I mean Detective Christianson in?"

He leaned down. "I'll go check for you," he whispered. He straightened and said, "I recognized the shoes."

Oh, yeah. Once again I'd embarrassed myself. No wonder Sebastian was so friendly. I'd forgotten I'd dressed to get noticed. And shit, here I was, waiting to see Nick. He was going to think I wanted him. Well I did want him, but not like that.

Officer Beal left and was back before I realized he was gone. He only came halfway through the door. He waved me toward it without speaking. I followed his direction through the door. Beyond the first door he led me to a side room with cubicles aligned along the far wall. There was only a slim aisle, so he stood at the door and pointed to the right.

"Last desk on the right," he said. To Nick he said, "DB, you got company."

Nick peeked around the corner, then immediately moved back behind the partition.

The room was a blue-grey color, with dividers only slightly lighter in shade. Each cubicle held two desks, with loads of files and paperwork. Photos and notes were tacked on the partitions. I eased toward Nick's desk to find him on the phone. He motioned for me to take a seat at the desk opposite his. I did.

He leaned forward on his desk, with his hand over the speaking end of the phone. I guess he didn't want me to hear his side of the conversation. I didn't want to hear it anyway. I was sick to death of this murder. I'd met a friend who may not be a friend at all, a boyfriend who wasn't a boyfriend and who wanted to let me know he was definitely single, and I'd picked up a serial caller. Throw in Henry, who wasn't telling me the whole truth; Lauren, who was more concerned with her writing career than her assistant's murder; and the office I'd left in shambles, I needed a drink.

Nick hung up the phone. He turned to face me when another detective came over to his cubicle.

"Yo DB, who's this lovely lady?" The detective was tall, trim, and had the dry, creased skin of a lifetime smoker. He smelled like stale tobacco.

"She's not as lovely as she looks," Nick said. "This is Mimi Capurro, owner of the Gotcha Detective Agency. Ever heard of it?"

The detective winced. "Oh, yeah. I think my wife hired you about a year ago."

"Oh," I said. "Were you cheating on her?"

"Funny thing, my mistress is my job, and when she realized it, she wanted a divorce. I think a real woman she could have understood. Crazy, huh?"

I had to admit it was crazy. "Yup," I said. I stood to shake his hand. "I'm Mimi, and you are?"

"Detective Sergeant Ronald Haussler. Ron." He shook my hand.

"Nice to meet you, Sergeant," Nick said. "Now Mimi and I have some private business to discuss."

"Excuse the fuck out of me," Detective Haussler said. He turned to go without further comment.

Appalled, I said, "That was rude."

Nick looked at me. "Uh-huh."

"What's the DB?" When I heard Beal say it I didn't quite get it."

"Defensive back. They still remember me from the good old days." Nick was referring to his professional football career.

"Do they know the whole story?" I treaded lightly.

Nick growled. "Who doesn't, it was all over the papers. The media never lets anyone with any money live down the mistakes they make. Hell, it was front of the sports page when I joined the SFPD."

The headlines featured Nick's trouble with drugs and alcohol. Nick had been an outstanding defensive back. In his short career in the NFL, he'd maxed out his chances to clean up. Back in the day, they called it a Three Strikes Rule, even though it was football. Along with the third drunk driving charge, he also had a number of other issues with teammates and the public. On strike three, Nick was released from the San Francisco team. On the bright side, he'd garnered three Super Bowl rings with two teams in those four years.

I didn't want to pry, but I couldn't help it. "So how has life been since football?"

"Not as good as it was when I was in the NFL. But being a cop has mental and physical challenges I could never have imagined. I like it most days. But to be honest, I really miss the money from pro sports." Nick sounded nostalgic.

"Life goes on," I said. "At least you can still get out of bed in the morning."

"True."

"You ever talk to Tomey? He has to take six different meds just to get through his day."

Nick smiled. "Wow, I haven't thought about Tomey in years. Is he back in Salinas?"

"It doesn't matter how big you guys get in the sporting world, you all come back home."

Of the class we went to junior college with, there were at least two players who went to the pros in basketball, baseball, and football. And other than the guys still coaching professional teams, the others had all come home to roost. And now Nick had come home too.

"This isn't really home, you know." Nick reminded me.

"That's right. Your mom still live in Cleveland?" I'd never met his mom, but I'd heard a lot about her in the years when we were still talking.

"She's buried there. She died of brain cancer before I left the NFL."

"Oh, Nick, I'm so sorry, I didn't know." I felt like shit for asking.

"At least she didn't live to see my disgrace."

I just nodded. What did a person say to that?

"How about you? You said your husband died." Tit for tat.

"Yeah, a few years ago in a plane crash. But there was no burial, since they never found his body." I felt as if a blood pressure cuff had been put on my heart, and was being pumped. This wasn't my favorite conversation. Time doesn't heal as quickly as I'd like.

"How did you end up working as a PI?"

Thank God, he knew when to change the subject. "I had no desire to get my Master's, and that's what it was to take to get a decent job as a trainer, so I jumped at a chance to join the Secret Service."

Nick laughed. "And I always thought I'd see you working with the Olympic athletes. I even looked for you during the televised games. I remember you'd had a phone interview with someone in Colorado Springs."

There I was, back to Dominic's death again.

"Funny how life gets in the way of our plans," I said. "When Dominic died, I decided to go into business for myself. I'd quit the service a few months before the crash, and used the hours I'd worked servicing papers for the Sheriff's department to get my PI license. Do you have any idea how many hours of private eye service you have to put in to get this damn license?"

I smiled, trying to lighten the mood. I wished I could see what he had on his desk. I blurted, "I have some information for you."

Did I say I'd had it with this case? So I lied.

"It couldn't possibly be information related to Esme's murder because I've already told you to stay out of it." His voice held a stern warning, which I promptly ignored.

"That Sebastian is a cutie," I said. "Okay, I'm sorry to bother you. I'll be going." I stood.

"Sit." Nick snapped his fingers and pointed to the chair.

"I'm not a dog, Nick." Now I was pissed and not sure I wanted to tell him anything.

"I didn't mean it like that. I can't believe you were able to talk to Sebastian."

"Do you want to hear about my meeting or not?"

Nick acquiesced. "I'm all ears."

So not true. He was all man, in many ways, but that was beside the point now. So I told him all about my meeting with Sebastian, up to and including the Camarilla, the dinner meeting, which Nick already knew about, and the way Sebastian came on to me.

"Well you aren't exactly ugly." Nick stated this in a matter-of-fact way.

"I think that was a compliment. Even coming from you."

Nick pulled at his tie. It was the first time I'd noticed what he was wearing. The man dressed rather dapper. He wore chocolate brown, flat-front slacks with a nicely pressed crease and loafers in a similar shade. His argyle socks were a pattern of brown and pink that complimented his pale pink shirt and lavender tie. The man had worn brown, pink, and lavender, and made it look masculine and sexy. He and Charles could share a closet.

"You've always been very cute. And now that you are a woman you are very sexy. Just because I'm not happy to have you snooping in my case doesn't mean I'm not happy to see you again after all these years." He leaned forward and touched my hand.

Holy pheromones, it was getting hot.

Then he said, "And you smell divine."

Thank you, Donna Karan.

Don't blush, don't blush, don't blush, I kept telling myself. It didn't work. I heated up enough that I could feel the fire in my cheeks, and spreading.

"You too," I said. And he did smell good. A hell of a lot better than Haussler.

"So Sebastian wants to do you, huh?" Nick asked. He took his hand away but still sat close.

"Why do you have to be so crass?" I liked Nick knowing a younger guy was interested.

"By what you told me, he wants to see you again." Did he sound jealous? Nah, Nick didn't know the meaning of the word.

"Maybe he just wants to get together for drinks and talk."

"Wake up, Mimi. He's a guy. He wants to have sex with an older woman."

Ouch, the older woman thing stung. "Whatever. Maybe I'd like to have sex with him, too. It's been a long time." Oh, shit, how did that last statement slip out?

Nick chuckled. "If you're looking to get laid, here's my card. Call me. I'd be happy to take care of it." He flipped his card at me.

This was the Nick I knew and regretted having sex with in college. To him, women were for sex and sex only. He had very little respect for females then, and even now from the sound of it. But the offer was tempting.

What was wrong with me? I hadn't thought about sex with a man since Dominic had died, and now, after a few minutes alone with Sebastian, and his body, his voice and the flirting, I was ready to jump Nick. I needed a cold shower. Then I remembered I'd be hitting the bar after this. I had a client to meet, or rather a client's cheating husband.

"I'll probably get a little tonight without any help from you or Sebastian. Thanks." Even though I knew I wouldn't.

"Is that why you came here, to tell me that Sebastian has the hots for you?"

"No. I wanted to tell you I have serious doubts about the story they're telling."

"Why's that?" Nick swiveled in his chair.

I swiveled too. "Henry says he stayed behind to work on the PR project. Sebastian says he stayed to get drunk before Lauren came home."

"So maybe that's what Henry told Sebastian. Besides, he probably figured Sebastian wanted to be with Esme, and he didn't want to hear the grunts and groans coming from down the hall."

"According to Sebastian, he and Esme were no longer a couple."

"Oh? That's news."

"Sebastian said they were still friends, but the relationship was over. Something about static cling."

Nick laughed hard. "I get it."

I wasn't sure what was so funny. "Okay, good."

"Where does this lead us?" Nick was thinking aloud.

"Do you have any suspects?" I needed to know his angle on this investigation.

"I can't share that information." He was adamant.

"What about Esme's mom? You talked to her, didn't you?"

"Actually, we talked to her mom and her aunt."

"So you know she was living with her aunt, not her mom," I said.

Nick nodded. "It was a strange set up. But Esme's mom hasn't seen her in a long time, and the aunt is an invalid. I don't see either one of them wielding a sword and slicing off Esme's head. Have you ever lifted one of those things?"

I had to admit I hadn't. Swords weren't really my thing.

"They're heavy. The person who did this was strong. Even if Esme was drugged and complacent, the person had to have the strength to lift that thing and swing it hard. A little half-hearted swipe wouldn't take a head clean off."

I saw the image of Esme's body sitting in the chair. The slice was clean. No one had hacked at the neck. The deadly blow was one solid swipe.

"What about Sebastian? He said they'd broken up, yet Esme wouldn't leave him alone. What if she threatened him in some way? He seemed serious about keeping his business and personal lives separate. He even said he didn't want the people at work to know about his involvement in the Camarilla game thing."

"But is that motive to kill the girl?" Nick sounded skeptical.

"Not so much," I had to agree.

"I can't find an angle I can get my teeth into." Frustration filled his voice.

"How close were Esme and Henry? You don't think maybe she and Henry had a thing, do you?"

"Didn't you say she was with Sebastian, left the dinner with him?"

"Yes, but maybe she flaunted Sebastian in front of him. Henry could be jealous. Maybe he and Esme had gotten close while she lived there. You know Lauren traveled quite a bit over the last few years. And Esme was always home to take care of the correspondence, the blog, email, you know. They could have gotten carried away."

Nick thought about it. "There's a possibility. A very slim possibility. Maybe we'll have to take another look at Henry. But I really don't see it."

We could banter back and forth all afternoon. I looked at my watch. I had to get back to the office before I headed out for my decoy stint. I got to the point.

"So look, here's the deal, do you want to go take a look at the Camarilla game tomorrow night?"

Nick smiled at the abrupt change of subject. "Sure. Where and what time?"

That was more like it. "How about we meet at my office, and we can drive over together?" I suggested.

"Let's play it by ear. I have more than just this case at the moment, and I'm working alone until I get my permanent partner."

"Okay." I was disappointed. I'd wanted to spend some time getting to know Nick again. At least we were being civil to each other.

"Then we'll talk tomorrow. Set it up. Does anyone know we'll be there?" Nick asked.

I was excited about seeing the game. I stood to leave. I watched him watching me and I liked the expression on his face.

"No, we'll only be watching from the periphery," I said. I started out of the office.

"Tell you what. They know us, but they don't know Charles, right?"

This sounded promising. I waited, not answering.

"They want to have a positive profile. So let's say we have Charles pose as a reporter and go in, take photos, and ask questions. He can throw in a few about Esme and see what kind of reaction he gets."

"Nick, you're brilliant. At least we can get a neutral perspective on their attitudes toward Esme."

Now all I had to do was talk Charles into it.

CHAPTER 14

By the time I got back to the office, Charles and the temps had all of the papers picked up and stacked in piles. Not an inch of the conference table could be seen beneath the weight of paper and folders. He stood with shirt sleeves pushed up past his elbows and was sorting through one of the piles on an extra table for the sorting process.

"Hey," I announced myself. "Looks like you've got yourself a system."

He looked up. If ever Charles looked flustered, it was now. "Since when am I a secretary?"

I smiled. I could relate to his frustration. Paperwork wasn't my strong suit, so why did I open a business where every case had reams of reports? At first, I used to put off the reports, but then it became overwhelming. Now I forced myself to write it all down at the end of the day. Just like a lawyer, when you are billing by the hour, keeping track means the difference between a steak dinner and macaroni and cheese. In my first year I probably worked at least a hundred hours for which I never got paid. Having Charles has made a difference. He makes sure I get every penny.

"How about I give you another task?" I hurried over and kissed him on the cheek. "You know how much I appreciate you, right?"

"Yeah, you only appreciate me when you need something. I'm a computer forensics tech, not a freaking file clerk." Boy, he was in a bad mood.

I handed him Esme's phone, hoping to mollify him.

He snatched it from me, turning it over and back. "What's this?"

There wasn't anything special about it. It was a typical thin, Blackberry. "A cell phone," I said.

"Really?" Charles's sarcasm increased with his temper. He really was in a bad mood.

"Esme's cell phone." I beamed.

Now Charles looked at the phone again with a new appreciation. "How did you get this?"

"Sebastian gave it to me."

"How did he get it? Didn't the police take it when they searched the house?"

"Sebastian said he thought she dropped it in his car on Monday night. He was going to give it to the police when they stopped by, but since I got there first, he gave it to me. Lucky me." I was almost giddy.

Charles flipped the phone open. "It's dead."

"I know. Do you have a charger that will fit it?"

"If not, I'll go buy one. This should be interesting." He abandoned the papers he'd been sorting and left me standing there to assess the magnitude of the mess we had.

I walked around to the other side of the conference table and looked closer at the piles. No matter how I tried to process the information, I couldn't make sense of how he had everything organized. I picked up one set and flipped through one page at a time. There was no rhyme or reason to the stack that I could find.

Charles came back as I set the papers back on the table. "We're in luck, I have a charger. We'll give it about an hour or so and then I'll take a look. When I get the number, I'll call the cell phone company and get a copy of the records for the last few months. I'm sure we'll be able to match every number to those in her PDA."

"Good," I said, and then pointed at the table. "Is there a method to your madness here?"

"Madness is a good way to put it," Charles scoffed. "The temp and I just tried to clean things up. It looked bad when clients came in. I wouldn't give my business to a company with papers strewn across the floor."

I had to agree. "So this is just random stacks?"

Miffed, Charles said, "Yes, Mimi, I can't work miracles. Every piece of paper we had in this office was on the floor."

"I wasn't criticizing. I was asking. This is a lot to absorb."

"This is taking away from our clients, you know."

The thought made me sick. We could ill afford to neglect our clients in order to clean this up. When I got my hands on the person who did this, I was going to make a mess of my own on his face.

I said, "Do you think we should hire a few more temps and have them work with minimal supervision, so we can get back to work?"

Charles frowned. "That's all well and good, but we have to hire bonded temps. The stuff in these files is confidential. And what happens when we need to have something for a current case, and we can't get to it?"

"All the more reason to have extra help putting everything back in order," I said. My phone rang. "Hold on."

I didn't look at the caller ID. "This is Mimi."

"Are you really that stupid? I told you to leave this alone. If you don't, you'll be in worse shape than your offices." It was that voice again.

Now I was annoyed. "Look you idiot, cell phones can be tracked. I'll know who you are within minutes."

"Throw away phones aren't traceable." The line went dead.

And that's where the caller was very wrong. The disposable phones that come with prepaid minutes are easily traceable. All I, or rather Charles, needed to do was track the activation time and place. From there, I admit, it was a crap shoot. We'd have to get lucky enough that the seller had video surveillance. Most places with electronics have some sort of camera system in place.

"Who was that?" Charles asked.

I sighed. "Not sure. I've been getting calls all week telling me to back off. Since the only thing I've been working on is Esme's murder I guess maybe it's related to that. I haven't really thought much about it. I mean what coward hides behind stupid cell phone threats?"

"Maybe the kind that kills people." Charles looked concerned.

"I guess I should be worried, especially if someone has my cell phone number. It's not a number I give out to everyone."

"It's on your business cards, Mimi." Charles reminded me.

"Shit, that's right. Hell, it could be anyone."

"Does anyone related to this murder have your card?"

"Lauren, Esme, well I guess she doesn't count now, Sebastian, Henry, Lauren's publicist Pat, and I guess Nick." I couldn't remember everyone I'd given my card to.

"Give me your phone. We'll see if it's your hot boyfriend or not." Charles grinned. He thought he was so funny.

"One, he's not my boyfriend. Two, what will I do for a phone?"

He grabbed my phone from by hand before I could react. "It won't take that long. I'll have the number traced before you can get through a single pile on this table."

I looked at the daunting task. No thanks. "Tell you what. You trace the number and I'll call Manpower to get two or three temps here in the morning. Until then we'll forget this pile is here. What they don't get to we'll work on this weekend."

"I don't work weekends." Charles turned on his expensively loafered heel and left the room.

"Since when?" I yelled after him. He didn't bother to answer me.

I went to my office and looked up the number for Manpower temp services. I had the number and was dialing it when Jackie walked in. I looked up and put my hand up for her to wait.

My call was short and sweet. They'd have three employees at the office in the morning. Yes!

"How was your day?" I asked Jackie.

She plopped in the chair across from me. "Long. Sorry I didn't get to help much with the paperwork. I had three appointments today, and I chose to meet the clients at restaurants instead of here. I'll pad my expense reports."

"Haha." Thinking about the state of the office, I said, "Smart."

"You have a decoy appointment tonight, don't you?" She raised her brows.

Even though I appreciated the business, I blew out a breath and complained, "Yes."

"You want me to take it?" She sounded like she wanted me to say no.

"Yes," I said. Then I added, "No, I need a break from this case. I'll go. Besides, I had it planned into my schedule today."

Jackie relaxed. "Good. I haven't seen my kids in a few days. I was hoping to have dinner with them tonight."

"Jackie, you need to tell me when you're taking on too much." Last thing I needed was to lose a good employee from being overworked.

"You know I'd work any and all hours if you needed it. I don't get paid for sitting on my butt. We bill by the hour, remember?"

"I've got this tonight. You go home and enjoy your kids." Her kids were a joy. She was lucky.

Jackie stood. "Thanks. Have fun tonight."

I watched her leave, thinking aloud, "What a sleazy business we're in." Then I thought about it. I'd rather stalk cheating spouses than track down murderers any day.

Charles appeared in the doorway. "How many calls did you say you've gotten?"

I said, "Three, I think."

He came all the way into my office. "Are you sure?"

"Give or take," I said. I wasn't absolutely sure. "Why?"

"I tracked the incoming calls and there are four different numbers with unknown. Did you get your message from Sebastian?"

"Sebastian? What message?"

Charles put my cell phone on speaker and dialed my voice mail system. After the prerequisite dialing and passwords Sebastian's voice came on.

"I've been thinking about you since you left today. I really need to see you again. Call me." He left his number and repeated that he really needed to see me.

"How could I have missed that?" I picked up the phone and started to dial.

"Wait," Charles closed my phone. "His was one of the unknown numbers."

"Do you think he's making the calls?" I didn't believe it.

"I think it's weird that you got a call, and then immediately after he left this message."

"Are they the same number?"

"No. But he's an IT guy. I don't think he'd be dumb enough to call and threaten you, then call back and leave a message from the same phone."

Sebastian was no dummy. "Fine. I'll call and see what he wants."

Charles waited.

I dialed and noticed it wasn't the number for Deriw. He answered on the second ring.

"Mimi. Thanks for calling." He sounded winded.

I kept my voice neutral. "Hi, Sebastian. What did you need?"

Not sounding as self-assured as he had earlier in the day, he said, "I need to see you."

"What about?" Couldn't he tell me anything I needed to know over the phone? It's not like we were talking about National Security here.

"I just need to see you," he repeated.

This line was getting old. "Look Sebastian, I'm really busy."

"Take me off the speaker phone." He spat the words out.

I did. I picked up the phone. "What?"

"Please, I just want to get together and have drinks. Besides, you weren't straight with me earlier."

"Not straight about what?" What could I have possibly lied to him about?

"It's not important. Meet with me tonight," he pleaded.

Will the real Sebastian please stand up? His tone wasn't the secure, "I can have any girl I wan"t one that he'd had while I was there earlier. It sounded childish and desperate.

"I can't. I have a previous date tonight." I did, no matter that my date was a married man that didn't know he was meeting me.

"Cancel it." He demanded.

"No, Sebastian. Look, I have to go. I have a lot to do before my date tonight." Then, to ease his impatience, I said, "Maybe we can get together tomorrow after the Camarilla."

Eager, he said, "That would be great. I can't wait. I'll call you."

I wanted to say, "I'm sure you will." But I said, "Okay, bye."

I disconnected. Charles stared at me.

"What was that?"

Still puzzled about the call, I said, "I don't know. He wanted to get together with me. He sounded desperate."

"How did your meeting go with him?"

"Well, I told you he gave me the cell phone. He was very open." I gave Charles the play by play of my conversation with Sebastian, and how it did or didn't mesh with what Henry told me. I also told him how cocky and flirty Sebastian acted.

"So you think he's got the hots for you?" Charles wiggled his brows.

Oh, brother, he really wanted me to have a man.

Charles asked, "What's this about meeting him after the Camarilla?"

Now I needed to be savvy. I had to get Charles to say yes without a fight. I didn't have time to beg.

"It's this live role-playing game they play in Santa Cruz."

"Like Dungeons and Dragons?" He sat on the edge of my desk, curious.

"Sort of, but it's vampires. Ever heard of the Masquerade?"

"No. Vampires, huh?" He was curious.

"Yeah, Esme was a part of the game, and since our other lead has been wiped out, we're going to look at the players. Henry and Sebastian are players too. It's just too good a lead to pass up."

"Where is the tie-in with Esme's murder?" Charles sounded skeptical.

So was I, to be honest, but it couldn't hurt to take a look at how the game worked. "I'm not sure. But Lauren's books, the sword, and the game are tied to vampires. There has to be some sort of connection."

Charles raises his brow. "I have to agree."

Okay, here we go. "You want to come with Nick and me tomorrow night."

Charles popped up. "Sure. What time?"

"Are you sure?" Charles never wanted to go anywhere. Other than work, he usually stayed home in his cocoon.

"Yes, and don't ask why," Charles said.

"I won't. But you can't change your mind. Nick wants you to go in and act like you're a reporter. Take pictures, ask questions, you know." Here was the rub, and I knew he'd change his mind.

"You want me to bring our digital camera from the office?" His cooperation was really out of character and puzzled me.

"Okay, what gives? You have never agreed to go out without asking if you're getting paid for it. And now you just say, 'Okay, you want me to bring the digital?'"

"I didn't say it that way. And if Nick's going along, why would I argue about it?" Charles winked.

"Nick is not your type. Besides he's a little old for your taste." Charles was usually interested in the All-American look. Come to think of it, sans tattoos, Sebastian would be right on target. Too bad Sebastian liked girls.

"I'll find out what's up between you two. And if you won't talk, maybe Nick will."

I groaned. Now I was sorry I asked. My secrecy was about to bite me in the ass.

CHAPTER 15

I was at the CV Ranch by seven o'clock. CV Ranch is a resort and conference hotel that sits several miles down in the valley from Highway 1. The view from the hotel overlooks a stunning view of the resort's golf course, and when the sun is setting it's a sight to behold. No wonder people from all over the country, and the world, planned their business conferences here.

There was something about business and golf. Most of the conference hotels in the Monterey Bay area were affiliated with a golf course. But they also had great bars. The bar at CV Ranch had an open floor plan. The white walls were capped with a wood-slatted, vaulted ceiling and open concrete beams. The décor featured clean, straight lines with upholstered white barstools, black-and-green seating, and ivory tables. Seating was arranged for groups of four or more, and each area had its own low table. I sat at the bar, waiting and sipping my drink.

Here's how the decoy thing works. This one in particular was referred by another detective agency. The woman hired the company to see if her husband was cheating on her while traveling. Since his travels brought him to California, it's cheaper and easier for that company to hire a subcontractor, and the two businesses split the fee. It's not as much money as it would be if it were my client, but if I ever have a client in their neck of the woods, they reciprocate.

Acme Detective Agency set up the gig. They sent me several photos of the man I'm to interact with, and the information on his whereabouts. There may be a chance I don't even see the husband, but with most business conferences, they all end up in the bar after the last meeting. I knew the last meeting ended at five, and they were having a group dinner. I figured they'd hit the bar for drinks by seven, seven-thirty.

The man I was looking for, Albert Niess, was six feet tall with a medium build. From his photos he looked handsome enough, but not "ooh la la" handsome. Albert would be easily recognized. The hardest part of the gig was to not call the man by his name until he told it to me. I wish I didn't know it ahead time, but it keeps me from hitting on the wrong guy.

The bartender knew me and thought what I did was similar to being a hooker. I took offense at first, but in a way it was true. Only I didn't have to have sex with the man in order to get my money. I've been called worse, especially the time I led the husband to think we were going to do it right there in the bathroom of the bar. I flirted and touched, and flaunted my goods, then said, "Hey, wouldn't it be fun to fuck in the bathroom?" It sounds crude, but men love that kind of talk. He agreed. And when we walked into the bathroom, with his hands all over me and trying to kiss me, his wife was standing at the sink. I think he peed his pants.

The wife calmly walked out. I innocently asked, "Who was that? And what was she doing in the men's room?" He stood stunned for a moment then said, "You bitch, you fucking set me up." He lifted his hand to smack me, and then got another surprise. I don't take well to violence, and before he knew what had happened, he was facedown on the floor, on his belly. I placed my knee in the center of his back and whispered in his ear. "I'm not the bad guy here, you are." Then I left him. The wife filed for divorce the next day.

Yes, it's a sleazy business, but someone has to do it. And in reality, it's only a small portion of our income. Most of our jobs are for people cheating their employer or insurance company. So next time you complain about high insurance rates, you can thank the low-life that cheats the company out of money by filing a fraudulent claim. My job is to keep that from happening. My rates are high, but not nearly as high as the cost of fraud each year.

Like I said, sometimes I never even see the husband. But tonight, I would be working for my money. Albert came out of the dining room with three other men. All were laughing, joking and patting one of the shorter men on the back. Either the joke was on the poor man, or he'd done something great for which he was being congratulated. I'd guessed the latter since he seemed quite jolly too.

The next part was tricky. I had to infer myself into their little group, focusing in on Albert without being obvious. I didn't want them to think I was a prostitute, or worse, desperate. They bellied up to the bar, and as luck would have it, Albert sat in the middle. This made me think his wife might be on the wrong track. A man looking to pick up a woman would sit on the end, so there'd be a chance of meeting with someone.

I sipped my club soda with lime, and said, "You guys look like you're having a good time."

The man next to me looked with his eyes, but didn't actually acknowledge me. Was he rude or shy? The looker next to him said, "Yeah, we are. Want to join us?"

"Well, I'm waiting for someone." I looked at my watch. "He's late. You want to move to a table?"

Looker, a tall man with board straight black hair combed forward and light green eyes, stood. He took off his suit coat, revealing a toned physique, and tossed it at a chair by the closest table. He walked back to the bar as I stood. "I'm Danny."

Oh, boy, this would make things much more difficult. I'd have to find a way to engage Albert in our twosome. "I'm Alison. Come on guys, let's go to the table."

As they grabbed their drinks from the bar and moved to the table, I excused myself. Danny asked, "Where you going?"

"Powder my nose. I'll be right back." I deliberately brushed up against Albert.

Danny may have thought he was hot shit, but Albert was much better looking. He was a little generic with his brown hair and eyes, but much better looking than in his photos. He blushed when he said, "Oh, sorry about that."

When I touched his shoulder, he flinched. "It was my fault."

He hustled to the table, and I walked to the bathroom. Once in there I walked into a stall, shut the door and leaned against the wall. I sighed. Why couldn't it just be easy? I was tired from working Esme's murder, I wanted a full night of sleep for a change, and I wanted to be home with Lola. I'd seen so little of her this week. Usually I did stakeouts and Lola got to come along. She curled up in the back seat and snored. She never interrupted, asked questions, or berated me. She just listened and snored.

I opened the stall door and went to the mirror. I fluffed my hair a little, pulled out a tube of In the Buff lipstick and painted on another layer. Ready for the next round, I headed back to the table.

Did I mention you never leave a drink at the table if you leave? Date rape drugs aren't just for the college set. I made sure I left my drink at the bar, and the bartender knew to dump it. When I sat at the table someone would ask what I was drinking. I'd say, "Gin and tonic with a lime." And the bartender would pour me a tonic and lime without the gin.

And that's exactly what happened when I got back to the table. My luck had changed too. Albert was sitting on the couch, while the others had taken the chairs. I sat next to him.

I tried not to focus just on him at first. I looked around at all of them. "So you aren't from around here are you?"

Danny said, "Casper, Wyoming. We're here for a business conference."

Pretending I gave a shit, I said, "Really?"

Albert said, "Business and golf."

I said, "Oh, I love golf. This place has an excellent course. Did you play today?"

Danny laughed, "Yes, but we promise not to bore you with the details."

And they didn't. We talked about Monterey, John Steinbeck, the weather and even rodeo. Casper had a big rodeo, and so did Salinas. One of the guys was actually a professional saddle bronc rider. He had a family, so he worked a regular job and traveled to rodeos on the weekend. He'd even won a buckle at the rodeo in Salinas. I wasn't so much interested in the rodeo part, but I did like cowboys. Who didn't?

We'd been laughing and talking for about forty-five minutes before I looked at my watch and said, "Well I guess my friend isn't coming. Do you mind if I hang out with you guys tonight. I drove all the way here; I hate to turn right back around and drive home."

Albert looked at his watch. "I've got to get back to the room."

"Why? We're just getting to the fun part." I leaned in close to him.

He smiled, looked at his watch again and said, "Maybe a while longer."

His wife had nothing to worry about. I'd been touching his leg or his arm regularly while we talked. He made no advances. I didn't see a wedding ring, so I didn't ask if he was married. I'd let him say something if he wanted.

The others were talking amongst themselves, so I moved closer to Albert. "Do you travel much?"

"Only lately." He shifted but didn't move away. "We've been having to push our technology a bit harder lately, with the influence of foreign markets affecting sales."

"Sounds stressful." I felt for him. He looked tired. And he looked like he was a nice guy.

"You have no idea," he sighed.

Time to make my move. "Maybe we could go back to your room and I could give you a massage or something?"

His eyes widened like a deer in headlights. "Are you talking to me?"

"Who else would I be talking to?" What a strange reaction.

"Usually the women are picking up Danny, not me." He was tense.

"I'm not all that interested in Danny."

"I wish you were."

"Okay." I'd never had this reaction before. Most men say, "Bye guys, we're going back to the room."

"It's just that I'm married," he said. "I'd love to take you up on your offer, but then I'd have to explain it to my wife, and I'm not a really good liar."

Now I'd need to push him. "We don't have to tell your wife. It's just a massage. Besides, it'll feel good. I've been told I have great hands."

Albert jumped from the couch. "I've got to go back to the room." He turned to me, "Thanks for the offer, but I don't think my wife would understand."

"I'm not married. You want to take me back to my room?" Danny interrupted.

As cute as Danny was, I had absolutely no interest. But before I could say anything, I heard a voice behind me. "Mimi, there you are."

The voice was male, Charles was the only person who knew where I'd be, and it wasn't him. I turned to look, then immediately turned back to the table. It was Sebastian.

He looked fresh, as if he'd just showered. He wore long sleeves, so he looked like any other business man in the hotel. In reality, he looked better. With his height and build, he commanded attention. And he had it. All of the men at our table stared as he leaned over behind me and kissed me on the cheek.

I froze. This was too weird to be comfortable. I couldn't even force a fake smile. My stomach turned. He had to have followed me to know I was here. This was no coincidence. He'd given me enough time to get comfortable, and when it seemed I might be on my way out, he pounced.

He came around the couch and sat where Albert had been sitting. He kissed me again.

Danny said, "Well I guess your friend showed up after all. Bummer."

"I guess." I didn't even try to act happy about it. I didn't want anyone to leave. I didn't want to be alone with Sebastian.

My mental telepathy was on the fritz. They all got up in turn. "Hey, Alison, or Mimi or whoever you are, it's been fun. Have a nice night."

I turned to Sebastian. "What are you doing here?"

"I told you I had to see you." He touched my leg.

As much as I wanted to deny it, a warmth went through me. This guy was scary, and yet my hormones were working overtime. He was just different enough to wake up my dormant libido.

"I thought we agreed to meet tomorrow night after the Camarilla." That's how I remembered it anyway.

"We did, but I couldn't wait." He moved closer and whispered, "The police came to see me shortly after you left."

Damn that Nick, he had to go talk to Sebastian himself. But then, it *is* his job. "So?"

"So? They asked me a lot of the same questions you did, about Esme, and the Camarilla, and about dinner. They asked the questions differently, but they were the same. They think I had something to do with Esme's murder."

And there it was. He was scared. He'd been avoiding the cops, and now they'd caught up with him.

"Well, you are her ex-boyfriend and you are a part of the vampire role-playing-game. Did you read Lauren's books?"

"Are you kidding? If I want porn, I'll go online, or buy a Penthouse. I'm not into that kind of fiction."

I didn't have the heart to tell him that Penthouse paid for the erotic content. Yes, writers made a living writing erotic letters for magazines. "Do you have an alibi?"

"That's just it. I don't. And I was at the house that night."

CHAPTER 16

Sebastian's statement came as a shock. "You said you just dropped Esme off. You said you didn't go into the house."

"I lied. She invited me in for a glass of wine. I thought it would be harmless. It wasn't." He'd lost some of his bravado.

"What?" I hated being lied to. It happened a lot in my business, but I didn't have to like it. So I did a little lying too, but it was my job.

"We had sex on the table in the kitchen. We had a few glasses of wine, and then next thing I know she's got my clothes off. Oh God, it was the best sex I've had in awhile. Esme could really get me off." He looked down as he said this.

Remember the heat I felt earlier? Well, that statement was like getting an ice cold shower. Sebastian was disgusting.

"That falls under the category of too much information, Sebastian." I was repulsed.

He must have felt my revulsion. "That's why I didn't tell you. When I saw you, I really wanted you. I've never had an older woman, and you are so sexy. If you knew I'd had sex with Esme recently, you wouldn't be interested."

I put his mind at ease. "I wasn't interested before. I don't find younger men that sexy." Lie, lie, lie. See, it's okay for me, but not for others.

"But now I not only want you, I need you," Sebastian said, and grabbed my hand.

I tried to pull it back, but he was stronger. I could pull a move on him, but I was prepared to wait. We were in a room full of people, so I felt relatively safe for the moment. "You neither want nor need me. You have to leave me alone. Like I said, I'm not interested." Then I pulled a statement right out of my backside. "You know I'm dating the homicide detective investigating this case, right?"

Sebastian dropped my hand like it was holy water. "Are you going to tell him about me and Esme?"

"I don't know." Why was he telling me this?

"But I really need you. What am I going to do?"

"About what?"

"Esme. I had sex with her right before she was murdered. If they test for that stuff, they'll find my semen. They're going to come to me and ask for a DNA swab."

"So? Just because you had sex with her doesn't mean you killed her." Or did it? "Does it?"

He jumped up from his seat, "No! But like I said, I have no alibi, and I was probably the last person to see her alive."

"Was she alive when you left the house?" I wasn't sure where I was going with this, but maybe I'd catch him in a lie, or find something out.

"Yes. She was putting her clothes back on, and I was getting the hell out of there. She screamed at me from the back door as I practically ran to my car." His eyes were focused on me as he spoke. I didn't see any hesitation, but then maybe he was a good actor.

"Why such a hurry?"

"I shouldn't have gone in the house. I shouldn't have let her seduce me. I'm sort of with someone else right now." He looked down.

"You screwed her on the kitchen table, you're coming on to me, and you have a girlfriend?"

Incredible. I liked Sebastian less and less. What a self-centered bastard.

"I don't have a girlfriend. Just a girl I'm, well, sort of using for sex. But she's nowhere near as good as Esme was," he quickly added, as if that made all the difference.

I looked him in the eye. "Did you have a reason to kill Esme?"

"No."

"Does your new girl know about you and Esme?"

"Yes and no. She knew we were over. She didn't know I was still having sex with her."

"Did you see your girlfriend that night?" Maybe she smelled Esme on him and went to confront her.

"She's not really my girlfriend. And no. We had planned to hook up, but it didn't work out. So you see, I have no one to back up my story that I was at home and left early Tuesday morning."

He was right, he didn't have anyone. "Does your girlfriend know Esme?"

"Yes, she does." Sebastian wasn't going to give me the information willingly.

"So who is she?" Now I was too curious.

"She's got nothing to do with this, so I'd rather not tell you."

"How do you know? Maybe she's the jealous type and followed you? Maybe she saw you with Esme at dinner?"

"She knew that I was having dinner with people from the LRPG."

"LRPG?"

"Live role-playing game." The "duh" was evident in Sebastian's tone. "But really, neither of us had anything to do with Esme's murder."

"Maybe you need to tell Detective Christianson this information, not me."

"You believe me, don't you?"

I didn't know what to believe. I had no theory on the subject. But if it would get him out of my life, I'd lie. "Sure, I believe you."

Sebastian plopped back down. He took a deep breath. "Oh, thank you. Now you have to convince Detective Christianson that I'm innocent."

I got up to leave. Not sure how I'd extricate myself from Sebastian, I stepped back and leaned over to pick up my purse. "No, Sebastian, that's your job. I have nothing to do with it."

I turned to walk away, and I could feel him several paces behind me.

I kept checking the headlights in my rearview mirror on my way home. When I was younger, I could tell you the type of car behind me, since I was a car fanatic. I'm not so fanatical anymore, but I can tell if the same car is behind me for any period of time. I didn't see anything to confirm it, but I had a feeling I wasn't alone.

CHAPTER 17

I practically ran to my front door with the key ready in my hand when I got home. I hustled across the house to the back door and checked to be sure both locks were engaged. Lola had stirred from her slumber and followed me around the house as I went to each window and checked the latches. At the same time, I pulled all of the blinds and curtains closed. Once I was safely cocooned, I went into the kitchen and flipped the switches for the outdoor lights.

I wore my usual T-shirt and underwear to sleep in, but I added a pair of sweats and put slip-on shoes by the bed. I lay in the dark of my bedroom, with Lola sharing my pillow, listening and watching for any unusual movement. I must have fallen asleep during my vigil, because the next noise I heard was my alarm clock.

The stress had taken its toll. I awoke exhausted. Lola stirred from the alarm and immediately put her head back on the pillow. Within moments she was snoring. I left her there while I got up to take a shower.

I padded into the kitchen with my hair wrapped in a towel and my body wrapped in a robe. Still weary, I went to the kitchen cabinet and pulled down a canister with my stash of Kona coffee. I flipped the lid off my pressurized coffee pot and poured the grounds directly into the container. I filled the pot with water, pushed the top portion with the grounds into the open top of the pot and pushed the button. Watching the water boil up into the grounds, I spaced off. As the water, now in the form of coffee, was sucked back down into the pot, I regained consciousness. The aroma of good coffee was like an elixir. I inhaled and looked around the room. Something on the kitchen table caught my eye. It was an open book.

I walked over to see what it was. My breath caught when I read the title at the top of the exposed page. Prey.

I hadn't read any more of the book since the other night, and I'd put it on my bookshelf in the living room. Now I was second guessing myself. Had I left it on the table? No, I was absolutely sure I had put in on the shelf. I couldn't remember if it was there last night. But here it was now, opened to chapter three, the scene of the slaying highlighted in bright pink. A yellow Post-it note read, "You will be next. Stay away."

I froze. Someone had been in my house. First my business had been violated, and now my house. Bile gurgled in my gut. I reached for the phone, my hand shaking.

Did I call 911? I had Nick's number somewhere. In my cell phone. Instead of calling from the house phone, I went back to the bedroom and called him from my cell.

"Christianson," Nick answered.

"Someone was in my house." My voice cracked. I didn't sound like the strong woman I like to portray, and I didn't care.

"Mimi?" he asked. "What do you mean?"

"I mean someone was in my house last night. They left a message." I didn't know if the quiver in my chest was coming through in my voice, but something alarmed Nick.

"Are you alright?" I could hear him moving.

"Just a little shook up. They left me a copy of Lauren's book." I took a breath to keep from crying. "It's open to the killing, and it's highlighted."

"Do you have your gun?"

"Yes."

"Right there with you?"

"No, it's in my nightstand." I reached into it as I answered.

I wrapped my hand around the cold metal, thinking it would calm me. It didn't. I checked the barrel of my little snub-nosed .38 to be sure it was loaded. A futile move since I lived alone and always kept it loaded. I shoved it into the pocket of my robe.

"Get it now. Keep it with you until I get there." I heard a car door shut. "Don't answer the door to anyone but me. I'll call the crime scene unit from the road."

"Nick," I screamed into the phone. "Don't hang up."

I didn't want to be alone. Even though I was standing by myself, I felt like Nick was with me as long as I could hear his breathing. In a flash I was pissed. This person had reduced me to a pile of shivering goop.

I'm not a weak person. Why did I suddenly feel so vulnerable? In looking at the last few days, I realized I'd never been on the receiving end of a burglary, never been followed, and never had my private space violated. The last time I'd felt this alone was right after Dominic died. I swore I'd never let myself feel that way again, and here I was acting like a blithering idiot.

"I have to. I'll be there within a few minutes." The line went dead.

I said aloud, "Stop!" No one answered.

I looked around the room, but I couldn't move. Whoever had killed Esme knew where I lived. He was targeting me. Why? I wasn't the only one investigating. I had to be on to something. The phone calls weren't enough, and now he'd been in my house. A shiver ran through me as I realized he may have been watching me sleep. I couldn't decide if the book was there before I got home or not. I was so focused on the doors and windows I didn't even turn on the lights in the kitchen.

At that moment, Lola decided to trot into the room, looking around as if she might have missed something. She came up to me and put her front paw on my foot. I held her head against my thigh, and we stayed like that until Nick arrived. It was then that I decided the book was there before I got home. Lola would have at least growled if someone was in the house while I was there.

So did that rule out Sebastian? He showed up at CV Ranch quite awhile after I did. But he had to have followed me. No one but Charles knew where I'd be. Had he been to my house? If only I knew exactly when the book was left on the table.

I heard rushed footsteps on the porch and ran to open the door.

"Where's your gun?"

I pointed to my robe pocket. It made one side of the chenille fabric hang heavily. I looked down and tried to adjust the robe. Lola stood behind me, away from Nick.

"It's okay honey, he's a good guy." She didn't care, she stayed right there.

"Where's the book?" He stormed past me.

"In the kitchen, on the table."

I followed him into the room. He stood, staring at the highlighted passage. "Zeke is on his way."

As Nick said this, there was a knock on the door. "I'm coming in," Zeke said, by way of hello.

"Hey Zeke, take a look here." Nick motioned him to the table.

Zeke pulled a pair of latex gloves from his black CSU windbreaker. He gently lifted the edge of the Post-it note, then he placed his finger tip on the corner of the book. The book was held open by the weight of a coffee mug on the left side pages.

"I'll get my dusting kit." Zeke turned to leave, then turned back. "How did the perp get in?"

Nick looked at me, and I looked back, blank. I hadn't even looked. I'd been too stunned to look for the mode of entry. "I didn't look around."

Nick went back to the front door and looked for any sign of violence around the door. Next, he walked around the perimeter of the house, looking for windows that were ajar or broken. Nothing. Nick went back to the door. He scrutinized the lock.

"Whoever did this had a key. Who has a key to your house Mimi?"

"No one." I thought about it. "My mom, but that's it."

I thought back to any copies I had of my house key. The house had been a rental that Dominic and I owned. I moved in after selling the house we lived in before he died. The house had been empty when Dominic died because we were replacing the foundation. He'd had all the locks changed when the last tenant moved out. Then it struck me. There was a copy of the key at Dominic's office, and that would be the current offices of Gotcha.

"Whoever broke in here also broke into my office. They got a key when they trashed my offices." The revelation really spooked me.

"Are you sure?" Nick was taking notes now.

"Yes. The only other key was at the office. This used to be a rental house, and Dominic kept a key at work in case he had a possible tenant who was looking to rent. He had so many keys, he didn't like to keep them on his keychain. It was in the kitchen cabinet at the Gotcha offices." I was positive.

"After we eliminated the prints of the people who belonged there, we couldn't tie the rest to anyone in our database."

Zeke was back. Upon hearing our conversation, he said, "I'll stop by your office and print the kitchen cabinets."

"Someone would have had to know there was a key," Nick suggested.

"Not necessarily," Zeke said. "Did you see the place? They did a thorough job of trashing it. In all the mess the perp probably opened the kitchen cabinets and saw the keys. He took them and got lucky."

"He likely didn't know which key it was. He could have stopped by while you were out of town and tried all of them. Cocky, he came in while you were home."

The word cocky made me think of Sebastian. He'd known where I was. He'd followed me to Carmel and maybe even followed me home. My sense of unease last night had been justified. I had no desire to have my head in a bowl on the kitchen table.

"We need to find this guy," I said. "And I think the guy may be Sebastian."

Nick spun around to look at me. "What?"

"I was going to call you when I got to the office. Sebastian showed up at my decoy gig last night. The man I was working on had just gotten up to leave when Sebastian came up behind me and kissed me on the cheek."

Nick's eyes widened. "He what? What the hell?"

Something in me hoped Nick was jealous. But I couldn't think about that right now with my life at stake. "He told me you came to see him, and that you think he killed Esme."

Nick smirked, "That's not what I said. He heard what he wanted to hear."

"Well, you freaked him out. He was in a panic because he has no alibi."

"And he came to you about this?" Nick paced a four-foot path between the kitchen and living room.

"I guess he thought I could help. And he wanted to let me know he'd lied to me. He said you'll probably find his fingerprints in the house, and on the bottle of wine I told you about. Said he'd had sex with Esme on the kitchen table that night."

"Holy shit. If this doesn't beat all." Nick turned to Zeke. "He's trying to tie himself to the scene, leaving a possibility of doubt."

Zeke nodded.

I wasn't really sure Nick was right. Had Sebastian admitted it to cast doubt, or to show he was willing to work with us and be honest on all accounts? I didn't like Sebastian, but I also couldn't say for sure that he was the killer. But if I let myself think too much, I could see him wielding that sword.

"Get your locks changed today. Immediately. Have locks put on the windows too. I'll have twenty-four hour surveillance started by this afternoon."

He looked at me. I stood bare-footed, in my bathrobe, holding Lola's collar like she was my lifeline. He stared at my chest, not even coy about it. I looked down. Somehow my robe had pulled open. I wasn't flashing a nipple or anything, but close.

Nick looked back to Zeke, and then he stepped toward me. I thought he was going to offer comfort by hugging me and I started to lift my arm. But he just pulled the fabric back over my chest. Embarrassed, I touched his arm and said, "Thanks."

"Go get dressed. We'll get out of Zeke's way and let him do his job. You can call the locksmith from your office. I'll have an officer here to meet with him." He shooed me toward my bedroom.

"I'll be fine. I'll call you when I get to my office."

"I'll wait," he insisted.

"Please go. I'm going to take my time getting ready. I need to soothe my nerves. If you wait, I'll feel obligated to hurry and I don't want to." I all but stamped my foot like a child having a tantrum.

"Fine."

When I walked into the bathroom, Lola close on my heels, I looked into the mirror. Oh good heavens, I still had the towel on my head. I turned the water in the shower on and climbed back inside.

It was forty-five minutes before I was ready to leave the house. I let Lola ride in the passenger seat of the Land Rover and walked around to my side of the car. As I climbed in my cell phone rang. I flipped it open.

Before I could say anything I heard, "Do you understand?"

CHAPTER 18

I'd never been so happy to have a busy day. With the calls to and from the police station, the locksmith, and the security alarm company I planned to hire, I barely had time for my regular appointments. When I looked at my watch, it was already seven o'clock. I had an hour to get ready to meet with Nick.

Lola's head was resting on my thigh. It didn't look comfortable, but she's fallen asleep standing up that way, so maybe it was.

Charles stopped in for only the third time all day. Earlier he'd asked about my morning, gotten his head snapped off, and decided he'd best leave me alone. Now he peeked in and asked, "We leaving soon?"

At the sound of Charles's voice, Lola jumped. I looked up from my computer and said, "Soon. I have a few more reports to fill out. You ready?"

Taking a chance with his life, he stepped all the way into the office. "Nick stopped by earlier and asked about you."

"And he didn't talk to me himself?" I'd called him early in the day to let him know I'd set up the locksmith, and he'd updated me on the surveillance. That was the last I'd heard from him.

"I told him you were having a bad day." Charles leaned against the door frame. "He told me what happened."

"I figured he would." Soon everyone would know. It wasn't a bad thing, but I hated sharing my vulnerability.

"I realize you're shook up about it. But shutting yourself in your office and brooding over it isn't the way to handle things." Charles was getting braver by the second.

I didn't want to admit it, but he was right. "I know, but I needed to be by myself, to figure out why I'd been flattened by the situation. You know, it's not even a fear for my life. I'm not afraid to die. I'm more afraid to live in fear."

"We'll get this guy and there will be nothing to fear," Charles said.

I stood up, gathered my papers and shoved them into my briefcase. Charles came over, took my briefcase from my hands and put it firmly on the top of my desk. He wrapped his arms around me and held me tight.

"As long as I'm in your life, you'll never have to live in fear. I'll destroy the son of a bitch who lays a hand on you." My hero.

If only my hero liked women. If only my hero could be a homicide cop named Nick. I mentally slapped myself: He was the past. Regardless of him being in my present, he'd never be my future.

"Have I told you lately that I couldn't live without you?" I said into Charles's chest.

"No, but I know." Charles shook with laughter. "Come on, let's get some food."

"I've got to drop Lola with Jackie. Her twins are doggy sitting tonight."

I hated leaving Lola with someone else tonight, but she wasn't staying at the house alone. She was worried about me, and I could sense the difference in her. She probably sensed it in me too.

After a quick trip through the Taco Bell drive-thru on Main Street, we headed to the cop shop. Nick was standing outside talking to a young uniformed officer. He stood close, looking at her as if she were the most interesting thing on earth. His head flew back with a hearty chuckle, and he placed his hand on her shoulder. The officer leaned into him, laughing along with him. I willed her perfect little face and body to leave. And my willpower must have been strong because she touched his forearm and walked away.

When Nick saw my Land Rover pull up, his body stiffened. He no longer smiled. Charles hopped out of the passenger seat, taking the bag of Taco Bell garbage with him, and got into the back seat.

Nick looked at Charles, said nothing and climbed into the passenger seat. "I'd planned on taking my car," he said.

Charles said, "Sorry man, but I'm never going to be caught riding in a Crown Vic. Back seat or front, this is a much nicer ride."

He was right. My Land Rover had a lot of leg room, and the back seats were elevated, so the person stuck in the back could see out, and not just see the headrest of the seat in front of him. I looked at Charles in the rearview mirror. It was weird seeing him in the backseat.

"Who was that?" Now what on earth possessed me to ask such a stupid question?

"Who?" Nick responded.

"The officer. I've never seen her before." I tried to keep my voice neutral. I wasn't jealous, but curious.

"Affirmative action at work. She's new. Both Hispanic and female. Human Resources kills two birds." Nick looked in the direction the Hispanic officer had gone.

"She's a hottie," Charles said.

"You look at women?"

Charles never missing a beat, said, "And you look at guys. The difference is that I openly comment, and you're afraid to say another man is hot."

Nick smiled and shifted to look at Charles. "Right and wrong. I wouldn't use the word hot to describe a man. But I'm secure enough with myself to admit if another man is good looking."

"Really?" Charles was skeptical. So was I.

"Yes. As a matter of fact, I think you are one of the more handsome men I've seen in my life. For someone who likely never played a sport, you have the look of an athlete and the face of a model. I'm sure your body would be perfect for their underwear ads."

I'm sure I saw Charles blush, but he recovered quickly. "Right back at you, Nick."

"Thank you."

"Okay, before you two start making out, are you ready to go?" The sappiness was nauseating, kind of cute too.

I stomped on the gas a little harder than needed. Maneuvering into the Friday evening traffic on Main Street wasn't as bad as when I was a kid. Growing up, South Main Street had been the main drag. I can't begin to imagine the gallons of gas we wasted driving up and down the street. I drove my mom's station wagon and everyone knew me. The car may have sucked, but the stereo rocked. Back then, it took at least twenty to thirty minutes to drive the two-mile stretch. Now that it was a "No Cruising" zone, we were headed out of town toward Highway 1 in no time.

Charles broke the silence. "Hear anything on Mimi's break in?"

"Zeke didn't pull any prints we could use. The book was wiped clean. Not even prints from the bookstore where it was purchased."

"You know where it was purchased?" I was excited. Maybe we could track it.

"No, but I'm sure he had to buy it somewhere."

"He, huh?" Charles asked. "You know the perp is a guy?"

Again Nick said, "No." Snappier this time. I could tell he didn't like not having the answers to the questions. "He is just easier to say, rather than he or she, or even they."

"I get it." Charles flipped on the DVD player in the headrest and put the headphones on. We had been dismissed.

"It's related to the phone calls," I said. "I have no doubt."

"True. But we don't have anything more than that," Nick said.

Charles must have been listening music because he was humming and dancing in his seat. Both Nick and I looked at him.

Charles opened his eyes. "What?"

We both turned back to the front without comment. I saw Nick smile.

"Do you think anything will come of this? Zeke sent a guy to print the kitchen. I'm pretty sure he'll only find prints from Charles, Gemma, Jackie, and me. No one else really goes in the kitchen. Well, he may get a few paw prints if he dusts fairly low."

Nick smiled. "Lola has her own cabinet or something?"

"Or something."

"Where are you staying tonight?"

Startled, I mumbled, "Home."

"Are you going to be alone?" Now Nick was getting personal.

"Maybe. Why?"

"I know you'll have a cop outside, but I think you should have someone in the house."

"Really?" I was being silly. I was worried about going home tonight.

"Maybe Jackie can stay with you, or Charles."

"Just don't worry about it. I'll work something out." I wanted to ask him if he had plans, but that would have been a mistake.

Nothing else was said until we reached Santa Cruz and turned onto Laurel Street, then right onto Pacific Avenue. We drove around and finally found a parking space off of Front Street. The space was perfect because the meet up was at the clock tower at the intersection of Front and Pacific.

As we got out of the car, I could see several cape-clad characters approaching the Clock tower.

I turned and put my hands up in front of Charles and Nick. "Stay here. I want to ask a few questions, as a tourist, before Charles goes in." To my surprise, they stopped.

"Fine. I want to get an overall picture and see if I can pick out our players without being noticed." Nick looked around.

I walked up to a woman in a black cat suit. Her fleshy rolls were partially concealed by the hip-length cape she wore. On her head she wore a black hair band, covering her forehead and keeping the edges of her ponytail in place.

"Hi, may I ask you a question?" I put on my pleasant tourist voice.

Unsure, she said, "Okay?" Her pale flesh creased as she smiled.

"I realize this is Santa Cruz and all, but what's with all the vampire looking folks?" I tried for a Midwestern accent, drawing out my vowels.

"Oh, it's a game." Her tension eased.

"What kind of game?"

"We call it the Camarilla. It's a role-playing game."

"A game of what?" Like I didn't have any clue.

"We're vampires. The Camarilla is based on a group of Kindred, whose goal is to hide the existence of vampires from the Kine." She looked sheepish. "Kine means humans, but is literally translated as cattle." She giggled.

Harsh, I thought. "So are the non-players the Kine? You mean I'm a cow?" I spoke in jest, not anger.

She grinned. "I guess you would be considered a cow. No offense."

"None taken. So how does the game work?"

She looked over her shoulder. "We meet at the clock tower and the Storyteller gives us the scenario where we left off the week before. The characters are able to earn merits and flaws as the game progresses. We have an ongoing feud with the Sabbat, who believe we are inferior to Kine. But as we are the Camarilla, we are far more moral and humane than the Sabbat. It's all really very complicated unless you play."

"So you play every week?"

"Yes. It's great fun."

"Sounds a little eerie to me." I wasn't sure what else to say.

She kept looking over her shoulder as the other players gathered at the clock tower. "I'd better be going."

I watched as she walked away. Charles, with recorder and camera in hand was already mingling. I looked around for Nick but didn't see him anywhere. So I walked to the corner near my car. Someone tapped my shoulder. I jumped.

"It's just me," Nick said, grinning.

"You know what kind of day I've had. That wasn't funny," I snapped.

Nick's smile faded. "I wasn't trying to be funny."

I kicked him lightly in the shin. I wanted to kick much harder, but he was a cop after all.

He straightened. "Hey."

"No more sneaking up on me, please?" I walked over to a park bench and sat.

"I wasn't sneaking, but fine."

By nine o'clock it was getting fairly dark. I could see images thanks to the streetlights and storefronts, but the black clothing made picking out details difficult. One person I could definitely pick out was Sebastian. He stood much taller than the other players, and he was also much broader. I couldn't hear any of the chatter amongst the players, and I definitely couldn't hear the Storyteller, but I could see that he seemed to be handing out sheets and indicating directions. It wasn't long before the group disbanded and began to amble about the streets. Several disappeared down the side streets and into parking areas.

As I followed a female into the bookstore, I listened to the tunes of the street corner musicians. A bubble maker dipped his wand and I walked through a shower of bubbles. The girl's stride was swift as she entered the store. She spoke with others of her kind, apparently preparing a strategy.

I slithered in close. "Excuse me. May I ask you a few questions?"

The woman who turned around had a peach complexion with black eyes and blood-red lips. Her hair flowed across her shoulders in a cascade of curls, ending just above her ample cleavage. She wore a black lace corset which heaved her boobs to her chin and left her necklace of amulets buried between her mounds of flesh. She smiled. But before she said a word, a man stepped in front of her.

She pushed him aside. "Oh, Syd, she means no harm."

He took a half step to the side. "Yes, ma'am."

In a low, sugary voice, she said, "How may I help you?"

"I wanted to ask you about the Camarilla." My body language was as at ease as I could make it.

"What would you like to know?" She lifted her hand to let the other players know she was out of character for the moment.

"Who are you?"

"Really, or in the game?"

"Both," I said.

"In real life, I choose to plead the fifth. Too many narrow minded people in this world. In the game I'm Isabella. I'm a longtime player with a lot of power. I'm a status monger. I can make or break another character by word of mouth alone. What I say is held in high regard."

"And why is that?" Another aspect of the game for me to learn.

"As of this week, I'm the most senior female player. This makes me the richest player, with the most merits. Richest female player anyway." She pushed out her chest in defiance.

"Wow. Did someone quit to make you number one?" Apparently this was an impressive position.

"Sadly, no. Someone died." Her chest deflated a little. Her expression turned sad.

"I'm sorry. What happened?" Oh, oh, I was going to get somewhere with this one, I knew it.

"It's really not my business to discuss. I'm sure the elders would prefer to keep it between the Kindred."

Shit, another brick wall. Where did I go from here? "You mean the Prince?"

"Oh, you know Eugene?" Her mood brightened.

"Only for a very short time. That's why I'm here. He mentioned the game to me, and I wanted to come down and see how it worked. He said it was okay to talk to the players if I didn't interrupt the game." Lie, lie, lie.

"As the Prince, he rules the city, and if he says we can talk to the Kine, then we can." She stopped talking as another character approached.

Her whithering look could have stopped a cougar in its tracks. I know it made me step back.

She giggled. "I'm good, huh? I'm not nearly as impressive in real life. But as Isabella, I've earned my status. I love it." She waved her hand at me. "Yeah, I know, you probably think I'm whacked, but this is great fun."

"I get it. It's the allure of being someone else." To quote another wannabe vampire.

"Yes, that's exactly it." Now we were pals.

"So how well did you know Esme?"

She blanched. "You mean Eugene?"

"Oh, I'm sorry, I meant Eugene. He and Esme are friends and that's how I met him. They both start with E." Hand to forehead. I nearly blew it. "You know Esme too?"

"I know Esme." She was less friendly now.

"Lovely girl."

Stiffening, she said, "Of course. She and I were the first girls to join the game. We weren't exactly friends outside the game, but as a part of it we were allies."

"Know anyone who didn't like Esme?"

"Look, I don't know anything. If you want information, talk to her boyfriend." She put her hand back down and resumed her character. She turned and handed out a lavender colored business card to another player, then vanished.

Okay, she didn't really vanish, she walked around the corner to another stack of books. Before her bodyguard followed after her, I asked, "Where can I find the Prince?"

The dark man pointed to a man nearly as tall as Sebastian, standing a little apart from the group, wearing rustic garb. The Prince wore a beard, and his brows were as thick as the beard. He wore black boots, torn pants and a leather duster. His hair was nearly as long as Isabella's.

Before I could approach him, Charles had moved in to start his interview. The Prince turned away. Darn, I really wanted to see if he was the same guy who was in Henry's hotel room. Or more precisely, leaving Henry's hotel room.

As I walked back to where Nick stood, I saw a pale, ornately dressed man walk toward Charles and the Prince. The man wore a hat with a bright green feather and had an imposing manner. But I was distracted when Nick walked up.

"Find out anything good?" Nick asked. He was eating some sort of chocolate candy.

"Not really. But Charles is really getting into this. He's interviewing the Prince right now." I pointed to the trio.

"Which one is the Prince?" Nick licked his fingers.

"The rugged looking man with the long beard."

"He doesn't look like royalty to me." He wrapped up the rest of his candy and licked his finger a little more.

I reached into my handbag and pulled out a wet-nap. "Here."

Nick snatched it and tore the package open. "Gee, thanks Mom."

"Let's go back to the car and wait for Charles to finish." I walked toward the car, but Nick stayed put.

"Come on," I said.

"I want to know more about this Prince guy. I'm going to keep him in sight. If he drove here, I can get his plate number and run it. If no one wants to give him up, I'll figure out who he is on my own." He stood his ground.

"His first name is Eugene," I said as I walked away.

Nick jogged up to me and cut me off. "Eugene who?"

I stopped abruptly to keep from colliding with him. "I only got his first name, sorry."

"We'll just have to wait until the game is over, then follow him." Nick didn't move.

Nick and I watched the players and people in general for the next hour and a half. Finally Charles returned with a huge smile on his face.

"This is incredible. I'm coming back next week to play. These are some really intelligent people. A lot of them have really stressful jobs, like working for a detective agency with a bitchy boss." Charles looked at me. "Just kidding. I mean real stress. One guy is a neurosurgeon."

"That's great, Charles. Did you find out anything we could use?" Nick didn't share Charles's fascination with the game.

"Oh baby, did I." Charles flipped through his notes.

"I thought you brought a recorder." I wanted to hear what was said.

"Yeah, but no one wanted to be on tape. So I took notes. Good thing my mom made me take shorthand. No one even uses it anymore, but she said it would come in handy in college, and she was right. Who knew it would come in handy in real life too?"

"Right, so what do you have?" Now I was getting impatient. Nick could rub off on a girl.

"The guys I was just talking to, the Prince and the Emperor, were fascinating as well."

"Walk and talk. We need to keep an eye on this Prince." Nick started toward the clock tower.

"The Prince is the guy in the leather duster. The Emperor is the guy in the feathered hat. It's crazy. He's the Emperor of the Imperial Government of Norton. And he's a vampire alright. Has to be. He came to California during the Gold Rush. And get this. He lost all of his money, so he printed his own. Look." Charles held out a hundred-dollar bill with the Emperor's face on it.

I stared. "That's Henry."

Nick grabbed the bill from Charles. "It is. So this is Henry's character."

"What's his role in the game?" I asked.

Charles snatched his bill back. "It's mine." He pocketed it, saying, "He's a Malkavian, from a harmless clan of Kindred. I think he's really a drifter. The Prince hates him."

"And who exactly is the Prince?"

"You want to know who he is?" Charles said.

"Yeah, we'll get his plate number and run it." Nick spoke over his shoulder.

"His name is Eugene Winkle. I don't know his address, but I guess it would be easy enough to find on the Internet." I could tell Charles was pleased to offer this tidbit.

I smiled at him, and he winked. Nick stopped. He turned.

"You, my dear, are good." Nick reached out his arms. "I could kiss you."

Charles stepped forward, "Oh, please do."

I stepped between them. This was enough. If anyone was going to be kissing Nick, it was me. "Okay boys, let's follow him anyway. We might get something."

And boy did we get something.

CHAPTER 19

As we got closer to Eugene, we settled down and stopped talking. In serious stalking mode, we split up and approached from different angles. Since we too were in black, we blended in with the background. Eugene was parked in the same lot as I was which would make for an easy getaway. Little did we know we'd be there longer than we'd planned.

Eugene approached a car, but didn't get in. He stood alongside the vehicle, slowly pulling off his bushy brows. He put the hairy caterpillars on the hood of a Volvo SUV and began tugging at his beard. Once he had the beard off, I recognized him. It was Brad. Eugene was Brad freaking Pitt from the hotel. I knew that in real life Eugene and Henry were friends, so the Prince hating the Emperor was only part of the game. As we soon found out, Eugene and Henry definitely didn't hate each other.

"Hey, handsome," Eugene called as Henry approached. "Can you believe they sent a reporter?"

Henry pulled off his hat. "It's great. I hope he writes the story in a positive way."

Charles whispered, "I will." I shushed him.

"I think this will be good for the game. I'm excited." Eugene reached out and hugged Henry.

Henry pulled back and looked around. "Let's get inside."

Eugene unlocked the Volvo's door. He pulled off his duster and tossed it in that back seat. Then he stripped out of his boots too, and climbed in. Henry looked around. Fully dressed, he climbed in with Eugene.

"Oh. My. God," Charles said in three breaths. "My gaydar must be way off. I never guessed."

Of course we were speculating, but normally two grown men didn't get in the back seat of a vehicle together. Especially not when there was plenty of room in the front seat. I could see movement from where I stood, but I wasn't sure what it was. If I let my imagination take over, I'd guess someone was getting a little something in the backseat of that Volvo.

So that's why Henry didn't want me in the hotel room that night. He'd had his lover over. Too bad I wasn't a few minutes earlier, I could have witnessed the goodbye kiss.

Charles said, "I'm going in."

I grabbed his arm. "No."

"We have to have proof." He shrugged away from me.

If I fought him, they'd hear us. As Charles moved in closer, Nick sidled up beside me.

"Did you see that?" Nick stared at the Volvo.

"I saw more than I needed to. Eugene has a great body." Well, he did.

"You realize this gives us motive," Nick whispered.

"How?" I thought I knew, but I wanted to hear it from Nick.

"Let's get in the car." We tiptoed back to my car.

Instead of using my remote opener, which made noise and turned on the lights, I stuck my key in the door. I motioned for Nick to get in first, through the back door. The interior light didn't illuminate when the back door opened. He got in and adjusted the overhead light to off. Next, I opened my door and climbed in. Nick shut the back door, then got in the passenger seat. We closed the doors lightly.

Before we could say anything, Charles jumped in the backseat and slammed the door.

"What the hell?" Nick whisper-shouted. "They'll hear you."

Charles grinned. "No they won't. They're making so much noise, they wouldn't notice an earthquake."

"Really?" I wasn't sure I wanted the details.

"So looks like we may have motive." Charles strutted in his seat.

"You think Esme knew?" I asked.

Together, Nick and Charles said, "Of course she did."

"That's fine. But did she know enough to get killed? And which one did it?"

Charles said, "I take it back. There's always a chance she didn't know. If you think about it, she was probably doing the same thing after the game, but with Sebastian. I'd doubt she followed the boys back to Eugene's car after the game."

Charles had a point. Esme may not have known. Henry and Eugene's affair may have nothing to do with Esme's murder. But both men would have had access to Lauren's book before it was on sale. And both men would have something to lose.

"So what next?" I asked.

"Drive by the car and I'll get the plate number. We'll run it and get Eugene's address. Then tomorrow I'll stop by and pay the man a visit."

"You mean we." I was adamant.

"No, I mean I," Nick admonished. "You are not going."

"Hey, I've helped out a lot. We, Charles and I, got you a good deal of information tonight."

Charles leaned over the passenger seat, his chin near Nick's shoulder. "You better let her go with you, or you'll be the next body."

CHAPTER 20

My knickers were still in a twist when I dropped Nick at the police station. I wanted to go inside and wait while he ran the plates. He refused to let me out of my car, even threatening arrest if I followed him into the station. In silence, I drove back to the Gotcha office to take Charles to his car.

"I'm going inside to check on things." Charles stepped out of the back of the Land Rover.

"You want me to wait?" I asked, hoping he'd say no.

"Go home. Your home security is probably wondering why they are watching an empty house." He shut the car door and walked up to the front door of the office.

I watched long enough to know he made it inside and had flipped on nearly all the lights in the place. I saw him head toward the back as I drove away.

Being busy and being with people had made me forget about the book left on the kitchen table and the phone calls. There was no doubt the two were related, but how? I'd had my cell phone on silent all night, and I'd forgotten I had it with me. When I pulled into the driveway of my house, I pulled the phone from its holder.

I had six missed calls and three voicemail messages. Of the missed calls, one was from my mom, four were a private number, and one was Nick. I dialed my voicemail before getting out of the car.

The first message said, "You don't look stupid. What is it about back off Esme's case don't you get?"

The second message was about twenty minutes later. "Don't forget you promised to have drinks with me and Luke tomorrow night." My mom. And I had forgotten. I'd have to put it in my Blackberry.

The third message said, "You fucking bitch. Stay away from the game and its players. One of them will kill you."

My hands shook as I saved the messages for Nick to listen to. I'd call him in the morning and give him the information. I pushed the command button to call Charles now.

My phone said, "Say a command."

I said, "Call Chuck." He'd be pissed if he knew I had his name as Chuck on my phone.

My phone said, "Did you say call Chuck?"

I said, "Yes."

Phone said, "Calling." I waited.

"Miss me already?" Charles answered on the first ring.

"I got another call." My voice trembled.

Charles got serious. "Look, I'm not remotely tired, and I have no one to go home to, so I'm going to stick around the office for awhile. I'll see what I can do to get you some answers. This is getting too serious. You need to file a complaint with the police, along with the B&E."

"They already know the scoop. Besides, this creep can't kill me through the phone." I tried to sound braver than I was.

"I'll call you as soon as I find anything out."

I pressed, "No matter what time it is."

Charles promised. I hung up and sat in the car another minute or so. I changed my phone back to vibrate/ring from the silent mode. I wasn't anxious to go back into my house, so I scrolled through the ring tones and changed my incoming call to the words from Big and Rich's "Save a Horse, Ride a Cowboy." Silly, but I needed something silly at the moment. I looked at my house, where I'd been violated and threatened. The good thing was that there were cops in a car across the street. At least I thought there were. Nick assured me I wouldn't be alone, but I sure felt alone, and vulnerable.

I forced myself to go into the house. Before I stepped into the kitchen, I turned on the light by reaching in the door and flipping the switch. I pushed open the door and peeked inside. Nothing moved and I didn't see anything treacherous on the counter or table. I stepped inside. Barely in, I locked my new lock, and the deadbolt. Now I felt like I was in prison. Alone in my cell, but afraid just the same.

I stood in the kitchen, assessing the room. Zeke had been nice enough to send a cleaning crew to wipe up the fingerprint powder residue. I appreciated not seeing the reminder of the morning's events. Just the same, they were fresh in my mind. I wasn't going to be getting to sleep anytime soon, so I put my briefcase and laptop on the table and set up to go over some files.

Before settling in for the work ahead I made a pot of coffee. I poured a large shot of Bailey's Irish Cream in the bottom of my coffee cup, then added coffee. I stirred until the drink was creamy, brown and took a savory sip. That action alone settled my nerves.

Well, I thought it did. But when the knock came at the front door, I jumped and sloshed the sweet, hot liquid all over my hand and down my arm.

"Shit." I grabbed a wet sponge from the kitchen sink and wiped my hand, arm and sleeve. I didn't hurry to the door, figuring it was one of the officers letting me know they were on the job. Nice, but not necessary.

I went to the front door, standing off to the side, and pulled the curtain away from the window. It wasn't one of the officers. It wasn't anyone I'd ever expect to see at my door in the middle of the night. It was Nick.

I opened the door wide and blocked the entrance. "What are you doing here?" I was still miffed about him not letting me in on the information from running the vehicle plate.

"May I come in?" Business-like and gruff.

I opened the door wider. "Sure."

"I got the address. Eugene lives in Santa Cruz."

"Since all of this is taking place in other cities, do we need to have permission from the other jurisdictions to talk to these people?"

Nick said, "Not just to talk to them. If there are any arrests, we'll have to work with the local authorities. But that shouldn't be a problem."

"So we're going back to Santa Cruz to talk to Eugene?"

"I am." Nick walked into the living room and settled on my leather couch. "This is nice."

For what it cost, it better be. I had splurged on my furniture. This was a dark brown leather sofa. The Italian leather was buttery soft, which was why I bought it. And it was easy to keep clean. Lola liked to climb up on the furniture and snuggle, and she wasn't particularly careful about wiping her paws before jumping onto the couch. Leather cleaned up nicely and didn't hold onto the hair.

"Make yourself at home." I oozed sarcasm.

"Thanks. What's in the mug?"

"Bailey's and coffee. Want some?" I pushed my mug toward him.

"No thanks, but coffee sounds good." He crossed his legs.

"Great. There's some in the pot. The mugs are in the cabinet on the left of the sink." I sat in the club chair across from the couch. It was leather too, but red instead of brown.

"Some hostess." Nick stood.

"I didn't invite you over." But I stood just the same. "Sit, I'll get it."

By the time I returned to the living room, Nick had several reports and photos spread across my coffee table. I moved a coaster into place and put his coffee down. I went around the other side to sit across from him.

"No. Come over here and sit. I want to go over these with you."

I couldn't believe it. Nick was sitting in my living room about to go over Esme's murder book. I came back around the table and sat next to Nick, making sure there was a good distance between us.

He pointed to the photos. "These are from the murder scene. Do you see anything that stands out?"

I looked. These photos were in color, and graphic. The sword lay across the dining room table with a swath of blood across the middle. The rest of the room looked much as it had when I'd been in it early on Monday. I looked at a close-up shot of Esme's body. Her hands had been cupped in her lap, catching the blood running from her neck. But now I saw something else. The charms. Esme had a necklace of charms laced in her fingers. From the photo it looked as if the chain had been deliberately woven through her fingers.

"I thought we found Esme's charms in her bedroom." I saw them. And this necklace was identical: the ankh, the shen, and the vial of blood.

"There's more than one. You know most, if not all, of the players have these necklaces."

"I thought so. But whose blood would be in the vials? Is it human, or animal?"

Nick pulled a sheet of paper from the file. "The blood from both the vial in Esme's fingers and the one in her room had human blood. And we know the blood is from two different people. What we don't know is who."

This bit of evidence was new to me. "When will you know?"

"DNA takes time. And we have to have samples to compare it with. So far I have Lauren's, Esme's, Sebastian's, and Henry's. I hope to get a sample from Eugene tomorrow."

As a P.I., I got to do a lot of snooping, but I didn't usually have to piece together a puzzle. This was a complicated puzzle, with more and more pieces showing up as the days went on. I didn't know how someone could be a homicide detective without going crazy.

I sat back from the coffee table. "Do you like your job?"

Nick looked confused. "Why?"

"It just seems like a lot of pieces that don't fit. I'd think it was frustrating."

"No more frustrating than other parts of my life."

I wondered what he meant by that remark, but I was afraid to ask a question that was none of my business. I didn't have to.

"Look Mimi, it's been years since we've seen each other. We may look like the same people. A little older, but the same. You know?"

I did know.

Nick continued, "But we are very different. We're shaped by the events that occur around us. Your events were different from mine. But we can relate because we have a shared past. And we both have skeletons. Yours happen to be literal."

I knew he was talking about Dominic. "Actually, there are no skeletons. Debris from the accident was scattered everywhere. The only thing found was a shoe he'd had packed in his suitcase. Not even a piece of the suitcase was found."

I went on to tell him how I'd met Dominic in the produce industry. He'd worked for his family in a brokerage. Brokers were the middle man between the vegetable shippers and the grocery stores. Wining, dining, and travel were a huge part of his job.

"So you haven't really had closure." Nick had dismissed the paperwork and focused on me.

"Yes and no. It's hard to explain. Before he died, Dominic gave me Lola, and without her, I don't know if I'd still be alive. I feel a little bit of Dominic when I'm with Lola. I took Dominic's death very hard."

Nick nodded.

I wanted to change the subject. "So what about you? How did you end up back in Salinas?"

"You know about the drugs and alcohol. But what you don't know is that it got worse after I was removed from the roster." Nick looked down between his feet.

"Worse?"

"Oh, yeah. I was lucky enough that I didn't receive any felony conviction for my drunk driving charges. And I was able to get on the police force in San Francisco. Being a former NFL player gave me a lot of clout. Clout I didn't deserve. But all the guys wanted to be my partner, and they wanted to talk about the good old days. What they didn't understand was that I wanted to leave those days behind me and get on with my life."

I agreed. "I know the feeling."

Nick smiled. "You'd think being a cop, and seeing what drugs and alcohol did to people, I'd clean my act up. I didn't. You'll never believe this."

"What?" I was curious to know about his life since college.

"I had to sell one of my Super Bowl rings to pay off a drug debt."

"Wow." I couldn't think of anything else to say. That was a whopper of a confession. This was beginning to feel like our college days, when Nick would pour out his heart to me, and then we'd end up in bed.

"That was my rock bottom. I've been clean and sober for seven years."

And here I'd offered him a Baileys and coffee. What an idiot. I picked up my coffee mug and started toward the kitchen.

Nick stood to stop me. He grabbed my wrist. "No, you're okay. I'm okay with it. Drink your coffee. I'm the one with the addiction, not you."

He stood so close I could smell the coffee on his breath. I looked in his eyes and saw nineteen-year-old Nick. I saw the Nick who stole my heart. Suddenly my heart ached.

His hand moved from my wrist to my coffee cup. He took the cup and put in on the table. Then he turned back to me. He put his hands on either side of my face and pulled me close. He said, "I've missed you."

And he kissed me.

I melted like a chocolate bar on the dashboard in summer. Every cell in my body gravitated toward Nick. My mind tried desperately to get a grip and pull my body away. But the feel and taste of Nick's soft lips enveloped my senses. I kissed him back. I pressed hard against him, and my tongue followed his in the dance of emotions. I wanted this, and then I didn't want it. I needed this, but I didn't. At the very moment I didn't care what I did or didn't need or want, I was kissing Nick. I was kissing the man who'd broken my heart, and I wanted more.

Nick pulled back. "I've wanted to kiss you since I saw you Monday night. I know it sounds crazy, but I've been trying to concentrate on this case to keep from thinking about you."

My saner side took over before I could confess anything I'd later regret, and I kept silent. I looked at him, willing him to kiss me again.

"I've always wondered what it would be like if I saw you again. And I knew, when I transferred to Salinas, I'd see you sometime. I just didn't know it would be so soon."

I overcame my sanity. "Oh, Nick. I've missed you. I've missed talking and laughing. I missed our friendship."

"Me too." Then his mouth opened and covered mine.

I wrapped my arms around his neck and pulled him closer. I wanted his body touching mine. As I pushed my breasts into his chest, I felt his muscles tense. From the eagerness of his kissing, the tensing was a good thing. I tried not to think. Thinking would only make me need to stop this madness. It had been so long since I'd been with a man, or wanted to be with a man. Seeing Nick, and having Sebastian flirt with me had awakened a need I'd forgotten.

I told myself, even if it was only for one night, I wanted it. I wanted to feel Nick's skin on mine. I wanted to feel the sweat of hot sex, and I wanted that sex to be with Nick.

I brought my hands down to unbutton his shirt. I didn't care if the cops outside could see us. I tore myself away from Nick's kisses and worked my lips down his neck to his shoulders, as I tugged his shirt down. My mouth followed the ever lowering shirt until I found his nipple and gently sucked it into my mouth. He groaned.

"I want this, Mimi. I really want you."

And I wanted him too. I showed him how much by putting his hands on my top and helping him help me out of it. I backed away from him long enough to let him lift my shirt over my head. When the shirt hit the ground I heard a noise.

"When I saddle up my horse…" It was my cell phone. I could feel it vibrating at my hip. And it wasn't the only thing I could feel on there. I now knew just how bad Nick wanted me.

He kissed me through his words. "Do you need to get that?"

I ignored him, and the phone, helping him unhook my bra.

My phone rang again. It was late, and it was probably a private number. I fumbled with the buttons to ignore the call. Big & Rich stopped singing.

I don't know how long it took, or how I got there, but we were on the couch, Nick on top of me. His hard body pressed up against me. I had what I'd longed for, his flesh against mine. His skin felt like silk. As he moved on top of me, I felt as if we'd moved past whatever had torn us apart. Part of me wanted the kissing to go on forever, and part of me wanted more, and now.

Bang, bang, bang. A rapid succession of thumps on the door.

"Mimi, are you okay?"

Oh shit, it was Charles.

I struggled to get out from under Nick. Where was my bra, my shirt? By way of small wonders, we both still had our pants on.

"Hold on, Charles, I'm coming."

I picked up my phone and looked at the time. Wow, we'd been necking for twenty minutes. How did I last that long?

Nick sat up. "Not now, you aren't."

I turned to Nick. "Shut up." I threw his shirt at him. "Get dressed."

"Why? It's just Charles." Nick moved leisurely.

"Because it's Charles, you nitwit. He has a big mouth." I tossed my bra behind the couch and pulled on my shirt.

"Nitwit?" Nick laughed as he pushed his arm through a sleeve.

I looked at him and rolled my eyes. I put my fingers in my hair and fluffed it. Then I wiped my mouth with the back of my hand.

I opened the door. "What's up?"

"What the hell's the matter with you? I called and no one answered. I was scared to death something happened. And here you are with Nick." He clipped the last word, then repeated, "And here you are with Nick."

"Come on in. Want some coffee?" I tried to cover my embarrassment.

Charles, never one to leave when he should, said, "Sure."

"We were going over the murder book," Nick said.

Charles sat across from him. "I may have something more for your little murder book. That's why I called."

I came back with a Bailey's and coffee for Charles.

He sipped. "This is good. But not as good as what I have."

I sat next to Nick on the couch, careful not to touch. "What?"

Charles pulled out a stack of photos. He spread them across the table, over Nick's papers. "These will make more sense after what we saw tonight."

Laying on the table were three photos of Henry and Eugene. The first photo showed the back of them walking away. The significance of the photo was in their relative positions. They were holding hands. The second and third photos pretty much confirmed what we had expected was going on in the back of Eugene's Volvo.

"Where did you get these?" Nick said, eyes wide.

In that moment, I wished I was telepathic. I stared hard at Charles, willing him not to say anything. I hadn't told Nick that Sebastian gave me Esme's cell phone. If I'd ever had a wish come true, I needed it now.

"Esme's cell phone," Charles said.

If wishes were horses…looked like I'd be looking for a different cowboy to ride.

Nick looked at me. I looked him in the eye and saw a completely different man than the one sprawled on top of me only minutes ago. Nick's blue-grey eyes were dancing with fury.

He looked back to Charles. "How did you get Esme's phone?"

Completely innocent, Charles said, "Mimi gave it to me."

I scooted to the far edge of the couch, wishing it was longer. Nick leveled his gaze at me. I smiled, lips closed, brows high.

"Explain." Nick spat the words.

"Sebastian gave it to me. He said he found it in his car when he got back from his business trip. He said it was Esme's, but it was dead, so he had no way of checking it. He didn't have the same kind of charger hers had. Besides, he thought it was best to give it to the police. He gave it to me, and I decided to have Charles charge up the battery before I gave it to you." I was talking as fast as a native New Yorker.

Nick stood. "Are you brain dead?"

Stunned, I said, "Excuse me?"

"Why else would you hold onto a piece of key evidence that didn't belong to you in the first place? What possessed you to think you had any right to accept that phone from Sebastian?"

He was right. I had no defense. But he'd just called me brain dead. I stared at him, silent.

"And why didn't Sebastian think to tell me he'd given it to you?"

I thought before speaking. Sebastian had done it again. This was another way to cast a shadow of doubt. I had walked right into his scheme. First, his confession of being in the house the night of the murder, and then he gave me the phone. I was an idiot.

"Look, instead of having a conniption fit, why not be happy I got these photos from the phone?" Charles asked. "And guess what, they match the garbled photos I was trying to clean up from Esme's computer. This means we really do have a motive."

We both looked at our moderator, Charles. "Hello, are you hearing me?" he said.

I spoke first. "So Esme did know about Henry and Eugene."

Charles aimed a finger pistol at me and pulled the trigger. "Bingo."

"Where's the phone?" Nick snapped.

"It's at the office. I just brought the photos over."

Nick gathered up his papers and walked to the door, held the handle, and said, "Come on we're going to go get it."

Charles said, "I still want to look at it closer. I haven't had a chance to take down all the phone numbers. I got so excited when I saw the pictures I transferred them and printed them out."

"You're not going to touch that phone again. This could blow our whole case to hell." Nick shook his head, disgusted.

"Before you scuttle out of here in a huff, I have something else." Charles gathered up his pictures and stood. "I traced the phone calls Mimi's been getting. I tracked the activation to the MallMart on North Davis Road."

Nick stepped away from the door. "Really. When?"

"Tonight." Charles gloated.

"I mean when was it activated?" Nick's irritation was raw.

Charles shrugged. "Oh, it was activated on Monday afternoon. I wrote the exact time, but I left it at the office."

"So, what now?" I asked.

Nick looked at me. "This is great. MallMarts have surveillance cameras. We can get the tapes for the time when the phone was activated and see who bought the phone."

"Won't you need a warrant?" Charles asked.

Nick turned to Charles. "I've never wanted to hug a man as much as I want to hug you. But I'm too pissed about the phone to do it."

Charles blushed.

Nick added, "I'll see if they'll cough up the tapes without a warrant first. It'll be quicker. The threatening phone calls may not be enough for a warrant anyway. Depends on the judge, and I haven't dealt with any judges yet. I've only been with the SPD a short time."

The tension in the room seemed to ease. "Come on Charles, I'll meet you at the Gotcha office."

Charles looked at me. I nodded.

I was glad to be rid of both of them. I needed a cold shower.

CHAPTER 21

The weekend was spent putting needles back in the correct haystacks. The temps had accomplished quite a bit, but there were going to be miles to go before I slept. I had to beg out on dinner and drinks with my mom and Luke. Charles was true to his word and didn't work the weekend. But he'd done a lot on Friday night, and I didn't blame him.

Since I didn't have any cases to work over the weekend, I needed something to keep my mind busy. Every once in a while we do something that embarrasses us even when we are alone. And every time I thought about Nick on top of me on my couch I got embarrassed. I'd concentrate on the work at hand and stop thinking about it, but a pinch in my heart would set my mind back to Nick with his shirt off and his pants unzipped.

It was during one of those moments that I was having on Sunday afternoon when my cell phone sang. I looked at caller ID. I'd stopped answering any calls with "unknown" or "private." It was Nick.

My stomach did a flip and I pressed the button. "This is Mimi."

"Hey, what are you doing right now?"

"Twiddling my thumbs. You?" I didn't want to sound like I was glad to hear from him, though I was.

"I'm getting ready to head to the MallMart on North Davis. Want to go?"

No! I didn't want to see Nick again for a very long time. At least long enough to forget that I'd let him seduce me. And yet I really wanted to go with him.

"You want to stop at the office and pick me up?" I tried not to sound too anxious.

"Lock up and let's go. I'm at the curb." I could hear the smile in Nick's voice.

I smiled to myself, giddy with the thought of doing something other than shuffling papers. My hair was up in a knot at the back of my head, and my face was sans makeup. I hadn't expected to see anyone, so why get all dolled up? And I had my favorite yoga pants on. I don't do yoga, but I love the clothes. Somehow I didn't care what I looked like. I didn't even take the time to check myself in the mirror as I grabbed my handbag and jogged to the door. I even jogged to Nick's car.

He wasn't in his Crown Vic. He drove a convertible Porsche Boxter. I didn't know what year it was, and I didn't care. The top was down, and the sun was out. I felt a little underdressed until I looked inside and saw Nick.

He looked better than I imagined. He wore faded jeans and a very old San Jose State football sweatshirt. I swear, casual is sexier than dressed up any day. I hopped in the passenger seat and vowed to enjoy the ride.

And a short ride at that. We only had to travel up Market Street to Davis and head north. The MallMart was part of a newer shopping complex off the 101 Highway. As usual the parking lot was packed, and Nick parked his car as far from the store as he could, hoping no one would park next to his car and ding it. This is usually an invitation to do just that for people who hate people with money. But to avoid that, Nick pulled a car cover out from the trunk and handed me a corner.

"You're kidding, right?"

"No, this car is my baby. It's the only thing left from my glory days. I intend to keep it pristine." Nick lovingly tucked his end of the cover under the front bumper.

I laughed and stretched my side of the cover toward the back bumper. I wish I'd had those kinds of glory days. But maybe I could start my own by helping solve a murder. I'd be proud of that accomplishment.

"So I just want you to step in if the manager is uncooperative. Then I want you to flirt, smile, promise him sex…"

"What?"

"I'm kidding." Nick chuckled. "I'll present my badge and explain. I just want you to be quiet and look scared."

"Scared? I don't have to act for that one. Having a stranger in my house without knowing scared the hell out of me."

"And just remember that feeling, so you can make the manager feel it."

We walked in through the automatic doors past the shopping carts. If they still call the senior citizen at the entrance a "Greeter" they need to change the name because no one greeted us. The old guy didn't even acknowledge us.

Nick made it a point to greet him though. "Hey, good afternoon." He beamed, taking the old fart off guard. He said nothing back.

"Greeters, my ass," I said.

Nick grinned.

He must've had business here before because he knew exactly where the management offices were located. I had expected we would ask a floor manager to get the store manager for us, and we'd spend a lot of time waiting. Nick opened the door and walked into a reception area of a small set of cubicles.

Nick pulled his wallet from his jeans pocket and flipped it open at the woman. "I need to speak to the person who is in charge of the store."

The woman, a short, plump thing of about forty, stepped forward and examined Nick's badge. She looked skeptical, but said, "What can I do for you?"

"And you are?" Now Nick was skeptical.

"Janine Lambert, regional manager." She pushed her hand toward Nick. "What's this about?"

Nick pumped the woman's hand. "Detective Nick Christianson, with the homicide unit of the Salinas PD."

The woman went pale. "Homicide?"

"As much as I hate to say it, we are investigating a recent homicide." Nick sounded so sweet and sympathetic.

Janine visibly tried to compose herself. "And how is MallMart a part of this mur-homicide?"

"It's not directly related, but a throw-away phone that may be linked to the investigation was purchased from your store on Monday afternoon of last week."

"Okay?" She sounded defensive now. She probably knew what was coming next.

I stood quietly behind Nick, knowing I would be no help. Flirting wasn't going to help our situation at this point.

"We've tracked the activation to this store. And we need to know what kind of records you keep when a person purchases a phone."

"We ask to see a driver's license and we enter the number into our registers, but that would be very difficult to track unless you have the receipt for the transaction." She paused. "But if you have an exact time, I can see what I can do for you."

"Four fifteen."

I thought this was going well. Janine was helpful, not stubborn.

"In the morning or afternoon? We are a twenty-four hour store." She spoke as if speaking to a small child who didn't quite understand.

"Sorry, it was in the afternoon."

"We don't sell as many disposable phones as we used to, so I can see if there is a cashier number with the activation. It may take several days to a week to get the information. Sorry I can't get it any faster."

"What about surveillance video?"

"What about it?" Janine frowned.

"We know the day and time. So is there any way we can view the video from that time period?"

Janine stood with her brows furrowed. She didn't say anything, then she turned and went to the desk behind the counter. She punched the keys of the computer on the desk and waited. She looked up to see both Nick and I staring at her.

"Oh," she said. "I'm looking to see where the video would be for that shift. Everything is digital now, so we transfer the data to another server so we can free up our hard drive for more recordings."

We all stood silent, waiting. Janine looked back at the computer again. "Got it."

"You've got the tapes?" I said. Then I shut up. I'd forgotten I was just for backup.

"Oh, you talk?" Janine looked up from a pad of paper where she was scribbling and grinned.

"Yup, but I'm usually better off when I keep my mouth shut." Did those words just come out of my mouth?

Even Nick turned to stare at me. I'd lost my mind, and Janine and Nick were there to witness it.

"I don't have the actual tapes. But I've put in a request for the time period of 2:15 pm to 6:15 pm. I think that should give us a wider range, just in case the activation time isn't Pacific Standard."

Smart woman. She was regional manager for a reason, I guess.

Nick's body language loosened up now that he knew she wasn't going to ask for a warrant.

"You do understand that to release the tapes, which will be on CD, you'll have to get a warrant?"

"Fuck" was written all over Nick's face now.

"Look, that's going to take extra time we don't have. Is there any way we can do this without a warrant?" Nick wasn't pleading, he was flirting. He stepped forward and leaned against the counter.

"I'm not sure this homicide is worth losing my job over, but I'll tell you what, I won't give you the CDs. What I'll do is bring them to the police station when they come in, and I'll watch them with you. That way I'm not releasing them to you unless there is something significant on them. But if there is, and you need to keep them, I'll have to have a warrant to leave them with you."

Nick sighed. "Janine, I love you."

She blushed. "Don't thank me yet. I don't have the tapes."

I stepped in. "You really don't know what this means to us. When do you think you'll have them?"

She looked at her watch. "It's Sunday, so nothing will be done until tomorrow morning. I'll call the main office and get a rush, so if they messenger it, I guess tomorrow afternoon or Tuesday morning at the latest."

Nick walked around the counter and hugged Janine. "You are a gem."

I think she nearly fainted. She fanned herself for a second before she realized we could see her doing it. "I'll stop by the police station as soon as I have anything for you."

"Here," Nick said. He handed her a business card. "Call me to be sure we'll be able to meet up."

She took the card and scrutinized it. "Okay, I'll call you as soon as I have something, and we can set up an appointment."

"Thanks," I said. This had gone too smooth. Something had to give, but I didn't know exactly what it would be.

As we were walking out of MallMart, I said to Nick, "Guess you didn't need me after all."

"I didn't need you in the first place. I just wanted to have company." He winked at me. "Hungry?"

I was starving. Anything to keep from going back to sorting papers.

Nick and I had a hot date at Carls Jr. on the way back to my office. It's the only place I know that serves deep fried zucchini, which I love. So I stuffed my face with a chicken club sandwich and topped it off with fried zucchini and a diet soda. Oh, yeah, the diet soda made it all okay.

Nick ate twice as much as me and wolfed it down faster. I felt like a pig as Nick watched me finish my meal. But there would be no eating in his precious Boxter.

"Tut, tut, feels like rain," Nick said, looking out the window of the Carl's Jr. dining room. "We'd better get a move on so I can get my car back in the garage before it starts pouring."

It was cloudy, but it was always cloudy in Salinas. I didn't think it even looked like rain, much less felt like it. But Nick started stacking our food garbage on the tray. I rushed to shove the last two zucchini in my mouth before he threw them away.

"So your car is allergic to rain?" I said around the food in my mouth.

"Nice, why don't you spit a little bit of food at me while you're at it." Nick handed me a napkin.

I was tempted, but I refrained from blowing a raspberry at him, spraying him with zucchini, ranch dressing, and spit. So grown up, I know. But I actually felt comfortable with Nick when I wasn't trying to impress him.

"Did I tell you I got Eugene's address?" Nick said.

I climbed down into the Porsche. "Have you talked to him yet?"

"No, I thought I'd head over there and see if I catch him at home."

"Why don't you call first?"

"So he knows I'm coming? If he's a legit suspect, I'd rather catch him off guard."

"True that."

"From the address, he lives in a pretty nice neighborhood. I figure if I don't catch him at home then I can head over to the Boardwalk and get some fried artichokes, so the trip won't be a total loss."

I wanted to be a fly on the wall in that interview with Brad, I mean Eugene, but I didn't dare ask. Nick and I were getting along, and I didn't want to jeopardize that. But I wanted to solve this murder before he did. Call me competitive, or stupid, whatever, I wanted to catch the killer.

"Well, I'd best get back to filing papers. It feels like I'm never going to get through it all." I sank down in the seat at the thought of umpteen more hours of sifting and filing.

"I thought Charles had hired temps to do it?"

"He did, but the sooner we have everything back in order the better. I mean what if some paperwork is needed for a court case and we can't find it?"

"Don't you have all of your cases backed up on discs?" Nick shifted the Porsche down smoothly as we got to the office and pulled up to the curb.

"Yes, but I still like to have that paper in my hand."

"Doesn't mean you have to spend your weekend filing when you can afford to pay people to do it for you."

I opened the car door and stepped out. Leaning in the window, I said, "Thanks for taking me along."

"You want to go to Santa Cruz later?"

Did I just hear right? Nick asked me to come along. I'd get to be that fly on the wall after all. I shook my head, sure I didn't hear correctly.

"Huh?"

"Santa Cruz, Boardwalk, want to go?" He said each word distinctly and slowly.

"The Eugene interview?" Oh, I should have shut up while I was ahead.

"No," Nick drew out the word. "Beach, Boardwalk, maybe a late dinner?"

I tried not to show my disappointment. If he took me along, I'd find a way to get in on that interview. "Hey, dinner and a roller coaster, what more could a girl ask for?"

"Right. I'll put the car in the garage and we'll take the Vic over there. I'll pick you up at your house in an hour." Nick put the car in gear and peeled away from the curb.

I stood staring after him for at least a minute. I was asking myself where this was going, and should I stop it while I still had my heart fully intact?

What the hell, we only live once. And we aren't even sure how much time we have, so why worry about what might be when we can live what might be. Yes, Mimi Capurro, philosopher.

CHAPTER 22

The Boxter was definitely better than the Crown Vic, but at least with the state plates on the car, Nick could speed and we got there in record time.

Nick had changed into professional attire, with black slacks, a grey shirt and a monochrome tie. He looked good.

I didn't look so bad myself. I'd changed into black too, but I was in black pants and a black oxford shirt with the sleeves rolled up to my elbows. I chose black ballet flats which I could easily kick off if we went for a walk on the beach. I was thinking ahead.

Nick wasn't kidding about the neighborhood Eugene lived in. It wasn't even a neighborhood, with only one house every quarter mile. The only sign of a home from the road was the mailbox. We turned into a driveway lined with redwood trees as old as God. The driveway was paved in asphalt and lined on both sides with equally spaced pansy tufts.

When Nick parked in front of the split level home, I sat quietly, mesmerized by the views. The house was just high enough in the hills to overlook the forest of redwoods. I could see floor-to-ceiling windows along the side of the house where the walkway meandered to the front door. There was a BMW Z4 parked in front of the closed garage door.

I thought back to Friday night. Weren't they in a Volvo? I didn't remember seeing a BMW in that parking lot. Maybe the Volvo was Henry's, or maybe

Eugene had more than one car. At least it looked like someone was home.

Nick said, "Now be good. I don't know how long I'll be if he's here."

"I'm good. I brought my iPod. I'll just listen to music and relax." I dug into my handbag and showed him, then leaned my head back.

When Nick turned to get out of the car, I said, "Wait, look at me."

He did.

"Ack, your tie is off. Turn toward me." I reached out to him.

"I can do it." Nick snapped.

"Stop, you're wrecking it." I grabbed the tie, loosened the knot, and straightened it. And I slipped the bug nicely in the knot.

"Why did you do that?"

"I didn't want you to look too buttoned up. Slightly disheveled will give you an advantage, especially if he's as anal as I think he is. He'll give you less credit than you deserve."

When Nick walked toward the house, I pulled my recorder from my handbag, plugged the headset into it, and listened. I lay my head back on the seat and closed my eyes, just in case he looked back. I didn't want him to think I was too interested.

Nick knocked on a door that could have been the front or back door. With some houses you can't tell which is which. He waited, but not patiently. I could hear him sigh several times. Just when it seemed he was going to turn and leave, I heard the door open.

I would have loved to get another look at Eugene. Who cared that he preferred men, he was still nice to gawk over. I listened to the exchange of introductions, and then Eugene let Nick into the house.

"Nice kitchen," Nick said. "It's been a long time since I've been in a kitchen this well equipped."

"Oh, thanks. Cooking is a hobby. I never really get to do enough of it."

I could hear them walking down a hallway.

"What do you do for a living?" Nick was conversational.

"Computer stuff."

"What kind of computer stuff?"

"You name it. I work out of the house here, and travel to locations if necessary. But don't call me if you want something done right away. I'm booked several months out most of the time."

"Sounds like a nice gig if you can get it."

"Please sit," Eugene said. "Flexible. I'm able to travel quite a bit. So you are here to talk to me about Esme?"

"Did you know her well?" Nick had the interviewer voice now.

"Pretty well. I mean from the game, and from Henry. We were all working for the good of the game, you know. I guess the matter of whether the game succeeds or fails fell on our shoulders. No one else would've put the work into it that we did."

"What kind of work?"

"We were preparing a PR campaign. We had put together a proposal for the city so they wouldn't shut the game down. It's just like a city council to pass ordinances to keep us from being able to continue the Camarilla."

"A PR campaign?"

"Yes, and a little bit of money didn't hurt either."

"Speaking of money, that sword collection must have cost a fortune." I could hear the awe in Nick's voice.

"Oh that, I've been collecting for years. Hopefully it will be worth quite a bit more when I'm ready to retire. Safer than the stock market, I suppose."

He collected swords? Weird. But then he played vampire games too.

"Vampires are really a big part of your life, huh?"

Eugene was silent for a moment. "Stop beating me off. You're here because you want to know about Esme. So here it is.

"Don't even begin to think the girl is a saint who no one would have wanted dead. She's stabbed enough people in the back to attract a few enemies. Am I one of them? No. Could I be? Absolutely. She walked out on her roommate when she found out that Lauren and Henry would let her stay with them for free."

"But I thought her roommate was still living in the apartment. And all of Esme's furniture was still in there when we stopped by. Susan didn't say anything about being left with the rent to pay."

"She wouldn't. She's just happy to have a cheap place to live. But Esme would've moved all of the furniture out pretty soon if she'd had a place to keep it. She kept bugging Henry about letting her store it at the house, but Henry didn't think it was a good idea. There you go. When Henry said no to the furniture storage, Esme went and asked Lauren."

"What did Lauren say?"

"Kind of funny that. She said to ask Henry, since the house was his."

"Did Henry own the house before he married Lauren?"

"No, but that house is Henry's domain. He did all of the interior design, and he has a nice sword collection too. But his isn't on display. He keeps it locked in a cabinet. His is much more valuable than mine."

"So how well do you know Henry?"

I was waiting for the answer to this question.

"Actually, I met Henry through Lauren, in a roundabout way. You see, I quite like the vampire scene and I'm a fan of Lauren's books, so I started collecting signed first editions. Anyway, I was at a signing and Henry was there and we got to chatting. We had a lot in common, and then Henry joined the Camarilla."

"Yes, I saw the two of you in Santa Cruz on Friday night." Nick inferred seeing something he shouldn't.

"Oh really, where?" Not a hint of defense in Eugene's voice.

"At the Camarilla. I went over to check out the game and ask some of the players about Esme. She seemed well liked within the game."

"Yes, now that she's dead. She was the head vampire of her clan, and now three other women get to vie for the part." Eugene coughed. "How did you know it was Henry and me?"

"Well, I knew who Henry was from the night of the murder, and I recognized him in his Camarilla attire. And, well, I saw you leaving Henry's hotel room one night this past week. I recognized you too. Great costume, by the way. A prince, huh?"

Nick was egging Eugene on. It seemed as if he was trying to get under the man's skin and goad him into talking.

"Weird," Eugene said thoughtfully.

"What's that?" Nick didn't sound as if he really cared.

"Weird that you didn't talk to me Friday night. Why did you wait until now, coming to my house?" Eugene oozed suspicion. "Am I a suspect?"

"To be honest, Eugene, yes, you are."

I could hear Eugene stand. "Oh my God, are you kidding me? What on earth would make me a suspect? This is crazy." He was shouting.

"Look, we saw you with Henry. And I'm not talking about the game." Nick spat out the words.

"You're kidding, right? You think just because Henry and I are fucking that I killed Esme. Give me a break. It's not exactly a secret." Eugene had to be pacing, from the to and fro of his voice.

"Cool," Nick said. "If it's not a secret, I'll just have you come down to the station in Salinas with Henry and Lauren, and the four of us can have a talk."

Eugene spat, "Fine. Do that. Now unless you have some real evidence that I had anything to do with Esme's death, get the fuck out of my house."

Nick's voice went soft and smooth. "Eugene, why so defensive? I thought you were innocent."

Eugene lowered his voice this time. "Get out."

Nick grinned. "I'll be seeing you very soon."

I pulled the headphones from the recorder and plugged them into my iPod just as I heard the door slam behind Nick. I turned slowly to look at him, and I grinned.

Nick grinned back as he went round to the driver's seat and got into the car. He slammed the door shut. "He's hiding something, I just don't know what."

All innocent and sweet, I said, "What makes you say that?"

Nick looked me in the eye and said, "Well, you heard him."

My heart stopped. "Huh?" Oh, shit.

Nick lifted his tie and peeled the microphone from the back side as if it were an insect. He reached toward the passenger floor and tossed it into my handbag.

I'd like to say that Nick took me to the boardwalk and we had a romantic evening, but the whole microphone incident put an end to any good time we would've had. And the sad thing is that I didn't really learn anything. Nick didn't speak to me once on the ride back to Salinas.

I had wanted to drop the recorder off at Gotcha, so I could put it in the safe, but I didn't want to drive from my house to the office and back. "Can we stop by my office before you take me home?"

"Yeah." He didn't even look at me when he said it.

He whipped the Crown Vic around the street corners, and rolled up to the curb at the Gotcha office.

"I'll be right back." I got out of the car before Nick came to a complete stop.

As I jogged up to the Victorian house, I saw lights on toward the back of the house. This didn't seem right. I'd left when it was still daylight, and I didn't remember turning on any lights at the back of the office. I skidded to a stop.

I pulled my nine millimeter from my handbag and flipped off the safety. I slipped my handbag over my shoulder and made my way to the back of the house with my gun in front of me. When I got to the kitchen door, it was open just a crack. I heard noise inside.

CHAPTER 23

Laughing?

I peeked in the door and saw Gemma sitting on the kitchen counter. Charles was next to her, looking at her cell phone.

"What are you doing here on a Sunday night?"

"Even better question, what are you doing here?" Charles asked.

I looked at Gemma, "I didn't even know you were back."

"Just got in a few minutes ago. The car dropped me here."

To Charles I said, "And you?"

"I stopped by to see how much re-filing needed to be done."

"You were going to help?" This surprised me.

Charles smirked. "No, I just wanted to know how many temps to have Manpower send in the morning."

I should have known he wasn't there to help. "So what's going on?"

They looked at Gemma's phone. "Oh, we're looking at photos of one of the signings. I was just going to show Charles this crazy guy in the vampire outfit. He's different from the rest of the weirdo fans. This guy is serious. He was at two signings."

I went around to the opposite side of Gemma from Charles and took a peek. I looked up at Charles.

"Holy shit.

Charles grabbed the phone from Gemma.

"What?" Gemma pouted and stood on her tip-toes to get a look at what had Charles so interested.

"Is it?" I came around the other side and stood next to Charles, looking at the image.

"Yes, I would say it is." Charles started to walk away with the phone.

"It is what?" Gemma whined. She hated not being in the know.

I had my phone out to call Nick when I looked up and saw him in the doorway.

"What happened to I'll be right back?" He glared at me, then at Gemma and Charles.

I grabbed the phone from Charles. "Look at this."

I shoved the phone at him and waited for a response. The picture on Gemma's phone was the Prince, aka Eugene Winkle.

"This is awkward. He's doing her husband, and he's dressing up and attending her signings without Henry." He handed the phone back.

"You don't get it." I pushed the phone back at him. "He's the guy Lauren was talking about. The one who attends all of her signings."

"Okay." Nick still didn't understand what I was so frantic about.

"He wasn't at the signing on Monday night."

A dawning glimmered in Nick's eyes. "Oh, this gets better and better. He's her biggest fan, he's screwing her husband, so he probably got an advanced reader's copy from said husband."

"So he'd know about the slaying scene way before the book came out, and he'd have time to set up the murder. He probably stayed at the bar with Henry to get him drugged up, and then followed him home. With Henry tucked away, he lured Esme downstairs, if she wasn't already down there, and he killed her." I was giddy with the fact that I'd had the piece of evidence that solved this murder.

"Didn't he say Henry had a sword collection that he kept locked up?" Nick added.

"Yes. If he is Henry's lover, he probably had access to the collection." Then it struck me. "Henry has no idea."

"Or does he?" Nick said. "I'm going to figure out a way to get them into the station first thing in the morning. I want to talk to each of them separately. And maybe get a warrant for Eugene's house."

"Gemma, we need to keep your phone." I said.

"What?" I think Gemma was stunned at what she'd revealed, because she is usually much chattier.

"Charles, can you forward her number to my other cell phone?" I handed it to him.

Charles was silent too as he punched the numbers. He handed the phone back to me. "Just don't answer it, and it'll forward to the other number. Wow, this is crazy."

"You still want a ride?" Nick asked me. "I've gotta head out. I'm going to the station before I head home."

"Yeah, hold on." I pulled the recorder from my handbag and handed it to Charles. "Put this in the safe, please."

Charles looked at the recorder. "Okay." I think he was a little dazed at the idea of discovering the murderer, too.

Nick had driven the Crown Vic to the backside of Gotcha, so we went out the kitchen door. He walked around to the passenger side and opened the door. Before you think he was being polite, I remind you that the door only opens with a key. He left the door open and went around to his side.

I leaned down to adjust my handbag on the floor and Nick put the car in gear. I smacked my head on the dash, and my purse fell over.

"Shit." I swear he did it to be mean. I scooped my lipstick, tissues, cough drops and tampons off the floor before Nick could see all the crap I kept in my bag.

Nick looked over at me. "You okay?"

I was still hunched down with my head nearly under the dashboard. I mumbled, "Fine."

"What are you doing down there?"

"Nothing. My purse tipped over."

"Don't leave any condoms on the floor; they might think I'm accepting favors from the girls on Soledad Street." Nick laughed.

"Yeah, condoms, because I have the opportunity to use those." I was only half joking.

"What do you think about this whole thing with Eugene?" Nick said as we turned the corner onto my street.

"I haven't met him really. I don't know what to think. But from the looks of his house, and that he's able to travel at will, he isn't dating Henry for his money."

"Or maybe Henry is footing the bill. I mean look at him, then look at Eugene. That guy could have anyone he wants, and he's with Henry?"

I had to agree. Henry, in his forties with his slight build and comb-over, was such a contrast to Eugene's athletic, thirtyish good looks. "Do we know for sure the house he lives in is his?"

"I'll check with Santa Cruz City Hall tomorrow. But if Henry is paying out money to this guy, don't you think Lauren would know about it?" Nick pulled into my driveway.

"I'm at a loss as to motive, but opportunity and means are there. All of the evidence seems so iffy. I mean I don't know what all you have, but I just don't see enough to be able to arrest him." Oh, God, I sounded like a cop.

"I'll check on the test results of the wine, and the sword. But I'm willing to bet that the prints on that sword will belong to Henry. And if this is about the affair and Esme was about to spill the whole thing to Lauren, then Henry has motive, opportunity, and means. But why not just kill Lauren?"

"Kill the cash cow? She may have a nice life insurance policy, but keeping her alive was probably worth more." Lauren would likely sell millions of dollars worth of books over the next decade.

"Divorce her then," Nick said.

"Prenup?"

Exasperated, Nick said, "Do you have an answer for everything?"

I smiled, smug for the moment. "Not everything."

Nick pulled into the driveway and put the car in park. "I'm going in with you this time."

I didn't argue. I just pulled my handbag up from the floor and got out of the car. I hadn't done much other than file and sit in the car, but I was exhausted. It must have been trying to wrap my head around the idea that Henry would have Esme killed. But was it Henry? Did Eugene pull the murder off by himself?

As we walked to the front door, I said, "You know, the drugs could be an alibi for the murder. Henry says he didn't see Esme after dinner, but suppose he did. Maybe he drugged himself to be sure he had an alibi."

"Yeah, that's been an itch in the back of my mind since we found him Monday night." Nick scratched his head as he said it.

I stopped at the door. I wasn't inviting him in for another chance at the humiliation of the other night. "Okay, well I'm pretty sure I'm good."

Lola appeared at the door, lifting her lips in a smile.

"She doesn't like me." Nick took a step back.

I turned to look at Lola. "She's smiling at you."

"That's a snarl, not a smile."

"Lola doesn't snarl." I leaned to the side, patting her on the head. "But she's not in the mood for company."

"You sure you're going to be okay? I could come in and check out the house."

"I'm sure Lola and the cops outside would've run off any intruders." I stepped back and pushed the door. "Good night. Great date, thanks."

I closed the door and leaned against it. Lola tilted her head, looking at me like I was nuts. I was nuts.

I tried not to listen to Nick's footsteps as he walked back to his car. I heard the car door slam. I turned to open the door and call him back. Grabbing the handle, I stopped myself before I opened the door.

The last thing I needed was a dysfunctional relationship with Nick. Everything in my life was dysfunctional. It was time to getting started on finding a normal relationship.

I started to pull my arm through the sleeve of my shirt on the way to the bathroom, then remembered that police were watching the house. I pushed my arm back through and waited until I was in the bathroom to disrobe.

As the hot water ran over my body, I tried to replay the events of the last week in my mind, but the thought of Sebastian hitting on me kept coming back to my head. It was such strange behavior for a guy whose ex-girlfriend had just been murdered. And that thought brought me back to Nick. Creepy as it was, thinking about Nick reminded me of Esme's head on the dining room table. Not very erotic. I'd never make it as a ghostwriter for Lauren.

I didn't want to think about murder and vampires anymore. I jumped out of the shower, toweled myself off, and wrapped up my hair. A fresh, clean body needed some fresh, clean thoughts. I pulled on my nightshirt and went to my bookshelf for a good chick novel.

Before I settled in for the night, I wanted to set my alarm to be sure I got up in time to be at the cop shop for the interview with Henry and Eugene. Not that Nick would let me sit in, but I had a better chance if I was there and not here in bed.

I padded into the kitchen in my bare feet to grab my cell phone from my handbag. I reached into the side pocket, but it wasn't there. Shit. I dug around in the main part of the bag, but couldn't feel it. Dumping the contents on my kitchen counter didn't help either. The phone just wasn't there.

I stood with my hands on my hips, staring off into space, trying to retrace my steps. Ah, I dropped my bag in Nick's car. I'd bet it was on the floor of his Crown Vic. I looked at my watch. He'd likely be home, or back at the office by now, so I decided to call his cell instead of mine.

I sifted through the contents I'd poured onto the counter. Where had I put Nick's card? I unsnapped my wallet and looked through my card holder. No. I unzipped the side of my purse and shuffled through the business cards stashed there. No. Then with both hands I spread the crap across the counter. Ah, stuck to a bubblegum wrapper was Nick's card.

I took the card into the bedroom, crawled under the covers, and put the phone on my lap. I dialed the number and waited. By the fifth ring, I knew he wasn't picking up. Just as voice mail picked up I decided not to leave a message. Now I'd have an excuse to stop by the station in the morning.

The phone was nearly in the cradle when I changed my mind. "Hey, Nick. Sorry to bother you. My cell phone is probably on the floor of the passenger side of your car. Can you call me when you get this message?"

There, good enough. He probably wouldn't get the message until morning, and then I could say I at least tried to call. I put the phone back on the nightstand and picked up my book.

I must have fallen asleep while reading. I woke up to a noise, and Lola growling. When I sat up, the book dropped to the floor, startling me. I listened. Nothing. My sudden movement must have stirred Lola, causing her to growl. I leaned over the side of the bed and picked my book up. I put it on the nightstand and watched Lola reposition herself on her bed.

Satisfied that she'd still be on alert if anything was wrong, I settled back in bed and switched off my reading lamp. I lay quietly, listening again. What was that? Again silence, except the light snoring from the watch dog.

What had me so spooked? There were cops parked outside the house, for God's sake. I snuggled under the covers when I heard another sound. This time I was sure I heard something. As I reached over to grab my handgun from the nightstand drawer, Lola jumped from her bed growling.

As I grabbed for the drawer handle, someone grabbed for me. I was shoved back against the bed, my head slamming into the headboard. Though it was dark, I saw flashes of light as the pain zinged over my scalp. I flailed with my arms and legs, trying to kick or punch at whoever stood over me. This guy was strong, and quick. I couldn't land a single punch.

I should've been protecting my head because the intruder had grabbed my hair and slammed me back against the headboard again. Now my head was swimming, and I tried to focus my thoughts. Instead of reaching out to my attacker, I reached for the phone. As I did, the pillow was yanked out from under my head and shoved over my face. Oh God, I was going to die.

I couldn't find the buttons on the phone to dial 911, so I just hit one button and held it, hoping it was the redial button. It was all happening so fast, and yet it was in slow motion. Just then I heard Lola's deep bark, and then a scream. And then I heard nothing.

CHAPTER 24

I awoke to whispering. Awoke may be a strong word since my eyes refused to open and the whispering was muffled, as if I had a pillow over my head. At the thought of a pillow, I gasped.

"Mimi," my mom said. "Oh, Mimi, you're awake."

She scrambled to my side and grabbed my hand. "Oh, baby, can I get you anything?"

I still couldn't open my eyes. "Mom? Mom, where are we?"

I'd thought I yelled, but Mom said, "What honey?"

I felt her breath as she leaned closer to me. "Where are we?"

"We are at the hospital, honey." She rubbed my hand with her fingers.

"Hospital?"

"Nick brought you here last night. You were in really bad shape." The concern in her voice was palpable.

A memory came to me, but I didn't know if it was real or imagined. "Mom, is Lola okay?"

"She's fine honey, why?"

"I think she may have saved my life." The memories were coming faster. The noise, the fight. Lola barking.

"No, honey, Nick saved your life. You called him from the house and he found you."

"Actually, Lola was the one who saved you." It was Nick's voice this time. "Lola's barking alerted the officers outside the house and they came banging on the door. I must have gotten your call right before that because by the time I arrived, the ambulance was there and they had officers everywhere looking for the perp."

I used every ounce of energy I had to open my eyes. What a sight. Nick stood beside my mom next to the bed. His hair was ruffled, and he still wore the clothes he'd been wearing last night.

"But Nick, she called you." Mom admonished Nick.

"But Lola scared off the intruder." Nick grinned. "Mimi, you'd have been so proud. She bit the shit out of whoever was in your house. When I arrived, the back door was open, and Lola was sitting in the doorway with something in her mouth."

"The door was open, and she was still in the house?" Lola's habit was to bolt past me out the door. She'd grab a toy from the yard and insist on playing fetch.

"She didn't even growl or snarl at me when I walked up. Actually, she spit something out of her mouth when I walked in the door."

Groggy, but coherent, I said, "She wanted to play fetch."

Nick laughed. "No. She spit out a chunk of skin. Apparently she took a nice chunk out of the person who tried to kill you."

My mom gasped. "Mimi, this private detective thing is done. You need to find another line of work. No more of this dawdling around with seedy types. One of those husbands you snitched on was bound to come after you."

"Thanks, Nick. See what you started." I wished I'd stayed unconscious a little longer. Ah, the peace.

"Lydia, can I talk to Mimi alone for a few minutes?" Nick turned on the charm and Mom was mesmerized.

"Okay, but please talk to her about getting into another line of work." Mom sounded scared.

Nick placed his hand on my mom's back and led her to out of the room. When he came back, he closed the privacy curtain, pulled up a chair, and leaned close.

"From the look of it, Lola tore your intruder up pretty good. As much as I hate to say it, this is a good thing. I'm sorry you were attacked, but now we'll know who we're looking for. Not only do we have a nasty bite that had to have been seen by an ER doc, we have the morsel of flesh that Lola saved for us."

I sat up in the bed. "I really can't believe she didn't eat the skin she tore off. She usually sucks raw meat down without even chewing."

"She did all of the chewing she needed to do." Nick relaxed back into the chair. "Do you remember anything about last night?"

I scrunched up my face, thinking. "I remember hearing something, but when I was really still, the noise was gone."

I told him about Lola growling, and about deciding it was nothing. Then I told him what I remembered about the attack.

"So he was strong?"

"I don't know if it was a man or woman, but whoever it was made me look like a weakling. I'm no slacker, and this person was getting the better of me." I looked at myself in the hospital bed. "Fine, he or she got the better of me. Damn, that pisses me off."

"It's not like you were in a position to fight someone off. Lying on your back is a very bad position to be in when trying to defend yourself. Physics alone is against you, even if you are slightly stronger than the person on top of you."

I blushed as I thought of Nick on top of me earlier in the week. But my sinful thoughts were interrupted by the nurse pulling back the curtain.

"How are you doing this morning, Mrs. Capurro?" She looked to be about my height, but with thick ankles. Maybe it was the white pantyhose, but I'd bet the skin on those ankles looked stretched to the limit when bare.

"I'm great. What do I need to do to get discharged from this place?" I sat up and my head sloshed like the water in a goldfish bowl. I tried to hide it, but I think the nurse saw it.

"Why don't you lie back down? I'll have the doctor in here to take a look at you and we'll go from there." She smiled an insincere smile and turned to leave. She didn't close the privacy curtain.

"Look, if you can get out of here this morning, I have Henry and Eugene coming in for interviews around noon. I'm going to talk to them, and ask to see their legs. It has to be one of them who were after you." Nick looked anxious as he stood to leave.

"What if they refuse to show you their legs?"

"That would make me believe they are guilty, and hiding something." He patted his hip pocket on his pants. He reached in, pulled out what looked like a room key card, and handed it to me.

I flipped it over in my hand. "A visitor's pass?"

"I thought if you felt better, you might want to listen in on the interviews. You know, see what you think since you've been around these people as much as I have." Nick headed to the hospital room door.

I didn't know what to say. Did he feel guilty because I'd been attacked? It was my own fault. I should've left police business to the police. It was bad enough I had foes from my regular investigations. Now I was attracting extra enemies.

"Nick?"

"Yeah?"

"How did my attacker get into the house?"

"Whoever it was must have been watching the house for awhile. He waited for the shift change. The officers were distracted and right after that they heard Lola's barking and howling. The perp must have fled as soon as he was bitten, because the officers went through the entire house, and canvassed the neighborhood. No one."

"Oh." This didn't make me feel any better.

The doctor was happy to be rid of me after his follow-up exam, I made sure of it. Charles picked me up at the front of the hospital, and I went home to clean up.

I thought I'd be leery of entering my house, where I'd nearly been killed, but I wasn't. I was relieved to be home. As I walked in the back door, I realized someone had been here in my absence. I looked around. Everything was straightened and folded, and the chairs were positioned evenly around the breakfast table.

The message light was flashing on my machine. Three new messages. The first was from Charles early this morning.

"Nick just called. I'm on my way to the hospital." It was short and sweet, and I wondered why he hadn't come into my room.

The second was Jackie. "Hey, Charles just called to tell me you were in the hospital. He said you'd be out by the time I got around to calling. Call me, honey. I hope everything is alright."

The last call was a dial tone. I deleted that one. But I saved the others to listen to later, to remind myself that Charles and Jackie were all the relationship I needed.

In the bedroom, the bed had been made and you could've bounced a quarter off the pressed sheets. The pillows were stacked, and the duvet pulled back to reveal the crisp white sheets and violet blanket. I looked around the floor and saw that Lola's blankets had also been folded.

I just can't say how much I love Charles. And I know it was Charles because I don't know anyone else with OCD. Obsessive Compulsive Disorder is a good problem to have if it makes your life neat and clean, not so good if you develop rituals such as excessive hand cleaning or turning the key in the door 14 times before opening it.

I sometimes wished some of Charles would rub off on me. I guess we were the same in that we both liked men. But Charles had great relationship skills. He'd been with his partner for seven years. I couldn't even stay married more than one. Not that it was my fault or anything. I looked at the photo of Dominic on the dresser. God, I missed him. Most days now it was just a fleeting thought, but some days it hurt my heart physically and I just wanted to flop down on my bed and sleep forever.

Ah, enough of the pity party. I needed to get showered and cleaned up so I could get to the police station in time for the interviews.

CHAPTER 25

It was nearly one o'clock by the time I arrived at the Salinas Police Department. I parked on Lincoln Street and jaywalked across the street. I figured if I got a ticket, Nick could take care if it for me. I didn't think I had the energy to walk all the way to the corner, cross at the crosswalk, and then walk another half a block past City Hall, to the cop shop.

There were two uniformed cops at the front desk, and another in the lobby. The room smelled of sweat, mud, and dirty diapers. The wooden benches that lined the wall were filled with Hispanic women and their crying children. I swear if I understood Spanish, they were saying, "Why is daddy in jail?"

I didn't think this was where inmates were held. I was pretty sure they transported them to the county jail on Natividad Road. I didn't understand why these people were here, and I didn't want to. I just wanted to be let through the magic door to where it was quiet except for the normal sounds of everyday office work.

The officer in the lobby saw me and nodded his head toward the door. I smiled and pretended I knew what I was doing. I flashed my pass and walked past the front desk like I belonged there. In a way I did belong since I was invited by Nick.

Just inside the door to the right was the homicide division. I walked down the grey hallway and let myself inside the homicide unit.

A woman, roughly the size of an Amazon, sat at the first desk inside the door. She looked up at me with no expression, then looked back to the paperwork on her desk. I had been dismissed as unimportant.

"Hey, you don't look so bad." Natalie stood up from her desk behind the opened door.

"Thanks?" I wasn't sure how to take the comment.

She came toward me. "Nick told me what happened last night."

"Oh." I blushed. I was truly embarrassed that I'd not better protected myself.

"Come on." Natalie swung the sweater she had in her hand over her shoulders and shoved her arms in the sleeves. "Nick is already in the interview room. He has Henry cooling in one while he interviews Eugene in the other."

She waltzed past me and out the door, just expecting I'd follow. She was right. I didn't know where the interview rooms were located, so I was at her mercy. I followed obediently.

"So you think your attack had something to do with the Bailey case?" Natalie spoke over her shoulder.

"I think so, but in my line of business I piss off a lot of people when they get caught cheating. It doesn't matter if they are cheating a spouse, the government, or their employer, they get pissed when they get caught."

"So they know you snitched them out?"

I didn't like the way she put it, but the tone of her voice wasn't malicious. Besides, being a snitch is a good job, if you can get it. "Sometimes they find my business card and want revenge. But I've never been attacked physically before."

"Even if it was about the Bailey case, it doesn't make sense that they'd come after you. I mean, Charles has all of the computer information, we have all of the evidence, why go after you?"

"I wish I knew."

She stopped at a door painted a slightly darker shade of grey than the walls. "Okay, we'll go in here and listen in. It's not completely soundproof, so we need to keep our voices down, and preferably, we don't speak at all."

She opened the door to a room no bigger than a small closet. The floor, walls and ceiling were covered in navy carpeting. The wall directly opposite the door had an array of electronic equipment, and to the right of that was a flat-screen television. There was no two-way mirror to watch through. Natalie picked up a thin, black remote control and the television came to life.

Nick was speaking as we tuned in. "Look Eugene, if you're innocent, you don't need a lawyer."

Natalie whispered, "Looks like we're too late. He's lawyering up."

"But he wasn't arrested, was he?"

"No, but he's obviously got something to hide. I wonder if Henry will do the same."

Nick stood. "Stay here. I'll be right back." He walked out of the interview room.

Within seconds, the door to our little spy closet opened. "You made it. How much did you hear?"

"I just got here. I only heard him ask for a lawyer."

"Shit. Well, you can listen in when I talk to Henry. But I tell you, I'm beginning to think they have this all worked out. You'll see what I mean." He closed the door.

I felt like I should turn around and face the other direction to see Henry's interview, but Natalie just hit a button and we were watching Henry as he guzzled a swig of bottled water. Sweat glistened on his forehead. He wiped it with the back of his forearm. He jumped and spilled his water when Nick opened the door.

He was wiping water from the front of his shirt when Nick said, "Hey Henry, sorry to keep you waiting. We don't need to interview you anymore."

"What?" Henry shook visibly.

"We got what we need. We'll be booking Eugene in a few minutes."

Henry forgot all about the water on the front of his shirt, jumping from the chair. "Booking him for what?"

"What do you think? We didn't exactly bring you in here on drug charges." Nick spat out the words as if he was disgusted with Henry.

"That's not possible. Eugene wouldn't hurt anyone, much less kill them."

"Who said he killed anyone?"

"That's why we are here, isn't it? This is about Esme Bailey's murder. But I'm telling you, Eugene didn't do it."

"What makes you so sure?" Nick's slight smile was eerie.

"He was with me. We were at the restaurant until the bar closed." Henry stood, raising his voice.

"Sit down." Nick snapped.

Henry didn't sit. "This is crazy. I'm Eugene's alibi. We sat at the bar after dinner and had a few glasses of wine. When I got home, I grabbed another glass of wine from the bottle on the counter and headed to my bedroom to do some reading. I never saw Esme after dinner, and Eugene didn't come to the house. Eugene would never come to the house."

"You don't really know that, do you? You were out cold when Ms. Capurro found you in the bedroom. And my officers said you were unresponsive. Why kill Esme? Was she blackmailing you?"

"Are you kidding me? Blackmailing me with what?" Henry shouted at Nick.

Very slowly, Nick said, "For your relationship with Eugene."

Henry went red, then grey. He flopped down in the chair. "How do you know about that?"

Nick walked over and sat down in the chair across from Henry. "We saw you."

In almost a whisper, Henry said, "Where?"

"We were at the Camarilla game on Friday night. After the game we saw the two of you get into the Volvo." Nick had quieted too.

"That's not possible."

"Maybe you should go somewhere more private in the future. Oh, wait, there won't be a future. Eugene is going to prison. Well, guess there'll be a future for him, but not with you."

"You're an asshole." Henry slumped. "But here's the thing, Esme wasn't blackmailing me."

"Really?" Nick sounded skeptical. He leaned forward. "So she just makes a shit ton of money working for your wife? That's how she affords the designer clothes and the fine furniture in her apartment?"

Henry leaned in close to Nick and spat, "She worked her ass off for my wife, and she was well compensated. The furniture was given to her when Lauren decided to redecorate the house last year. What Esme didn't want, Lauren gave to the Salvation Army. She could have asked for more money, and Lauren would gladly have given it to her."

"So why would Eugene want her dead?"

Henry slammed his fists on the table. "That's just it, he wouldn't want her dead. Lauren already knows about Eugene and me. We just haven't decided how we are going to handle things. I'm her financial manager as well as her husband."

Nick raised his brows. He put his hands on the table and pushed himself up from the chair. "I'll be right back."

It was a matter of seconds before the door to our room opened. To me Nick said, "Can I see you out in the hallway?"

I got up from the table thinking, "Oh shit, somehow this is going to come back on me." I followed Nick into the hallway.

Before he could start yelling at me, I asked the first question. "Did Eugene really confess?"

"Hell no, I didn't get a damn thing from him. I'd barely been in the room with him a minute when he lawyered up. I told Henry he did just to get a reaction. Eugene really has no alibi, and I'm stumped. I need to see their legs, but I can't just ask without cause."

"So why did you call me out here?" Why not just talk in the room with Natalie?

"How much do you know about Henry and Lauren?"

"It's not like Lauren and I were buddies. Looking back, I've never seen them even touch each other, much less show affection. It seemed more like a business relationship."

Nick groaned. "I'm going to turn them loose. I don't even know where to go from here. Damn."

"Detective Christianson?" The officer from the front desk walked up behind Nick.

Frustrated, he snapped, "What?"

"Excuse me, sir, there's a woman here that says she's from MallMart, and she has a tape for you?"

Nick's attitude changed in a millisecond. "Escort her back, please."

"I hope her tapes have something on them. Are you going to release Henry and Eugene now?" I hoped and prayed the tapes would give us some proof that one of the two men was guilty. I was sure Eugene was the bad guy, and Henry was covering.

Janine Lambert was sitting in a chair outside Nick's office.

"Detective Christianson. I got here as soon as I could. I just got the tape this morning. I've narrowed down the timeline."

"Ms. Lambert, thanks for being so prompt." Nick put his hand on her shoulder and led her into the room I'd just left. "Please have a seat."

Janine sat in the chair next to Natalie. She reached into her bag and pulled out a disc. Natalie took it from her and put it in the DVD player. I stood behind Janine's chair, with Nick next to me.

Nick said, "Ms. Lambert, this is Detective Natalie Simon."

Natalie shook her hand, then picked up the remote. She pressed play, and we all sat in silence as the player booted up.

Janine Lambert shivered in front of me. She turned to Natalie and said, "Forward it about six minutes. That will put you at a few minutes before the activation time. We know which register it was because the clerk has to sign off on the activation. I've weeded out all of the other discs, and this one has the register we need to see."

Natalie pressed fast-forward, and we waited. I held my breath, and my heart rate soared. This may be the person who also tried to kill me.

When Natalie hit play again, you could have heard a badge drop on the carpet. We stared at the screen. Within seconds we had our first solid proof. I couldn't believe what I saw. The sound was bad, and the tape was grainy.

Nick grabbed me by the arm. "Let's go. Natalie, please book this into evidence, and make sure Ms. Lambert gets back to her car safely."

I followed behind Nick at a trot. As we passed through the patrol room, Nick said, "I need a patch through to the Santa Cruz Police Department."

CHAPTER 26

Nick slammed open the back door of the patrol room, and we were in the police parking lot. He jogged to his car, opened the passenger door, then jogged around to his side. I hopped in quickly, knowing if I was still standing next to the car when he got in, he'd leave me behind. I couldn't believe he was letting me come along.

I could still see the video of Susan wearing a hoodie, like the Unabomber, at the Mallmart checkout counter. It kept rerunning in my head like a nightmare.

No sooner had he started the car then dispatch came across the radio. "I have Santa Cruz PD for you."

Nick pressed the button on the microphone. "This is Detective Nick Christianson. I need police at 2309 Beach Street, apartment B."

"Copy." The Santa Cruz Police Department dispatcher didn't even hesitate. "I have two patrol cars on the way."

Nick pressed the button again. "No lights or sirens. We need to go in quiet. Just see if the occupant is home."

"We need a description of the suspect."

"Blond hair, blue eyes, skinny, with a dark tan. She probably won't answer the door. Don't leave the premises until we know she's not there."

"Copy that. What's your ETA?"

"We're rolling. Approximately 20 to 25 minutes." Nick hooked the radio mike back in its cradle.

I sat quietly, hoping Nick wouldn't change his mind and drop me off before heading to Santa Cruz. Tires squealed, and we laid rubber as he drove out of the lot. He reached out and put his light on the roof of the car and we flew.

I don't think I've ever driven faster than maybe 80 miles per hour, but Nick handled the car with ease at 110. It was pretty cool to see the traffic part like the Red Sea for Moses. That was until we got to Santa Cruz.

Our progress slowed down considerably once we exited Highway 1. But Nick didn't seem agitated, he was pumped. Lights and siren off, we cruised along Beach Street and up to the patrol cars in the gravel parking lot.

"Stay in the car for now." Nick rolled my window down, then got out to greet the officers.

After the initial greetings and hand-shaking, they got right to business.

There were two patrol cars and three cops. The oldest looked to be about 50, with military short platinum hair, broad shoulders and a flat belly. He probably looked heftier than he was because of the Kevlar vest. He stood half a foot taller than the other two cops who looked to be in their 30s.

The younger cops had their chests all puffed out and bellies sucked in. One had a shaved bald head, and the other thick black curls. They may as well have whipped out their nightsticks and marked their territory.

Nick started by asking, "Have you knocked on the door?"

The older cop answered, "We knocked, but no answer. One of the neighbors said he thought she'd left about an hour ago."

The bald cop said, "She's a waitress at Pebble Bay."

Nick was already getting in the car. "Can you guys stick around for about 20 more minutes? Just in case we miss her?"

Baldy and Blackie looked ready to say no when Father Cop stepped up and said, "We'll stay here as long as you need us. Just radio in when you have your suspect in custody."

Baldy and Blackie glared at Father Cop. What else did they have to do on a Monday afternoon?

Nick put the Crown Vic back on Highway 1, and we headed toward Seventeen Mile Drive. At the guard shack to the entrance of the Pebble Bay property, Nick slowed, rolled down his window and flashed his badge.

"What is your purpose?" the guard asked.

"I'd like to have your security people meet me at the entrance to Pebble Bay." Nick was polite, but not friendly.

"The purpose of your visit?" the guard asked again, not so politely.

"I'm here to question a suspect in a homicide investigation." Point blank, there it was.

The guard went back into the shack and got on the radio. He was gone for about two minutes before he returned.

"There'll be a security guard at the valet parking for Pebble Bay." The khaki clad security guard waved us past.

Driving through the shaded road to the hotel, we had to slow three times for deer. Apparently deer have the right-of-way on Mile Drive. The road was curvy, but not enough to make me car sick, and I was glad to see the long driveway entrance to Pebble Bay.

When we arrived at the valet parking outside the sand colored hotel, there was a welcoming party ready to greet us.

A handsome, twenty-something valet opened my door, and I was immediately greeted by a forty-something fop in a tidy black suit. He reached out his hand in greeting.

"I'm Fred Saway, General Manager. How can I be of service?" He bowed slightly as he shook my hand.

I looked over my shoulder to see Nick approaching fast. Fred dropped my hand like I'd bit him and gave all of his attention to Nick.

Nick shoved his hand at Fred. "I'm Detective Nick Christianson with the Salinas Police Department. We're looking for a suspect in a murder investigation. We were told she was at work today. She's a banquet server here."

"Yes, yes, my security division informed me of the situation. You see, I've contacted the Monterey County Sheriff's Department, and they've not been notified of this situation."

"Well, since we're just here to talk to Ms. Olson, I didn't see the need to bother local law enforcement. If the situation came to that, we'd have called ourselves." Nick's words were tight and crisp.

"An, now you won't have to be bothered." Mr. Saway looked over Nick's shoulder as he spoke. "Deputy Gomez is just pulling up."

Great, this was turning out to be a regular law enforcement circus. But then, if Susan did kill Esme, it was best to play by the rules and let the sheriff's deputy do his duty.

With all of the sand, khaki, and tan colors, everything seemed to blur. The building blended with the surroundings, and those blended with the deputy's uniform. Nick and I turned at the same time to see the tall, meaty man waving at Mr. Saway.

"Nick?" the deputy said.

"Joe?" Nick's tension released with the one word.

"How's the SFPD man?"

They did the shake, pull close and half-hug pat on the back thing that men do.

"I'm in Salinas now. I needed a change of scenery."

"You should have called me. You'd love the Sheriff's Department." They were still in a gripping handshake.

"Salinas is sort of home. I'm glad to be back there. It's an adjustment though."

"Yeah, I know what you mean. So what's going on?" Joe Gomez's brows crawled together to form a single caterpillar over his eyes.

"I have a murder suspect I'd like to speak with. She's an employee in the banquet department here. I need to see her ASAP." The men had taken a step back and were sizing each other up as they spoke.

"Okay, I'll escort you in, and from there, I'll stay out of it and just let you do your thing." Joe's body language stiffened, and he puffed his chest. "Mr. Saway, is that alright with you?"

He nodded vigorously. "Please, follow me."

I was a bit miffed that Nick hadn't introduced me, but I was more anxious to get to Susan than to be introduced, so I let it pass. We walked in a group, Mr. Saway in front, Nick and Joe next, and I brought up the rear.

Nick and Joe chatted about "old times" as we turned right at the hotel's entrance doors and trailed down a long, elegantly decorated hallway. The flower arrangements in that hall had to cost more money than I made in a month. We strolled about 50 feet and then made another right. We were in the foyer of the Grand Ballroom.

Mr. Saway came to an abrupt halt and turned to us. Behind him were a group of suits mingling in what looked like an early afternoon cocktail reception.

"Could you please wait here while I address the captain of the function? I would like to have him bring Susan Olson out to us, to avoid any confrontation in front of our guests." He didn't wait for an answer and strode toward a tiny man in a black tuxedo.

I watched the milling business men, and salivated over the hors d'oeuvres on the silver trays as the servers passed by. I even thought about grabbing a drink from one of the open bars, but I refrained.

Within a minute or so, Mr. Saway started back to us, and the tiny, tuxedoed man disappeared inside the ballroom doors. Mr. Saway's air of authority was intimidating, no matter how friendly he seemed.

"Ms. Olson should be out here shortly. I expect you will do this as quietly as possible." Not waiting for an answer, Mr. Saway stepped past me and disappeared around the corner.

"Not so stuck up and snotty here, are they?" Nick said to Deputy Gomez.

Joe's midsection jiggled as he laughed. "They aren't so bad. They just like things to go their way, and not upset their guests."

I couldn't just stand by and not say anything. "This place is all about money. And money doesn't like to bring attention to itself."

Just as the last word hit my lips, the captain opened the door to the ballroom. He held the door and behind him, Susan stepped into the reception area. She wore a uniform of black pants and shoes and an ivory cut-away tuxedo jacket over a white blouse and black bowtie. She held a silver tray in front of her.

As she turned and looked in our direction, the silver tray fell to the carpeted floor. It was a nanosecond before she bolted. So much for not making a scene.

Susan pushed and shoved thousand-dollar suits out of her way as she headed out the side door of the foyer. I may have imagined it, but I swore I saw her limp just slightly as she pushed through the double doors.

I felt a swoosh, as Nick and Joe took off after Susan. I thought about joining the chase, then thought better of it. I mean I'd had a rough night and a not-so-great morning. I shouldn't have been chasing after a deranged female in a pseudo-tuxedo uniform. Besides, I was pretty sure Nick and Joe could run faster than me.

I strolled to the double doors where the trio had just disappeared past the line of cars in valet parking. Susan had darted across the parking lot toward the row of tourist gift shops on the other side of the hotel. She grabbed the side of the planter as she rounded it, and disappeared inside a high-priced fashion boutique. By this time the guests were streaming out the doors to bear witness to the coming fiasco.

Nick and Joe looked like college hurdlers as they leapt over the same planter that Susan rounded. Nick slowed at the door to let Joe in the store first. It was Joe's jurisdiction after all.

By the time they were all in the store, I had strolled halfway across the parking lot. I rounded the planter at a slower pace than Susan had, and as it turned out my timing was incredible.

I reached out to open the door to the boutique when it opened for me. Susan Olson barreled toward me at breakneck speed. I had just enough time to realize I was going to be flattened by a human freight train before contact.

I was too close for the hit to have a major impact, but she did knock me on my butt. It was the first time I was ever happy to have the extra fat covering my butt bones. But there was no way this bitch was getting by me. She did a push-up off of me and started to take off again.

With both hands, I grabbed her black pants as she stepped over me. She wasn't going to be running very fast with my hundred and, uh, something pound body attached to her leg. She attempted to drag me for about three feet before she turned and began kicking at me.

"Bitch!" I screamed. She wouldn't be getting the better of me this time.

"Get off me." She wriggled and kicked, but didn't land anything.

I decided to save my energy by not yelling at her again. I tugged my way up her leg to get into a standing position. By the time I had my arms around her scrawny little waist, I was exhausted. I wrapped myself around her just to keep from falling back down.

Joe came up behind me. "Susan Olson, you'd better just stop now. It'll only get worse if you try to run again. You must know you won't get away for long."

"Fuck you," Susan spat. But she didn't try to run again.

Nick put his arm around my waist. "You okay?"

I had been dragged around like a ragdoll, no, I wasn't okay, but then anger took over. "Not yet."

I grabbed at Susan's pant leg again. This time I pulled up instead of down. And there it was, a gauze strip wrapped with pre-wrap and secured with athletic tape. It looked like a professional job.

"So how bad did it hurt when Lola took a chunk out of you?" I was so mad I hissed.

Susan yanked her leg away. "I don't have any idea what you are talking about, psycho bitch."

"Okay, that's enough with the trash mouth. Detective Christianson is going to read you your rights." Joe had Susan's hands behind her back and ready to cuff.

Susan spit at Nick and some of the saliva landed on me too. Yuck, yuck, gross yuck. I wiped the spit off the side of my face, but said nothing. The look on Nick's face said it all.

"So now we have assaulting a police officer, that's on top of murder, attempted murder, evading arrest, and God knows what else." Nick hadn't even bothered to wipe away the spit. He wasn't going to give crazy Susan the satisfaction.

I was standing on my own now, and I knew I should shut up and stay out of it, but I had to ask, "Why did you kill Esme? I thought she was your best friend?"

"You don't know anything." Susan relaxed slightly, then tried to yank her arm from Joe's grasp.

Joe finally slapped the cuffs on her, and not so gently.

"Ouch," Susan yelled more than whined. She turned back to me. "Esme only liked things that didn't belong to her. She got what she deserved. She took the wrong thing from the wrong person. Guess she won't be doing that again." She smiled without showing her teeth.

"What did she take?" Esme had money, couldn't she buy what she wanted? She didn't have to steal it.

Before Susan could answer, I had figured it out. "Sebastian."

"You're the new girl in Sebastian's life."

"I should've been the only girl. He was mine first."

Before Susan had time to say anything more, Nick stepped in and said, "You have the right to remain silent."

CHAPTER 27

And she reserved her right. She didn't say another word even after Joe and Nick put her in Nick's car. She sat quietly in the back seat as we drove back to Salinas. Don't for a minute think that the silence was resigned submission. The one time I turned to look at her, her gaze could have burned through metal.

"I'll drop you at the office," Nick said.

I wanted to go to the police station. But I didn't want to jeopardize the investigation by tagging along, so I let him drop me off, and I didn't make a fuss. Besides, I wasn't going to fuss in front of Susan anyway.

When I got to the office, I was greeted by a not-so-welcoming committee.

Charles met me at the kitchen door. "You have guests in your office."

I furrowed my brows at him, and he pointed to the open door. I was about to ask who it was when Lauren stepped into the kitchen.

"It's about fucking time. Explain to me what the hell is going on." Lauren turned on her heel and strutted back into my office.

I wanted to say, "What's up your ass?" But I thought I knew, so like a whipped pup, I trailed her into my office. What I didn't expect was that Henry and Eugene would be sitting in the room with Lauren.

Before I lost my temper at this invasion, I sat in the chair behind my desk, opened the side drawer and pulled out a bottle of water. It was room temperature, but I twisted open the cap and took a long swig anyway.

"You've made my life quite miserable without me even knowing it." Lauren sat on the arm of the chair that Henry was sitting in.

"And how is that?" I thought I knew, but I wanted to hear her version before I put my foot in my mouth.

"Henry tells me that you've accused him of having an affair with Eugene," Lauren spat.

"Okay." I was trying to keep from losing my temper, as I had to tell myself Lauren didn't know where I'd just come from.

"Henry is my husband because he's the best personal investor I know. We've been best friends since college. And as far as the world is concerned, we are married."

Oh, good God, just what I needed, another twist in this marital plot. Again I said, "Okay."

"Henry married me so I could become a US citizen," Lauren paused, then continued. "Henry is gay. He married me to help me out, and then we just got along. He's still my best friend, and the best financial planner I know. And Eugene is his partner. For better or for worse, we have to live together for awhile to keep the government happy. Your nosing around is going to get me deported."

Deported? "Where are you from?"

"South Africa." Lauren stated blandly.

"Shouldn't you have an accent?" Now I was just plain tired and wanted these people to leave. So what if I exposed Eugene and Henry's affair. I was done now, and they could go back to their funked up little world.

"I still do when I'm tired. But I want to be an American. I am an American. I'm an American author, with a bestselling series, and I love my life.

You digging into Henry's personal life, and having them dragged down to the police station to be interrogated is upsetting my careful plans."

"Oh, don't worry. Even though you hired me to do this, I'm done. One attempt on my life for this investigation was plenty. And apparently your little plans are so much more important than my life." I stood. "Now if you'll excuse me."

"What?" Lauren was genuinely puzzled. "Attempt on your life?"

Though I was really too tired to discuss it, I explained about the attack the night before, about finding Susan, and how my wonderful Lola had bitten a chunk out of her. I told her about Susan's statement when I confronted her about Esme.

Lauren's attitude did a 180. "I'd never have come here with the boys if I'd known about this. I'm sorry. And I thought I was going through hell. So what do they have on Susan?"

"For Esme, not so much, but they are putting the case together. Hopefully they'll be able to match the drugs in Henry's system with the ones in Susan's medicine chest. Not that it's ironclad, but it's a connection."

"Sounds like a lot of loose ends still," Lauren said.

"I really thought it was Eugene, because of the affair and all. But if you know about it, then there can't be any blackmail, and where's the motive?"

"So what about Susan?" Henry spoke for the first time.

"In Susan's case, I guess Sebastian was Susan's boyfriend before he was Esme's. And when Sebastian jumped ship, Susan had had enough of Esme getting everything. I don't have hard evidence, but I'm guessing that's what's going to come out of the interview."

"Incredible. I've never thought any man was worth fighting over, much less killing over. This is crazy. So what now?" Lauren asked.

"Even if they don't have enough evidence for the conviction on the murder charge, they have plenty for her attempt on me. Video of her purchasing the phone she used to threaten me. Lola didn't swallow the chunk of meat she pulled from Susan's leg, so we have DNA evidence that she was in my house and tried to kill me. So at the very least she'll go down for attempted murder. Better than nothing."

Lauren stood. This whole time, Eugene said nothing. Then he said, "I'm really sorry I didn't tell you the truth from the beginning, but Henry and Lauren really need this marriage thing to work. It's just for a few more years. I love Lauren too, and I'd hate to see her sent back to South Africa." Then Eugene leaned forward and smiled. "It was a fun ride, but I'm ready to get off now. I'd like to say I'm glad I met you, but it would be a lie." He looked at Henry. "Let's go."

Lauren stayed a few more minutes and thanked me for all I'd done, and apologized for Henry and Eugene's lack of appreciation. Then I packed up my briefcase and headed home. I was tired, and I was glad to have Charles as my chauffeur. He walked me to the door, and made sure Lola and I were comfortable before leaving.

Just as I had settled onto the couch with a blanket, Lola at my feet, there was a banging on my front door. Lola sat up, ears at alert, but she didn't bark or growl. I sat for a moment, not wanting to stir from my comfy spot. Then my cell phone rang.

I looked at the screen, it was Nick. "Hello."

"Open the damn door," he whispered into my ear.

Suddenly my spot on the couch didn't seem as comfy. I pushed Lola off my feet and jumped up. I was probably quite a sight in my fluffy slippers and housecoat, but I didn't care. I opened the door wide.

Nick grinned. "You feeling alright?"

"Better now."

He walked past me.

I shut the door and went back to my place on the couch, curling my feet under me. Nick sat on the opposite side. He kicked off his shoes and put his feet on the couch, facing me. Lola sniffed and went into the other room.

"She's not talking," Nick said,

"I figured that. She's a strong, stubborn girl."

"But we don't need her for the Bailey murder. We have an open-and-shut case on the attempted murder charge."

"We do?" I figured we did, but I didn't want to seem too sure of myself.

"Your dog is a genius. Oh, and Susan nearly hanged herself. She said something about how Lola should be euthanized, then before she could finish she realized what she was saying. Lola is safe for now."

My heart jumped into my throat. Lola was my baby. Safe for now? What the hell did that mean? "For now?"

Nick chuckled. "Sorry, I shouldn't have said it like that. Nothing will happen to Lola."

At the sound of her name, Lola came back into the room and put her chin on Nick's lap. His knees were bent, and she just rested her chin at his hip. She had her favorite stuffed frog toy in her mouth.

Lola has always been a good judge of character. And she really had to like and trust someone before she chinned them. And chinning them with her favorite toy? Unheard of.

Nick scratched her under the ears. Lola let out a low moan. Oh, yeah, this might work out after all.

###

About the Author

Jamie was born on the Central Coast of California where she spent her entire childhood entertaining. She started writing plays and charging admission to the backyard performances while she was still in elementary school.

Jamie has written a hiking book for Falcon Publishing, and has a short film currently in pre-production.

Jamie also writes screenplays for the large and small screen. She's currently adapting the Gotcha Detective Series for a TV pilot.

Jamie lives in Iowa with her husband, two dogs, two cats, and two horses. She writes with a view of their six acre farm.

Connect with Me Online:

Website: http://www.jamieleescott.com

Twitter http://www.twitter.com/jamie_ld

Facebook Fan Page:
http://www.facebook.com/jamie.jld

CPSIA information can be obtained at www.ICGtesting.com
Printed in the USA
LVOW131821130512

281526LV00001B/24/P